Blue Path

Path Series

by:
Neri Lopez

Blue Path

The Path Series: Book 6
Neri Lopez

Siren Book & Craft LLC

Other books by this author:

Path Series
Book 1: Red Path
Book 2: Unconquered Path
Book 3: Wagering Path
Book 4: Unexpected Path
Book 4.5: Double Trouble Path – Wedding Novella
Book 5: Twisted Path
Book 6: Blue Path

This work includes themes of sexual assault and rape that some readers may find disturbing or triggering. Viewer discretion is advised.

If you or someone you know experienced sexual assault, please know you are not alone and that resources exist to help you during this difficult time. If you are or have been a victim of sexual assault, you can contact your local police department or call the number below.

National Sexual Assault Hotline: 800-656-4673
Or chat online at: http://www.rainn.org

RAINN (Rape, Abuse & Incest National Network) is the nation's largest anti-sexual violence organization. RAINN created and operated the National Sexual Assault Hotline in partnership with over 1,000 sexual assault service providers across the country.

For victims of a roofie assault, please contact: 844-960-2939
    http://www.theedgetreatment.com
Help is available 24/7 on the Suicide and Crisis Lifeline. You can call or text in English or Spanish.

The number is: 988 or reach out to them online at http://988lifeline.org

American Indian Cultural Center

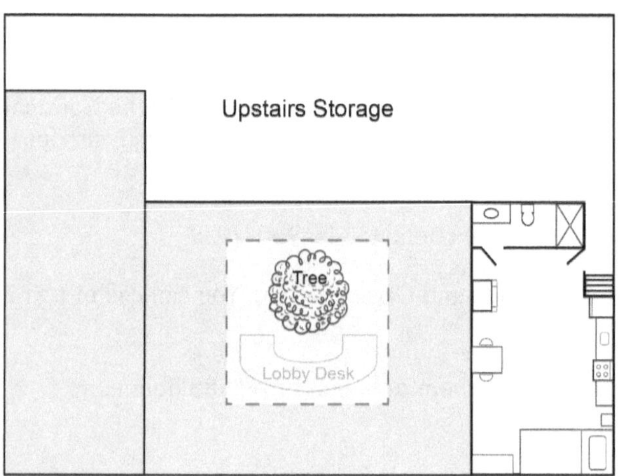

Second Floor

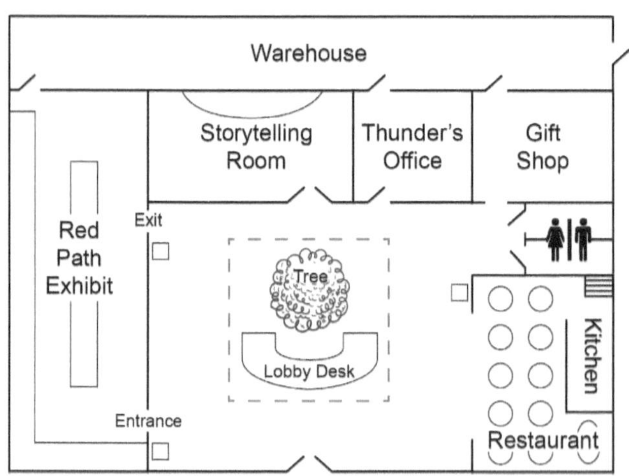

First Floor

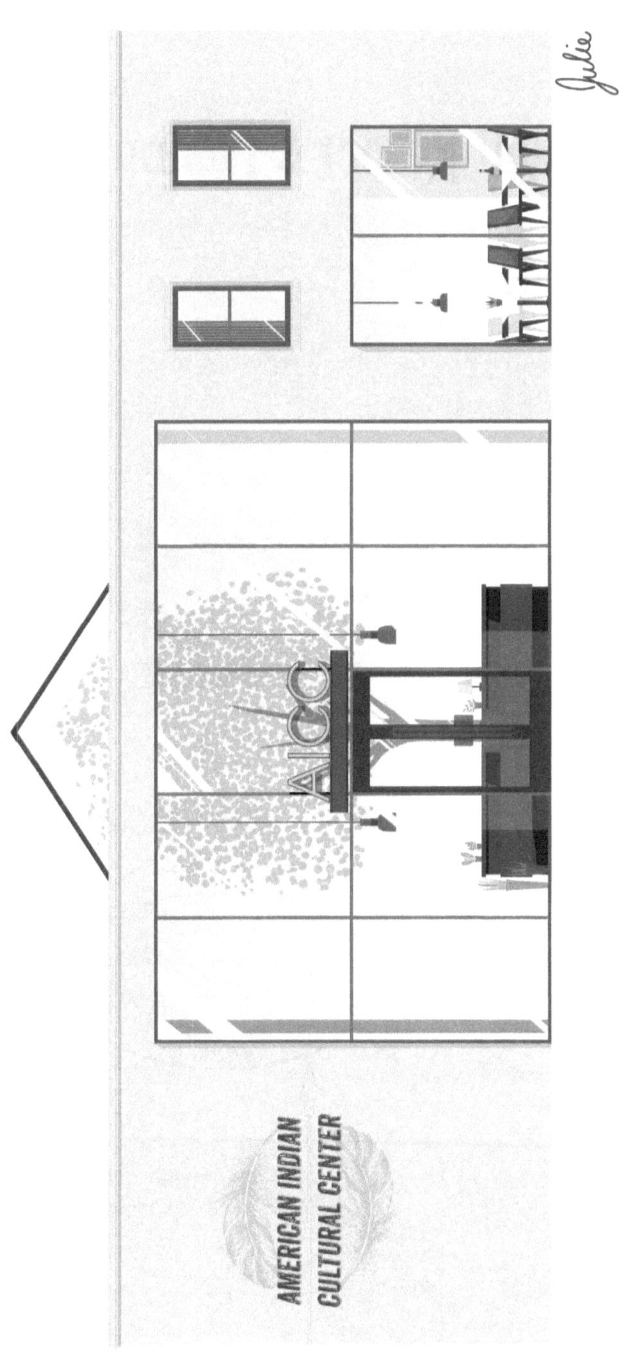

Visit Neri's website for the beautiful color version
https://www.sirenbookandcraft.com

Rock 'n' Roll Resort & Casino

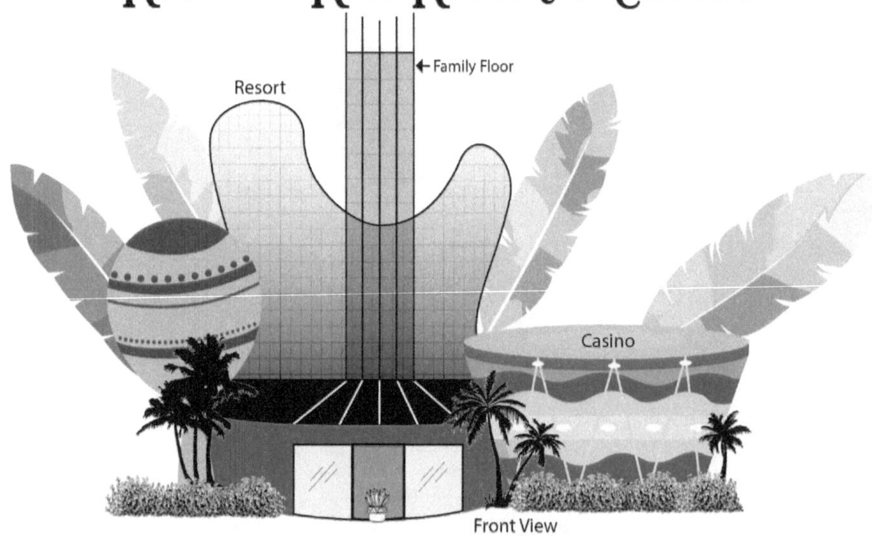

Path Series Family Trees

d.-deceased ❧ div.-divorced ❧ a.-adopted ❧ shaded box is a spouse

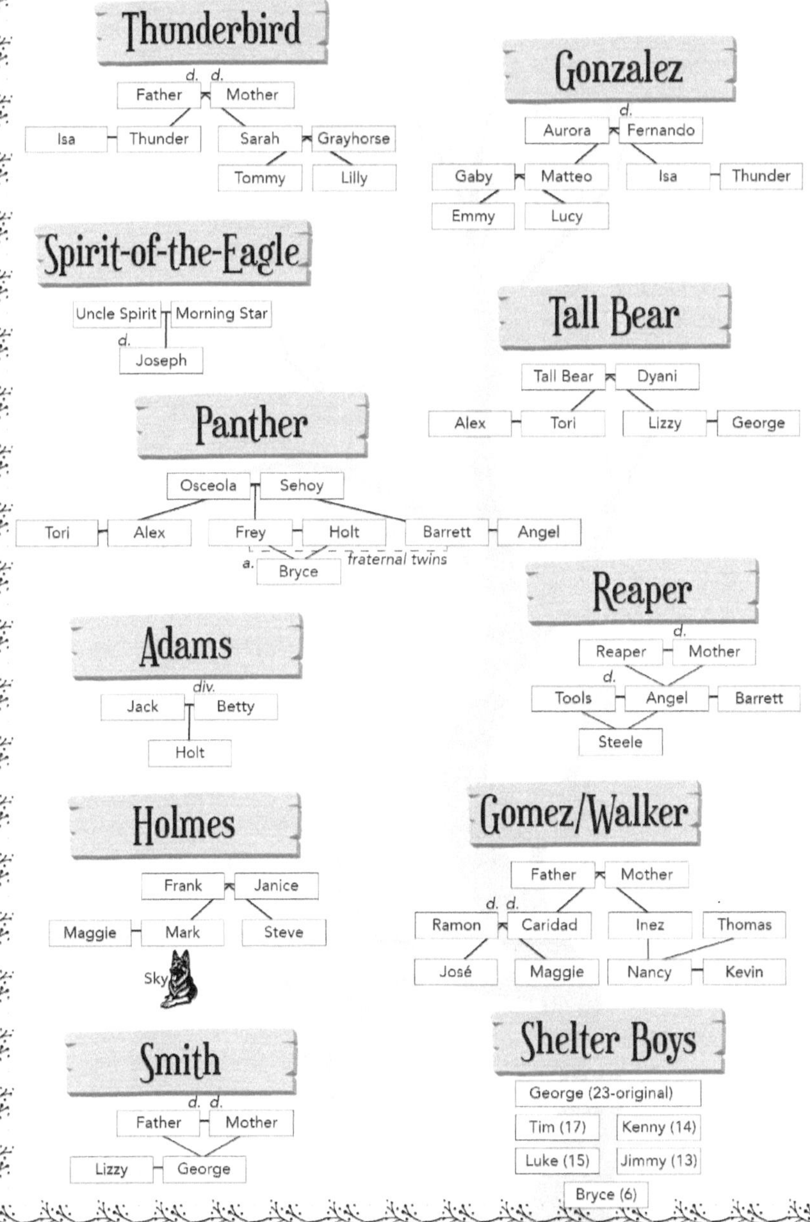

Translations

Lakota

até – father
iná – mother
lekší – uncle

Spanish

¡Mami, por favor, sácalo de aquí!" – Mom, please, get him out of here
¡Ay Niño, para afuera, sale! – Oh my boy, get out, let's go!
hermanita – little sister
gracias – thank you
Tío – uncle
Tía – aunt

Seminole

chatski - mother

Contents

Chapter 1

Who's There?

George

"Oh, my goodness," Tori screamed and stood frozen with her hand over her heart. "You scared me."

"Are you okay, baby?" Alex immediately approached Tori and hugged her.

As an extra security measure and to deter vandalism by Lucifer's Renegades, a local one-percenter motorcycle club that continued to give Thunder trouble, George had moved to the apartment above the kitchen at the American Indian Cultural Center. His police training had kicked in when he heard noises coming from downstairs. He'd slinked down the steps barefoot to surprise whoever was in the kitchen. Once he saw Tori and Alex, he immediately put his gun in the back waistband of his pants.

"I'm so sorry, Tori." George held his hands up in surrender. "I didn't mean to scare you. I've never seen you guys here so early."

Winston, a local drug dealer and Reaper, the president of Lucifer's Renegades Motorcycle Club, had kidnapped Tori a few months ago. Alex got there in time to save her before they escaped. George had helped make that arrest, and he knew how easily she got startled.

"My bad," Alex muttered. "I should've let you know."

"It's okay." Tori stepped away from Alex. "You just surprised me. How are you, George?"

"I'm good. Why are you guys here so early?" A few months ago, Tori and Alex had tied the knot. George was used to seeing them at the AICC because Tori worked in the office while Alex was their chef.

"We have a large student tour group coming today. I needed more prep time than usual." Alex was already getting out the ingredients for his fry bread.

"I told Alex I'd help him, so I came in early too." Tori gave George a hug.

"You may want to put a shirt on before Mark gets here and gives you shit." Alex pointed at him with the spatula in his hand.

The noises had spurred George to flee his apartment so quickly that he only managed to put on his pants.

"Good idea. Although I love to rile Mark, so maybe I'll go sit at his desk shirtless until he comes in."

"Stop." Tori lightly smacked George's shoulder on her way to the refrigerator. "That's not nice."

"Where did you find such a sweet girl, Alex." George smiled.

"I lucked out." Alex kissed Tori's cheek when she placed the rest of the ingredients he needed on the table.

"Alright, lovebirds. I'm gonna go shower and get ready for work. I'll see you guys later."

George was working the day shift, then had a couple of days off before switching to the night shift. The deputies worked twelve-hour shifts seven days out of every two weeks. It was a strange schedule to most, but he was used to it. When he wasn't working as a deputy, he helped Mark, the in-house security officer, along with his K-9 Sky, to monitor the cultural center.

George's mom and dad were drunk and higher than a kite the night they ran into a tree and died, leaving him an orphan at age six because he didn't have any siblings, and neither did his parents. George was an oops' baby. His parents, who were older and never wanted kids, accidentally had him after a reckless night of drug and alcohol use. Even at a young age, George sometimes wished he'd never been born, feeling neglected because of his parents' addictions.

Child services stepped in and placed him in several foster care homes. In one home, the woman's boyfriend beat him up, so he ran away. In the other, they starved him. After the third home and third run away attempt, they opted for the shelter for boys.

George was fine there. He had shelter, food, and access to education. Despite the bullying he endured at school because of his limited wardrobe, he was grateful for his situation—it was better than being homeless. He stayed out of trouble and kept his nose in his books. He pledged to himself that he would dedicate his time to helping others in the future.

His life turned around the day he met Johnny "Thunder" Thunderbird. Thunder was a native American man who moved to South Florida to start a cultural center. He believed in teaching non-natives about his Lakota culture, as well as other Native American cultures and history.

When George met Thunder, he was seventeen and had less than a year before he graduated and had to leave the shelter. Thunder took him under his wing and mentored him several times a week. After graduation, Thunder got him a job at Giovanni's Restaurant as a bar back and offered him a rent-free room at his house so George could save up enough money for his own place.

Impressed by his skills and strong work ethic, his boss at Giovanni's quickly promoted him to bartender. George loved bartending. He got to meet people from all walks of life and hear their fantastic stories. Another perk was that Thunder's house was a short walk from both the beach and Giovanni's. With Thunder's help, he saved enough money for a second-hand car and his own apartment.

A few years later, when George wanted to become a police officer, Thunder stepped in again and paid for his Police Academy classes. He appreciated everything Thunder had done for him, a deep sense of gratitude washing over him.

After his shower, he dressed in his uniform and headed downstairs, purposely stomping on the steps to announce his arrival. Tori and Alex were still in the kitchen, making fry bread and other goodies. Wanting to get out of their way, he went in search of Mark, who was already at the lobby desk with Maggie and Sky.

"Good morning," George announced loudly before he approached them.

"Hi, Deputy George," Maggie stepped out from behind the desk. "Don't you look handsome today?"

"Hey, Jessica Rabbit." Mark grimaced at Maggie. "Hands off. He always looks like that."

"I know." Maggie winked at George before turning toward Mark. "I just like to rile you up. Jealous much."

"Sassy woman," Mark grumbled. "George, I hope you meet a nice, sweet, young lady to date and not a sassy one like that one." Mark pointed at Maggie.

"Oh, you love me, and you know it." Maggie laughed and perched on his lap. She grabbed his face and planted a long kiss on his mouth.

"Okay then. I'm gonna go do a perimeter check. Sky, do you want to come with me?" George patted his leg and Sky immediately got up and stood by his side, waiting for further commands. Sky, Mark's blue-eyed German Shepherd dual-purpose K9 Officer, frequently teamed up with other officers. The primary focus of Sky's training under Deputy Bryan Wright was narcotics detection, developing her sense of smell to pinpoint illegal substances. So sharp was her mind that she became the go-to K9 officer for training in identifying suspicious objects and apprehending suspects.

Before the field trip children arrived, George patrolled both inside and outside several times. Then he and Mark sat behind the desk with Sky scanning for any issues while Maggie and Tori assisted Thunder with the activities for the students.

Chapter 2

Favor for Thunder and Tori

George

Around noon, George and Mark got some fry bread and were chatting at the lobby desk. George turned around when he heard the stomping of kid's feet as they ran to the restaurant for their lunch. They all looked so excited, their joy was contagious. George smiled at Thunder as he approached him and Mark.

"George, are you working at the police station today?"

"Not until five o'clock." George nodded. "Why, you need something?"

"It's all hands-on deck here. I need everyone to help me with this field trip and they don't leave until around three. But Lizzy, Tori's sister, gets in at one o'clock today. Can you please go to the airport and pick her up? I know this is really short notice. I tried to wait and see if they would leave earlier, but..."

George held up his hand, stopping Thunder. "Say no more. I'll head over there now. My shift doesn't start for another couple of hours." *Shit!* He'd forgotten Tori had mentioned Lizzy was coming into town. After their encounter the night of the shooting, he'd tried to text and call her, but she never returned his messages or phone calls. He knew after what they did it would be hard to date since she lived in South Dakota and he was in South Florida, but they could've at least talked it out.

"Thank you. I really appreciate this. You can get her flight info from Tori."

"I'll do that now." George finished the last bite of his fry bread and stood.

Tori never asked him about Lizzy, so maybe she didn't know what happened. Walking into the kitchen, he found Tori at the fryer with Alex.

"Hey, Thunder asked me to go get Lizzy. Do you want me to bring her back here or take her to the resort?"

"Oh, George." Tori hugged him. "Thank you so much. Alex can't make the fry bread fast enough to feed the kids from the field trip and the visiting tourists. Otherwise, I'd go get her."

"No worries." George grabbed a fry bread and Alex smacked his hand.

"Did she not say we are trying to feed tons of hungry kids and tourists?" Alex growled at him.

"Well, yeah, but I'm doing you a favor." George turned to Tori and gave her his best smile.

"Oh Alex, let him have one."

"He got one earlier." Alex glared at him.

"Another won't hurt anyone." Tori kissed Alex's cheek.

"Whatever," Alex grumbled.

"So." George gave Tori a peck on the cheek. "Can you text me her flight info and where you want me to drop her off?" George took back his fry bread and smirked at Alex.

"Can you call me after you get her?" Tori pulled out her cell and seconds later, George's cell dinged with Lizzy's info. "I'm not sure if we'll still be here."

"Going by the crowd out there, baby, we'll still be here." Alex took more fry bread out of the fryer.

"I'll call you anyway." George waved on his way out. "See you later."

George knew he was a good-looking man; the countless women who flirted with him while he bartended at Giovanni's had told him so, through their laughter and suggestive comments. He turned heads wherever he went, especially when he was in his police uniform. The women flocked. There was something about a man in a uniform that always drove women crazy, and he'd had some doozies. Skirting his way around the tables in the restaurant, he smiled and waved to anyone who said hello.

If he wasn't in such a rush, he would have stopped to chat with the children, their parents, and anyone else who greeted him, enjoying the sounds of their laughter. As a public servant, he always made time for the community engagement. Unfortunately, he only had thirty minutes to get to the airport. Several times, a woman would stop in his path, their hands brushing lightly against his as he eased them out of his way and continued to the front door. With the flight about to land, there was no time to stop and chat, only the urgent need to move on.

Mark was laughing at him when he walked by the lobby desk.

George stopped and pivoted back toward Mark. "Shut up, fucker." George mumbled only loud enough for Mark to hear.

"I didn't say a word." Mark shrugged.

"You could've helped me."

"And how could I do that?" Mark quirked his eyebrow.

"I don't know. Send Sky." George took another bite of his fry bread. "Women love dogs."

"Okay, Romeo, I'll remember that for next time." Mark nodded. "Go get Lizzy before those ladies heading over here delay you any further."

George turned toward the restaurant and saw a couple of ladies whispering among themselves and heading his way.

"Shit, I'll see you later."

George couldn't leave fast enough. It seemed the more he turned them down, the more they chased him. He wanted to do the chasing, not the other way around. Although, occasionally, he allowed himself to be caught. He was young, and this was the time to sow his wild oats, right? So far, he didn't have any stalkers or angry exes because he was always upfront with them. He knew he'd settle down someday, but for now, he enjoyed casual dating.

How was this going to work with Lizzy? For a moment after they were together, he thought they had something special, but how could they when they barely knew each other except for one passionate night before she left? Now she was moving here. George knew they would have to talk, but it was going to be uncomfortable as hell, since she had been ignoring him for the past several months.

Growing up in the shelter, he never had a girlfriend. He didn't want to be vulnerable; his parents' lack of love made him question if anyone could truly care for him. Then, after meeting Thunder and getting a job at Giovanni's, he didn't have time for a serious girlfriend because he needed to work every shift possible to move out of Thunder's house and get his own apartment. A place that was solely his was something he dreamed about since he was young.

No one to tell you what to do, no one to beat you or tell you, you're worthless. Not that Thunder did that. Thunder treated him like a little brother. Once he took George under his wing and later into his house, George learned what family was all about. It was the main reason he wanted to become a police officer. To serve and protect the innocent. He wished someone had protected him from his father's anger and his mom's indifference.

He strove to make Thunder proud, yearning for the approval of the only person he called family. He had to talk to Lizzy. The last thing he needed was for Thunder to be disappointed in George's behavior toward her. Thunder had told him Lizzy might live with them as soon as Isa, Thunder's wife, gave birth to their firstborn. *What if Lizzy told Thunder that he was an asshole? That he left her hanging? George reached out to her, but what if she never mentions that? He needed to talk to her before Isa had her baby.*

As much as George wanted Thunder's approval, he also loved having Isa in his corner. She always took an interest in his life and asked how he was doing or if he needed anything. Because of them, he'd met the Panthers, Mark, Maggie, Holt, and the rest of the crew. They were his extended family, always inviting him and his partner, Sean O'Reilly, to all their family gatherings and holiday celebrations. It would devastate him if Thunder and Isa, or any of his other pseudo-family members, hated him. Then he would be alone again.

Chapter 3

Airplane Troubles

Lizzy

Lizzy couldn't believe her dad had allowed her to move to South Florida and live with Tori. She had been pestering him since Tori's wedding, but Tall Bear wasn't ready to let her go until every member of Lucifer's Renegades was behind bars. After what they did to Tori, Tall Bear didn't want to take any chances with Lizzy.

Fortunately for her, the club had disbanded after a massive shoot out by the docks. The only member of the LRs that was still not accounted for was Numbers. Tall Bear had been told that Numbers had run out of town with his tail between his legs and was afraid of facing Reaper, their club president that was in jail.

It had taken many arguments, discussions, and pleading from Lizzy, but it had finally paid off. She was on her way to Tori. Tori lived in the resort that her husband and family owned. Lizzy wasn't sure where she would stay, but the prospect of a city excited her with vibrant nightlife, the promise of pulsing music and dazzling lights. Living on the reservation didn't give her many chances to go out and experience different bars and meet new friends.

She dreamed of a big city, where she could dance until dawn in vibrant clubs, savor diverse cuisines in countless restaurants, and enjoy activities like off-Broadway shows—experiences limited or forbidden on the reservation.

Before she boarded the plane, her mother and father shed a few tears and promised to visit soon. Tall Bear made her promise to stay safe and out of trouble. Lizzy never went looking for trouble, it just always seemed to find her.

During the flight, she sat beside a pleasant older woman named Karen, who faintly smelled of lavender and vanilla. Everything had been going great until they discussed Mount Rushmore.

"What do you mean Mount Rushmore doesn't have the most important presidents of our country?" Karen guffawed at her.

"I just mean that some of those presidents weren't so great. I think they should've put statues of Sitting Bull, Red Cloud, Chief Joseph, or Pocahontas. You know, mix them in. Maybe two of each or two mountains facing each other. Our leaders were as important to this nation as those presidents."

"How could you say such things?" Karen's face was turning red. "Those men on that mountain sculpted America. The artist purposely chose them to showcase the founding, expansion, preservation, and development of our nation."

"I'm not trying to make you mad. You have your opinion, and I have mine." Lizzy shrugged.

Lizzy didn't hate Mount Rushmore, she just thought it would have been nice to have a memorial of famous Native Americans carved out of the mountains. She loved seeing the Crazy Horse Memorial, but it was taking so long to finish, she might not get to see it in her lifetime. During their discussion, Karen got so incensed she pushed the button, asking the flight attendant to move Lizzy to another seat. The flight attendant informed Karen that the flight was full, and passengers had to remain in their assigned seats. Lizzy stared, mouth agape, completely dumbfounded by Karen's request. Didn't she have a right to her own opinion? She never told Karen she was wrong, just what she would like to see.

Karen's repeated calls for the flight attendant led to Lizzy being escorted off the plane by a federal air marshal upon landing. Well, that was fine with Lizzy, since she was the first one off the plane. The thought of Tori seeing her deplane with a federal air marshal escort filled her with dread; it would not be a pleasant reunion.

The federal air marshal gripped her arm and hauled her out of the terminal, heading straight toward baggage claim, when Lizzy heard a voice say her name.

"Lizzy?"

Lizzy stopped, causing the federal air marshal to stare down at her.

"Why are you stopping?" the federal air marshal glowered as he looked around.

"Because." Lizzy pointed toward George with her other hand. "He's my ride."

George stood there, his jaw slack, squinting at her with worried, furrowed brows.

Of all the people to send to pick her up, why did it have to be George? Probably because no one knew they'd had shared a sexy interlude several months ago after the double wedding. The chaos and adrenaline of flying bullets had caused her to want to have sex at least once before she died. George didn't know she had been a virgin because, as soon as it was over, she dropped her dress down and bolted. Literally leaving him with his pants down in a room he opened with his master key card.

She didn't question how he got the key card, but she was aware of George's ties to the Panthers and his security duties at the resort and the casino. Not because he told her, but because Tori couldn't stop raving about him. That night was so embarrassing that she wanted to forget it had ever happened. She was so stupid. Who would want to lose their virginity being fucked up against the wall in an empty hotel room by a stranger? Okay, so he wasn't exactly a stranger. He knew her sister, but not her.

After that night, George repeatedly called and texted, but she ignored him, ashamed and mortified by her desperate pleas for sex. She knew she'd have to pay the piper at some point because she wanted to move closer to Tori, but it was too soon. She wasn't ready for their first encounter; a shiver ran down her spine as she saw him. *This was going to be so awkward.* The federal air marshal twisted his head toward George and dragged Lizzy to him.

"Deputy, are you waiting for her?" He sneered.

"Yes, sir." George placed his hands on his waist. "Who are you?"

The federal air marshal released Lizzy's arm and pulled out his badge.

"I'm Federal Air Marshal John Finley. I was on the flight with this little lady when she caused enough trouble to warrant an escort off the flight and out of this airport."

"What did she do?" George looked between them.

Lizzy didn't want to get into it. She just wanted to leave the airport and go see her sister. *Where was her sister? Why was her sister not there? Of all people to send, why George? This day just got better and better.*

"I'm right here." Lizzy stomped her foot. "You can ask me, George."

"Okay." George turned to face her. "What did you do?"

"Can we talk about this later?" Lizzy looked around. "Where's Tori?"

"Sir, since you are an officer of the law, I will leave her with you." Federal Air Marshal John Finley nudged Lizzy toward George. "Please promise me you will take her directly to baggage claim and out of this airport."

"Of course." George nodded. "I'll take care of it."

"I am not an 'it.'" Lizzy stood proudly defiant with her hip cocked out and her hands on her waist.

"Great. You all have a nice day. Good luck with that one." The federal air marshal pointed to Lizzy and smirked before he left.

"What?" Lizzy pivoted, ready to give the marshal a piece of her mind, but George stopped her.

"Easy there." George put his arm around her shoulders and spun her toward the baggage claim walkway. "You know he can arrest you, right?"

Lizzy glared at George, but allowed him to guide her through the airport.

"Let's get out of here and you can tell me what happened. Your sister and Alex are waiting for you at the cultural center."

"Fine," Lizzy huffed. "But it wasn't my fault."

"Of course not."

Chapter 4

Lizzy was NOT like Tori

George

G eorge escorted Lizzy to the baggage claim area and pulled the luggage off the carousel as it spun past them. He knew they were going to have to discuss whatever happened on the plane and her ignoring his calls, but he wanted privacy when they opened up that can of worms. Gaging by her pursed lips and angry commands, she was steaming mad. Luckily, she only had two bags and George could haul it all himself because as soon as he pulled them off the carousel, she pivoted away from him, heading toward the exit. Not even thinking of helping him.

"Lord save me," George mumbled to himself.

"Is this your car?" Lizzy pointed to his patrol vehicle parked outside in the pickup lane.

"Yes," George answered her and unlocked the door. He came in his patrol vehicle because he had to head in to work after dropping Lizzy off. He'd learned early on that if he left his patrol vehicle parked in front of places, it served as a deterrent, so he left it parked out front instead of in the parking garage. Besides, he knew he would not be there too long.

"Can I sit in the back? See what it's like?" Lizzy pulled the back door open, but George slammed it shut.

"No, sit in the front." George didn't want her sitting in the back like a criminal. Thunder, Tori, and Alex would take turns killing him if they saw her back there. Besides, no one chose to sit back there. It wasn't like a regular car. The seats were plastic in case a suspect threw up or relieved themselves before getting to a bathroom. The smooth, non-porous texture of the design allowed for easy hosing. His seats were clean, but there was no way in hell she was sitting there.

"Ooh, can I drive?" Lizzy strolled around the front of the car.

"No." George quickly opened the trunk, then locked the doors so she couldn't open the driver's door. After he moved his equipment around, he fit her bags. He shut the trunk and strolled to the driver's side. "You are not authorized to drive this vehicle, so don't even think about it."

"Party pooper." Lizzy rolled her eyes and headed to the passenger side.

George got in and started the car. "Buckle up."

"What's this?" Lizzy pointed to the computer attached to his center console.

"My computer for my job."

George waited for Lizzy to buckle up before he pulled into airport traffic.

"Can I look?" Lizzy turned the computer to face her.

"Do you mind?" George glared at her. "That's not a toy." He should've known she would be a handful after the night he tried to be a gentleman, but she wasn't having it. In all honesty, he could've stopped her, but when she dropped to her knees and sucked his cock, his mind short-circuited with the electrical shocks that singed all the way up his body. She was trouble with a capital "T". He needed to take control of this conversation–fast.

"Can you turn it on so I can see how it works?" Lizzy ran her hand along the laptop. Was she looking for the on button?

"Stop that." George removed her hand and turned the computer back to face him. He was not booting it up while she was in the car...nope, absolutely not. She would probably start typing and clicking on private files.

"Tell me what happened on the plane. Federal air marshals rarely break their cover on planes unless there's a serious threat to the pilot, flight attendant, or a passenger." George couldn't wait to hear what the hell happened.

"Everything was fine with Karen, my seatmate, until we started discussing Mount Rushmore." Lizzy turned in her seat and pointed at George. "And let me tell you, she was definitely a Karen."

"What the hell does that mean? Karen is just a name?" George left the airport and got on the highway.

"You know, like those memes where they always talk about 'Karen'. She's a middle-aged, middle class, white woman who feels entitled and thinks she's always right. Although, my Karen was well past retirement age."

"Please stop talking. What you are saying sounds so racist and rude. I don't care what her name is, you don't berate an old lady on a plane no matter what she says. Did you stop and think that maybe to her, you're the Karen in the story?"

"Aha!" Lizzy pointed her finger in his face. "You do know what I meant by 'Karen'. Although her name really is Karen."

"Wipe that smug look off your face. I walk the streets. Of course, I knew what you meant by calling her 'Karen', but I was hoping I was wrong. Please, continue with your story."

"Whatever. All I did was say that instead of the U.S. Presidents on that mountain, it should be four famous Native Americans since we were here first." Lizzy crossed her arms and glared at him.

"And who would those be?"

"Well, duh. Chief Joseph, Sitting Bull, Red Cloud, and Pocahontas because Crazy Horse already has a memorial in the works."

"Why Pocahontas? She's a cartoon princess."

"No, she was real, and she helped the English settlers."

"Why not Sacagawea, Geronimo, or Quanah Parker?" George glanced at her.

"Fine." Lizzy threw her hands up. "Our mountain can have over four people on it, but there better be at least one woman representing us. Women were of vital importance to several tribes. If you want Sacagawea, then it can be Sacagawea."

"Go on." George said after a period of silence.

"What do you mean, go on? Don't you agree with me?" Lizzy sounded insulted.

"Personally, I prefer for it to be the same as Mount Rushmore. Four influential leaders: Chief Joseph, Sitting Bull, Geronimo, and Red Cloud." George knew that would get a rise out of her because she'd been so adamant about a woman on the mountain. She didn't disappoint. Her eyes got all squinty and the corner of her mouth raised up in disgust. She was adorable when she was all riled up.

"Of course you would," Lizzy huffed. "Men."

George laughed. "Okay, you have a valid point, but I also see her side. I will not die on that hill arguing with you about it." George pulled off the highway and was glad to be only five minutes away from the cultural center. Lizzy was a fireball, nothing like Tori.

"Well, at least you agree you would die on the hill, and I would win." Lizzy smiled at him.

"Couldn't you just play nice and agree to disagree?"

"I came up with an excellent compromise. I suggested carving Sitting Bull, Red Cloud, Chief Joseph, or Pocahontas into the existing mountain, perhaps on its side, or into a separate, nearby mountain, creating a majestic memorial to their legacy."

"Like I said, agree to disagree," George reiterated.

"Why should I? She didn't come up with a compromise."

"She's an old lady. Have some respect." George couldn't believe he was having this conversation. Lizzy was behaving like a spoiled child. Time to redirect. "On another note." George glanced at Lizzy. "Why haven't you answered any of my calls or texts for the past few months? We need to talk."

"I don't want to talk about it." Lizzy turned toward the window, suddenly interested in the passing scenery.

"We have to talk about it at some point. Why not now when no one is around?"

"Nope, not gonna."

"Would you please stop acting like a five-year-old?" George was slowly losing his patience.

"When you stop acting like my father."

"I am not your father. I just want to have a conversation about what we did the night of the shootout. I also want to know why you're ignoring me?"

"So, you want me to call you, daddy?" Lizzy smirked.

"No! Just answer the question."

"Okay, daddy." Lizzy turned toward him and batted her eyelashes at him. "Will you reward me with ice cream so I can lick it before I swallow?"

"Motherfucker." George squirmed in his seat and counted to one hundred backwards. This girl was going to be the death of him.

"No licking and swallowing for you?" Lizzy raised her eyebrow at him.

"Would you look at that? We're here." George pulled into a parking spot.

"Finally." Lizzy jumped out as soon as the car stopped.

George locked his car, grabbed her luggage, and dragged it after her into the cultural center.

"Hey, Lizzy." Mark came around the desk. "It's good to see you."

"Good to see you too." Lizzy hugged Mark. "Where's my sister?"

How could she go from acting like a she-devil to him to a sweet angel to Mark? George would've never believed it if he hadn't seen it. Meanwhile, he was walking around with his cock hard enough to drive nails into a wall. Clearly, he liked the she-devil side.

"Lizzy." Thunder's booming voice came from his office. "It's so good to have you here with us."

Lizzy ran to him for a tight hug. "I'm so glad to be here. I know you helped convince my dad to let me come. Thank you."

"You're welcome. Things are calm here now. I thought you were coming for a visit, but Tall Bear said you are moving here?" Thunder raised an eyebrow.

"Wait, you're moving here?" George interjected. He thought she was just coming to help Isa with the baby for a couple of months.

"Yes." Lizzy turned to him, beaming with the fakest smile he'd ever seen. "Aren't you glad I'm staying, or are my ideas and questions too much for you to handle?"

"Is everything okay?" Thunder's head bounced between George and Lizzy like a tennis match.

"Everything is great." George said through gritted teeth. He was a calm, laid back person, but Lizzy knew just the right buttons to push to piss him off. "Where do you want her luggage?"

"Uh Lizzy, Tori is in the kitchen with Alex." Mark motioned with his thumb.

"George, you can put her luggage in my office until our guests leave." Thunder turned and waved him to follow.

Great, now he had to explain their situation to Thunder, and he wasn't even sure what the hell made Lizzy hate him. He'd tried to talk to her. Hell, nobody hated him. He got along with everyone. It was what made him a great deputy. He could sympathize with people and stay calm under pressure—except with her.

Thunder shut his door for privacy as soon as George walked in. "Are you sure you're okay? I know Lizzy can be a handful."

"Thunder, she's more than a handful. She's a volatile ball of fire." George dropped into the chair opposite Thunder's desk.

Thunder chuckled, "I see you two have hit it off."

"Yeah, right?" George rolled his eyes.

"What happened?" Thunder sat behind his desk.

George recanted Lizzy's story about her confrontation with Karen, being escorted off the plane, and their discussion in the car. But did not mention the sex against the wall night. Thunder's face showed several expressions during George's story—understanding, shock, laughter, and confusion.

"So, what you're saying is that her stay is going to be full of adventures," Thunder sighed.

"She is definitely NOT Tori. Alex picked the right sister to marry." George nodded vehemently.

"Tori said Lizzy was spirited, but I did not know to what extent. Can you help me keep an eye on her?"

"Uh, are you serious?" George swore to himself. *This was gonna suck.* But it was Thunder. He couldn't tell him no. "You know what, fine. Sure. I'll do anything you want me to do."

"Thank you. Lizzy promised to move in with us to help Isa after she gives birth, which should be within a couple of weeks. How much trouble can she cause in such a short amount of time?" Thunder shrugged.

"I think a lot, but we'll see." George stood. "I'm gonna do another perimeter check, then head to work."

"Sounds good." Thunder walked around the desk and hugged George. "Thank you."

"You're welcome. You know I would do anything for you and Isa."

"Yeah, I know, as we would for you."

Chapter 5

Happy Sisters

"Torrriii!" Lizzy screamed as she entered the kitchen and threw herself at her sister.

"Ooff," Tori grunted, turning just in time to catch Lizzy for a hug.

"Hey, Lizzy," Alex smiled at her.

"Hi, Alex." Lizzy hugged him after Tori.

"Why didn't one of you come get me?" Lizzy gave them the evil eye. "I had to deal with that stick in the mud, George."

"You don't like George?" Tori eyebrows furrowed. "Everyone likes George."

"Wow, you are the only female on the planet that hasn't fallen for his charms." Alex went back to cleaning up his kitchen.

"Those females must be crazy." Lizzy knew he was sexy, muscular, and had beautiful blue eyes, but she wouldn't say that to anyone else–not even her sister, and definitely not Alex. She didn't want anyone to figure out how much she liked him and throw them together. They didn't need to know he was her first.

"Can I have one of your fry breads on that plate?" Lizzy pointed to the stack. She loved the way Alex made his homemade fry bread.

She had been so excited to get to the airport; she didn't eat breakfast. When the flight attendant offered Lizzy a bag of pretzels, Karen's anger was so intense that she crumpled her bag into a ball of crumbs before shoving it towards Lizzy. Lizzy glared at her while she opened the bag, tipped her head back, and poured the crumbs into her mouth. She was not giving Karen the satisfaction of not being able to eat her pretzels, even though it was more like eating breadcrumbs than pretzels. It didn't matter; she preferred fry bread to pretzels any day.

"Sure. Baby, can you and Lizzy check and make sure our guests don't need any more food so I can finish cleaning my kitchen?" Alex asked Tori.

"Yep. I'll see you later." Tori gave Alex a quick peck on the cheek. "Come on, Lizzy, let's check on everyone."

Lizzy followed her sister out into the restaurant. It always amazed her how kind her sister was with everyone. Lizzy feared Tori would never be the same after what Winston did to her. She guessed the drug Winston gave Tori had erased her memory of what he did, making the situation easier to manage. Still, her sister's empathy toward others was impressive. Growing up, she always heard how Tori was the nice one, the sweet one, the giving one, while Lizzy was the troublemaker, sassy, and too adventurous. After a while, she didn't care anymore and figured if they were going to accuse her of things, then she may as well do it.

Some days it bothered Lizzy, but most days, they were right. Lizzy enjoyed doing exciting things and didn't really care if others didn't like her. She was nice, but not a pushover like Tori. Her biggest problem was that she was very inquisitive and loved to debate ideas with others. Maybe she should've been a lawyer instead of working in a daycare, but her family didn't have the money to send her to college.

While her sister spoke to the guests, Lizzy grabbed paper towels and cleaner and began wiping down the tables as the guests left the restaurant. Behind her, she heard several women giggling, and turned around to see what was causing the commotion.

George was holding court with several women of all ages. They were swooning all over him as they flirted and touched his arms. He was laughing with them as he backed away toward the door. Lizzy couldn't believe it; women really did fall all over him. As she stared in awe with her jaw hanging open, George glanced at her and smirked before he left.

As George left, the women waved goodbye, smiled, and then started giggling.

"I see you witnessed the 'George effect' on women." Maggie used her hands to do air quotes. "They can't help themselves. He's so darn hot in that uniform. Not that he isn't hot out of it. He has an incredible eight pack."

"You better not let Mark hear you say that." Lizzy shoulder bumped Maggie.

"Oh, he knows how I feel about Deputy George," Maggie grinned at her. "He also knows that I only want to be with him. He is the only man that can handle me and love me like I deserve. I love that man with all my heart." Maggie stared at Mark and sighed. "Mark also looks hot in his uniform."

Lizzy and Maggie were laughing when Mark approached them. "You ladies look like you're up to something. Do I even want to know Nancy Drew?" Mark draped his arm over Maggie's shoulder and kissed her temple.

"We were just saying how hot you look in your security uniform." Maggie winked at Mark before wrapping her arms around his waist.

"You were talking about George, right?" Mark huffed.

"We were talking about both of you." Lizzy pointed between Mark and Maggie. They were perfect for each other. Maybe she would find a Mark, Thunder, Alex, or Holt while she was here. Those three men knew how to treat a woman. She'd had a crush on Barrett, but then he hooked up with Angel, and she lost her chance. That's okay, there were plenty more fish in this South Florida sea.

"Lizzy, with things so quiet around here, Maggie and I thought you might appreciate some extra space, so we moved out of our room at the resort. Besides, I was ready to move into our new house and let Sky run around in our backyard. Hotels are hard on dogs. You can stay in our old room that connects to Frey and Holt. But don't worry, they always keep that door locked–thank goodness." Mark rolled his eyes.

"Thank you." Lizzy beamed at them. "I was wondering if I'd be sleeping on the couch in Tori and Alex's room until Isa gives birth. I mean, I love my sister, but you are absolutely right. I would like some extra space."

"We figured as much." Maggie released Mark. "Our guests are leaving. I'm gonna go say goodbye with Tori and Thunder."

"I'll finish these tables and sweep." Lizzy moved to another table.

"Thanks, Lizzy. Tori and Alex will appreciate it and be able to leave earlier." Mark nodded. "I'm gonna check all the rooms and make sure everyone's gone."

By the time Tori came back after all the guests left, Lizzy had already cleaned the tables and was in the final stages of sweeping.

"Thanks, Lizzy." Tori gave her a side hug. "I'm gonna see if Thunder needs anything. If he doesn't, we can leave. Where's your luggage?" Tori looked around.

"It's in Thunder's office, I think."

"Okay, when you're done, take the broom to Alex? He wants to sweep the kitchen before we leave. I'll be back in a few."

Lizzy hoped George had left her luggage there because the last thing she wanted was to have another face-to-face with George today. Or god-forbid have to call him to find out what he did with it. Lizzy emptied the dustpan into the trash bin and walked into the kitchen.

"Alex, did you want the broom?" Lizzy called out.

"Yep, you can leave it by the doorway. I just need to turn the fryer's off."

"I can sweep for you while you finish up."

"Thanks, Lizzy. That would be great."

Lizzy swept while Alex wiped everything down.

"How are your mom and dad doing?" Alex asked, while he turned off the appliances for the night. "We haven't had a chance to go see them since the honeymoon."

"They're good. Same old, same old. They're thinking about visiting this summer."

Tori peeked around the corner into the kitchen. "I have your luggage. We can leave as soon as you guys are done."

"Sweeping is done." Lizzy announced as she emptied the dustpan into the trash.

"Let me take the trash out and we'll go. You ladies can wait for me in the lobby." Alex tied the bag and headed out the back.

"I'm so glad you're here." Tori hugged Lizzy. "It's nice to have my little sister with me."

"I'm glad too. I missed talking to you." Lizzy followed her into the lobby.

"Are you guys heading out?" Mark spun around in his chair.

"As soon as Alex comes back from taking out the trash." Tori leaned against the lobby counter.

"Shit, I would've done it." Mark stood.

"Too late, he's already gone." Tori smiled.

"Lizzy, we need to get together and properly welcome you to South Florida." Maggie stood and wrapped her arms around Mark's arm. "I'll text you. We'll plan a Girls' Night Out. Do you like to go dancing?"

"I love to dance." Lizzy would love to go out with the ladies.

Mark groaned and dropped his head.

"It'll be okay, Surfer Smurf." Maggie patted and rubbed his back.

Lizzy was about to ask why Mark looked so defeated when Thunder approached them with Alex. Thunder, Maggie, and Mark worked longer hours than Tori and Alex. But that was because when Alex left the cultural center, he went to work at 'RUSH', the casual dining restaurant at the resort. Tori would help if needed.

"Thunder," Lizzy said, needing to reassure him that Isa was her top priority. "I'll be staying in Mark and Maggie's old room at the resort since they moved into their new house, but please let Isa know I'm available to help her either before or after she has the baby, if she needs me."

"I'll let her know. Thanks, Lizzy." Thunder squeezed her in a tight hug. "It's great to have you with us."

"It's great to be here."

Alex took Lizzy's luggage to the car and drove them to the resort.

Chapter 6

My Luck is Changing

Numbers

Numbers and Red had been keeping a low profile in Jacksonville for the last three months. They fled town because Numbers' image was plastered across every South Florida news channel. Numbers had shaved his head and beard, but Red couldn't part with his hair, so he colored it black. They never wore their kuttes, and both had lost a lot of weight because they barely had enough money for food. Red stole food from either the grocery store or convenient stores. One night they counted their money and Numbers knew he had a decision to make.

"We only have fifty bucks left." Numbers pocketed the money.

"I can rob the store?" Red volunteered.

"No, we can't afford to have your photo out there too if you get caught." Numbers paced at the foot of the bed. "I say we get gas and drive to the clubhouse."

Red raised his eyebrow. "Isn't that kind of risky?"

"Yeah," Numbers sighed. "But we can't stay here. We don't have enough money for this shitty hotel or food. We'll leave at night."

"Okay." Red nodded.

"Let's take a nap and then go." Numbers laid down and shut his eyes.

They were going to have to be careful driving into their hometown. Red had ditched his cousin's car, and they kept hot wiring cars every couple of days. Numbers was tiring of that song and dance. He was ready to go home and get in the good graces of Reaper. Even though Reaper was still in prison, he had friends everywhere. The cops were the least of his worries.

A few hours later, at sundown, they drove south, adhering to the speed limit, hoping and praying no one had reported their car stolen. When they got close to the clubhouse, they drove around, making sure there were no cops around. Then they ditched the car several blocks away in the woods and walked to the clubhouse, staying away from the streetlights.

Numbers tried the door, but it was locked. He knocked and a few minutes later; the door cracked open. A female voice said, "Who is it?"

"Sandy, is that you?" Numbers said into the crack of the door. "It's Numbers, let me in."

The door opened wide, and Sandy threw herself into his arms. "I'm so glad to see you."

Numbers held her and walked in. Red shut the door behind them.

"Is anyone else here?" Numbers pulled Sandy back.

"None of the men, just me and the girls." Sandy gave him a wobbly smile. "You look different. Red? Is that you?"

"Yep." Red stepped around them and headed to the kitchen. "You got anything to eat?"

"Yes, help yourself." Sandy followed.

Numbers looked around. The place looked desolate. "Where are the girls?"

"The ole ladies are staying in their men's rooms and a couple sweet butts took a couple of rooms upstairs. Please don't be mad." Sandy looked down. "We didn't know if anyone was ever coming back."

"It's okay. Get some food for us. Is the club's safe still in the meeting room?"

"Yes, but it's empty."

"Empty, how?" Numbers screamed. "I had a shit ton of cash in there."

"I didn't want the cops to get our money, so I got the combination from Brick before you guys went out to the shootout and I divided the money among the ole ladies and a few sweet butts. We stuffed the money in our clothes. They didn't pat us down when they raided. Since the safe was unlocked, they saw it was empty and left it sitting there."

"Smart. So where's the money now?" Numbers held his hand out.

"We'll bring it to you in the morning, but you need to know some is missing."

"Why?" Numbers growled at her.

"I had to spread the money out fast and some of the sweet butts took the money and ran." Sandy wrung her hands and lowered her gaze. "I'm sorry, Numbers."

"Fucking Bitches." Numbers took a seat at the bar. "Get me a beer."

"We don't have any. Sorry, with the guys gone, we used the money for food and water."

"Fuck! Is anyone in my room?" Numbers stood. If he couldn't have a fucking beer, he was going to sleep. He'd worry about everything else in the morning.

"No, I don't think so."

"Tell Red to find a room. I'm going to bed." Numbers headed to the stairs. "In the morning, I want to see all the money that we have left."

"Okay," Sandy answered.

The next morning, all the ladies dropped the pile of money on the meeting table. Numbers kept most of it. He wanted to make sure it got spent correctly. But he was nice and gave them each a few hundred. The first thing he sent Red out for was beer and then to buy a gun.

Numbers and Red were now the last remaining members of Lucifer's Renegades because the others either left town, joined another MC, or were in jail.

The next day they began spying on the American Indian Cultural Center, waiting for the right time to kill Maggie, Tori, and Angel. Mostly, it was Red who did the spying because Sandy told Numbers the police were still looking for him. Numbers was insistent on killing those three women. Tori got their president, Reaper, arrested. The conflict between the LRs and Los Lobos de Muerte started because of Maggie's brother. And fucking Angel because she couldn't keep her mouth shut and had to go warn them about the shootout. Because she talked, almost all of his brothers were in jail. Reaper wanted Steele in the club and the little shit had turned traitor. Numbers should add his ass to the kill list, but he didn't think Reaper would agree.

He needed to get back into Reaper's good graces after he fucked up the wedding shootout. Even though Reaper was in jail, he could still make his life miserable. Plus, if the police caught Numbers before he could take care of those loose ends, Reaper would kill him slowly in prison.

They learned a lot from their spying. Not only were Maggie and Tori there, but it seemed like a young girl who looked like Tori was also working there now. Young blood, Numbers bet she was sweet in bed.

Chapter 7

A Day in the Life of a Deputy

George

For the past three months, George had been working the day shift from 5:00am to 5:00pm, but this week he changed from day shift to night shift. Now he worked from 5:00pm to 5:00am. He was used to working twelve-hour days, but the shift changes from day to night or vice versa always threw him for a loop. But he loved his job, so he sucked it up. Being a deputy was the most fulfilling job he'd ever had. He thrived on the daily challenges of being a Sunrise County Sheriff's Deputy; no day was ever the same.

The night shift was usually crazier than the day shift, especially on Friday and Saturday nights. It seemed everyone did stupid stuff on those nights. That's not to say, the day shift was a walk in the park or that the other days of the week were quiet. Every shift, regardless of the day, was action-packed.

While he drove around, keeping the streets safe, he couldn't stop thinking about Lizzy and her sassy ass mouth. He wanted to talk it out, but her silence about that night was driving him crazy. All he wanted to do was apologize. He'd messed up. Lizzy was Tori's sister; she didn't deserve to be fucked against a wall. Hell, he had never treated a one-night stand like that before. Why did he do it with Lizzy? In his defense, he'd never been so desperate to get inside a woman before. Their chemistry just sizzled the moment they found themselves alone in that hotel room. Thank God no one had walked in, because he didn't remember locking the door.

Lizzy had gotten him so horny, so quick, he hadn't been thinking straight. He'd tried to stop her several times, but once he saw the desperation and despair in her eyes, he knew he was going to give her anything she wanted. When they finished, she ducked out from under his arms so fast he didn't have a chance to stop her before she slipped into the bathroom and slammed the door. Instead, he gave her some space. He was glad she was on the pill, because he wasn't ready to be a dad. Pulling his boxer briefs back on, he noticed some blood mixed in with their orgasm. *Oh fuck! Was it from Lizzy? Was she a virgin?* George dropped his head against the wall. He felt like shit. If that was her first time, he had really fucked up.

Unfortunately, he didn't have time to talk to her because Barrett called and when he placed the phone on his shoulder to pull up his pants; she ran out of the room. He would've gone after Lizzy, but Barrett sounded weak on the phone. Then Angel, the woman who interrupted the wedding and left with Barrett, told him to hurry because Barrett was bleeding out. George called the paramedics on his way to Barrett's room. Once the paramedics stabilized him, George followed the gurney with Barrett all the way to the ambulance before he went to assist the officers who were arresting the members of Lucifer's Renegades MC (who were shooting up the wedding venue and their guests) and Los Lobos de Muerte MC (who were shooting the LRs as they defended the wedding venue and their guests). It was a shitshow of epic proportion.

When he reached the station, it had taken him half the night to give his statement since he was at the wedding from start to finish. Well, except for the twenty minutes he was with Lizzy. He told the deputies, taking his statement that he took Lizzy to a safe location and calmed her down. *Fuck! Twenty minutes, he never finished in twenty minutes.* He was an asshole who didn't see to his girl's needs first. He really needed to apologize. But catching Lizzy alone had proven to be an impossible task before she went back to South Dakota.

Now, months later, he still hadn't talked to Lizzy because she was ghosting him. Driving around, he heard a call go out to his partner, Sean O'Reilly, about a DUI. Even though Sean was the primary, he still drove out to lend a hand in case the driver got violent. It was best to have at least two officers on site in case they needed to subdue the suspect.

Upon arrival, George watched Sean ask the man to step out of the car and walk a straight line. Observing from a distance, George stood ready to intervene. Lieutenant Harris pulled up behind George's patrol vehicle and walked toward him.

"How's he doing?" Lieutenant Harris nodded toward Sean.

"Man can't walk a straight line to save his life," George chuckled.

"How many times has he tried?"

"He's started over about three times, but only gets a few steps in before he loses his balance."

They continued to watch as Sean asked him questions. *Where was he headed? How much did he drink?*

The man rubbed his head and stared at Sean without saying a word. Finally, Sean asked him to put his hands behind his back, put the cuffs on him, and read him his rights.

George knew the drill from training with Sean. The minute he cuffed the guy, George radioed dispatch to call a tow truck company to come get the man's car off the road. They had several companies that answered the call within minutes because the longer it took, the worse the traffic jam.

"Can you stay with the car until the tow truck arrives?" Lieutenant Harris asked before he left.

"Yep." George waited until Sean left and pulled his patrol vehicle with flashing lights behind the suspect's car. The best part of waiting was watching all the traffic, seeing his lights, and following the rules. The worst part was the rubberneckers that wanted to know what happened and might cause another accident. Sitting in his car with nothing to do wasn't fun either, but he didn't want to leave the suspect's car unattended in the middle of the road.

After the tow truck hauled the car away, George called it in and pulled out into traffic. As he was driving around, he got a call about a disturbance at The Dragon, a local nightclub. George was only five minutes away from the club, so he answered the call from dispatch and headed there with his lights and sirens blaring.

Fortunately, or unfortunately working as a police officer in this county, he knew all the bars, their owners, and their bouncers.

"Hey, Jake," George said to the bouncer at the door. "I heard you have a problem?"

"Yup." Jake opened the door for him. "Carmine took the drunk guy into Dave's office."

"Great, another drunk guy," George mumbled.

"Just another Friday night in paradise, man," Jake chuckled.

George nodded and headed toward Dave's office. Dave was the owner of The Dragon. The club had only been open a few months and like any other club in South Florida, you always got stupid people doing stupid things when they drank too much.

George knocked on Dave's office door.

"Come in."

George opened the door and stepped inside. Dave was sitting behind his desk while Carmine, his big ass bouncer, held the drunk guy's shoulders down to keep him in the seat.

"Deputy George, thank you for coming so quickly. It appears this gentleman had a little too much to drink. When Carmine asked him to leave, he threw a beer bottle at him." –George glanced at Carmine looking for cuts or bruising– "Luckily, Carmine ducked."

"Carmine." George approached him. "Is that what happened?"

"Yes, sir."

"Dave, you want to press charges for drunk and disorderly behavior?" George grabbed the man's arm and pulled him out of the chair.

"Heyyy, eazzy there, offfficccer." The man pulled his arm back and stumbled onto the desk. "He's lll...lying, I nnn...never threw anything at himmm."

It was going to be a long night. George leaned the drunk man against Dave's desk as he cuffed him and read him his rights.

"I'll take it from here. Give me a hand, Carmine?"

"Sure thing."

George grabbed one side while Carmine grabbed the other and they escorted the drunk guy into George's patrol vehicle. During the short drive, he heard the man wretch in the backseat. *Great, just great. Now he had to get a hose and wash his car out. Fucking Friday Nights. Bet Lizzy wouldn't want to sit back there now.* The smell was putrid as it permeated throughout the car. He opened his front windows because he couldn't open the back windows for ventilation because a drunk person might try to jump out. The guys at sally port, the single entry point to their jail where they booked all suspects, were gonna love him.

After he dropped the drunk guy off, who was still pleading his innocence, he went back to the station and had to scrub the vomit caked on the backseat of his car before he rinsed the lingering smell of stale beer. Whoever thought to make the backseats plastic was a genius. If that smell had permeated into cloth seats, he would've been smelling it for weeks if not months. He retrieved a couple of towels from his trunk—emergency preparedness at its finest—and dried the water-soaked seats. Then headed inside to write his report on the drunk man at The Dragon.

Chapter 8

Girls' Night Out @The Dragon

Lizzy joined Tori and Alex at work on Saturday because Isa didn't need her yet. She and Maggie hung out at the lobby desk for most of the day, swapping stories about their childhood. When guests arrived, Maggie or Tori would give them a tour. Lizzy joined the first couple of tours in case she needed to help. She knew all about the Lakota artifacts but wanted to learn the history behind the other tribal artifacts.

Mark also sat at the lobby desk, but he mainly did security with Sky. He patrolled the inside and outside of the cultural center multiple times daily, also monitoring the security cameras in each room. After the theft and kidnapping, Thunder and Mark were adamant about security.

"What are you two plotting?" Mark came back with Sky after doing an outside perimeter check.

"We're going to have a Girls' Night Out tonight." Maggie set her phone down. "I already texted all the girls."

"And where is this Girls' Night Out, princess?" Mark squinted at her and sat in his rolling chair. Sky laid down beside him, gazing out the front door.

"The Dragon." Maggie smiled.

"Uh, no." Mark shook his head. "No way. Don't you remember what happened last time you girls went there?"

"This time will be different." Maggie sat on his lap and wrapped her arms around his neck. "Come on, Surfer Smurf, you can always come with us like last time."

"Fuck no." Mark raised his arms out like he was being arrested. "It's time for one of the other guys to step up and keep you crazies out of trouble."

"Come on, don't be like that." Maggie kissed his lips.

"Don't be like what?" Thunder walked up behind them.

Lizzy whipped her head around. Where had he come from? She never heard his footsteps.

"The girls want to have another night out." Mark grimaced.

"What girls?" Thunder glared at Maggie.

"Angel, Frey, Lizzy, and me." Maggie beamed at Thunder. "Isa is very pregnant and wouldn't be any fun."

"Thank fuck." Thunder murmured and ran his hand over his head.

"Sarah and Gaby are going to your house to hang out with Isa and Tori doesn't want to go." Maggie jumped off Mark's lap and wrapped her arm around Lizzy. "Lizzy should have some fun before she starts her babysitting job for you."

"Lizzy always has fun." Tori joined the conversation.

"Not here I haven't," Lizzy whined.

"You've only been here a day." Tori's eyes widened.

"I know, but if Maggie wants to take me someplace where I can dance, why can't I go?" Lizzy shrugged.

"I think Barrett and Holt should go with you ladies." Mark pulled out his phone and shot off a text.

"Are you texting Barrett?" Maggie leaned over his shoulder.

"Yup."

"I'm just glad Isa is staying home. It's too close to the birth of our baby for her to be going out. You ladies have fun. Mark, I'm heading out." Thunder spun on his heel and left.

"Lizzy, please be careful when you go. Make sure no one spikes your drink, don't take drinks from strange men, don't leave with strange men...," –Lizzy put her hand up in front of Tori's face.

"Stop, Tori. I'm not an idiot. You're my sister, not my mom. I'll stick with the girls." Lizzy took her sister's hands, holding them between them. "I just want to go out and enjoy myself. I'm not looking for a hookup. I just want to dance."

"Okay." Tori pulled her in for a hug. "Sorry."

"Motherfuckers...ugh!" With a jolt, Mark shot from his chair, sending it spinning wildly behind him.

"What's wrong?" Maggie pulled his phone from his hand.

"Barrett and Holt both have to work tonight, so I'm the designated protector." Mark inhaled a deep breath and stared at Maggie and Lizzy. "You girls must promise me you're going to behave. It's four against one and I only have two hands."

"Come on now." Maggie rubbed Mark's arm seductively. "Who's my badass boyfriend that keeps me safe?"

Mark grimaced and pointed at his chest.

"That's right. You will protect us and kick anyone's ass that bothers us, right, Big Sexy?" Maggie winked at Mark.

"I'm so fucked." Mark closed his eyes and braced his hands on his hips.

Lizzy enjoyed watching their banter. Even though Mark looked like he was ready to throw in the towel, she could tell he would do anything to take care of them tonight. And watching him squirm was hysterical.

"All right, that's settled then." Maggie turned to Lizzy. "We'll come by and pick you and Frey up around nine. Give me your phone and I'll type in my number."

"Thanks, Maggie." Lizzy waited until Maggie gave her the phone back and stuffed it into her back pocket.

"Hey, guys." Alex came out of the restaurant. "What's going on?"

"Lizzy, Maggie, Angel, and Frey are going out tonight, and Mark is their chaperone." Tori wrapped her arms around Alex.

"Round Two, huh?" Alex raised his eyebrow at him. "Man, you're a glutton for punishment, but we appreciate you taking one for the team." Alex offered a fist bump, and Mark reluctantly returned it.

"Yeah, whatever." Mark dropped into his chair. "Why fucking me, again? What did I do to deserve this?"

"You're a great boyfriend?" Alex walked behind him and slapped his back. "Good luck with that."

"Yeah, thanks." Mark murmured.

"Baby." Alex squeezed Tori's shoulder. "I'll be ready to go in about an hour." Alex kissed her temple and left the group.

Lizzy loved to see the love between Alex and Tori. Alex was so good to her. Watching her sister's face light up, her eyes sparkling with happiness every time he touched or kissed her, filled Lizzy with overwhelming gratitude for his tender care.

"I need to finish some paperwork while Alex finishes up. Lizzy, do you want to come into the office with me?"

Lizzy watched as Maggie consoled Mark, whispering in his ear while she sat on his lap. Judging by his grin, she must have promised him anything his heart desired.

"Sure."

Lizzy followed Tori, and they worked in the office until Alex came by to get them. They always left before Maggie and Mark, who usually closed the center. Thunder usually left with them, but since Isa was nearing the end of her pregnancy, he left early if he didn't have any meetings or tours scheduled.

On their way out, Maggie reminded Lizzy to be ready by nine. She would text when she got to the resort so they could come down. Mark would be their designated driver for the night.

Lizzy couldn't wait to sift through her closet and find the cutest outfit she owned to wear for her first Girls' Night Out.

Chapter 9

The Dragon...again?

George

"Hey, Mark, what are you still doing here?" George finished dressing for work and was heading out for his shift.

"Maggie had to finish something up and I'm waiting for her."

"What are you guys up to tonight?" George bent down and pet Sky.

"The girls want to go out tonight and I'm the DD." Mark shut down his computer.

"Ah, the dipshit dumbass that gets stuck chaperoning them again," George laughed. "Didn't you learn anything from the last time?"

"It wasn't my idea, but Barrett and Holt have to work tonight, so I'm on duty."

"Uh, I hate to tell you, but Barrett isn't working tonight."

"What are you talking about?" Mark spun around and growled at George.

"I just talked to Barrett," –George pointed over his shoulder– "because Sean and I are working another beat, so we won't be around the casino if there's trouble. I just wanted to give him a heads up in case they call, and other deputies show up. He thanked me and said he was hanging out with Steele."

"Fuckers," Mark grumbled.

"Who are you cussing at now?" Maggie came up behind them.

"Did you know Barrett lied to me and he's not working tonight?" Mark braced his hands on his hips and glared at Maggie.

"How would I know that? I only talked to the girls." Maggie shrugged.

"I gotta go, but if you need backup, call Barrett." George said on his way out.

George remembered the last time the girls went out, Mark got into a fight with Maggie and the shit hit the fan when the LRs kidnapped her. Luckily for all of them, the club was disbanded, and Numbers was nowhere to be found.

George got into his patrol vehicle and logged in for work. There were some minor issues, but they were all being handled, so he patrolled his area and called his partner, Deputy Sean O'Reilly.

"Hey, man," Sean answered. "What's up?"

"Just got on. Let's hope for a quiet Saturday night."

"You just jinxed us. You know that, right?" Sean sighed.

"We'll see."

George hung up. After going through the police academy and graduating, George did three phases of ride-alongs with three different Field Training Officers. Sean was his primary FTO. He had several more years of experience and was a wealth of knowledge. They'd hit it off from day one. Once George was ready to patrol on his own, Sean had requested becoming his partner. They didn't do all their calls together, but when there was trouble, they had each other's backs.

South Florida's rush hour was a nightmare. Northbound and southbound traffic was completely congested. Cars honked, and people rushed past each other, everyone in a hurry to reach their destination. Sometimes, George would stop in the "police only access turn" on the highway and assist the Florida Highway Patrol officers by pointing his radar gun at the drivers, hoping to slow them down. Other times, he would park on the side of a busy road with his lights flashing intermittently, to prevent drivers from speeding. So many accidents happened when the driver lost control of their car. Preventing accidents and protecting his community was George's goal.

However, at other times when he was patrolling the streets—like now—he'd stop reckless drivers who were texting while driving. If that was the driver's first time being caught, George would issue only a warning, but he ensured each driver's information was in the database, including the warning and date. Florida law states that the first offense results in a $30 fine, plus court costs and fees. Subsequent offenses within five years of the previous offense results in a $60 fine, court costs, and three points on your driver's license. He wondered if the mom in the van knew the law.

George ran the plates to make sure there were no issues with the car or the driver, like expired tags, expired license, stolen car, warrant, etc. He turned on his lights and sirens and pulled the van over. Before he got out of the car, he radioed dispatch and turned on his body cam.

"Got a 10-50, getting out now." Dispatch could track their vehicles so any time an officer engaged with the community for any reason, they had to notify them of their actions.

"10-4," Dispatch answered.

Traffic stops could be dangerous because you never knew if the person had a firearm and/or hated cops. George had learned to be careful and speak to the driver in a calm voice. He didn't want to pick a fight; he wanted them to be aware of their surroundings and keep themselves and others safe on the road.

By the time George reached her window, she had already rolled it down.

"Well, hello there, officer." The woman winked at him. "What can I do for you?"

Each time someone hit on him during a traffic stop, George felt incredibly uncomfortable. Despite the many attractive women he saw, he remained professional while in uniform. Officers had to be careful not to be too flirty but remain friendly. He peeked in her van and saw she was by herself.

"Hello, ma'am." George grinned. "Do you know why I stopped you?"

"Because you wanted a date?" the woman laughed.

"Uh, no ma'am. I'm taken." George often lied so they would stop flirting with him.

"I don't see a ring?" the woman nodded to his left hand.

"I'm engaged. Ma'am, I stopped you because you were texting while driving. May I please see your license and registration?" George held out his hand.

"Of course." the woman leaned over to open her glove compartment. George took a step back and watched her movements, slowly resting his hand on his gun. Most people hid their guns in their glove compartment. Her hand came away with the documents he'd requested. "Do you want me to step out?"

"10-4." George heard the dispatcher's voice in his earpiece. Dispatch always checked in with their officers every three to five minutes to verify their safety.

George clicked the lapel mic attached to his shoulder and said, "10-4."

"No need, ma'am. I just need those documents." George pointed to her hand. The woman placed them on George's palm, sliding her fingers seductively along his. George pulled his hand back. "I'll be right back."

He double checked her information. She had a few speeding tickets, but no one had ever pulled her over for texting and driving. He entered the warning into the database and walked back to her car.

"Here you go, ma'am." George handed her the documents. "I'm giving you a warning today, assuming this is a onetime thing. Please, keep your eyes on the road and be mindful of other people. You can look at your phone when you reach your destination. This is on your record, so don't text and drive again, or you'll get a ticket and end up in court. Do you understand?"

"Thank you so much, officer. I promise I won't do it again."

George didn't believe her for a second, but he nodded anyway and headed back to his car.

"10-98, issued a warning." George radioed Dispatch from the car radio and turned off his body cam.

"10-4."

George pulled into traffic after the van and continued to patrol his area. His next traffic stop was an eighteen-year-old kid driving a beat up old El Camino. Kids from poorer backgrounds, like this one, typically drove old, unreliable cars and frequently fell behind on registration and insurance. When he looked him up, he noticed he didn't have any other infractions, other than an expired registration, and let him off with a warning. But he took the time to talk to the young man and warn him of the dangers of driving with expired information.

George did a few more traffic stops, one which resulted in a speeding ticket, before a call came in announcing a disturbance in progress at The Dragon. That place had more calls than the casino run by the Panther family. George wondered if it was another drunk patron he would have to escort out. Hopefully, this one didn't puke in the backseat of his patrol vehicle.

Chapter 10

Oops

Lizzy

Maggie and Mark picked up Frey, Angel, and Lizzy at exactly 9:00 pm and drove to The Dragon. When they entered, Mark led them to a bar and ordered their drinks. Lizzy didn't know a lot about mixed drinks, so she ordered a beer. Not wanting Tori to give her a hard time about taking a tainted drink, she watched the bartender pop open the bottle and place it in front of her.

Angel and Mark also got beers, but Maggie and Frey got Long Island Ice Teas, which Mark was none too happy about. Lizzy found out why when she asked, and he told her there were five different types of alcohol in one drink. Lizzy would've passed out before she finished the first drink.

Once everyone had their drinks and plopped Mark at a table by the dance floor, the girls went to dance while Mark watched their beverages. He looked miserable and kept giving scary stares to any man who approached them. Maggie thought it was funny and made it a point of dancing seductively in front of him. Several times, he got up and danced with her. Lizzy thought it was cute. Plus, Mark was an excellent dancer.

"Hey, baby." A brave man came up behind Angel and pulled her against his pelvic area.

"Ugh, I don't think so." Mark was instantly there, pushing him away from her.

Angel didn't even have to say a word. Lizzy thought it was great how seriously Mark took protecting them.

Then several men approached the girls all at once, and Mark had his hands full. Lizzy was laughing and having too much fun to stop the man who was grinding his groin into her ass.

"You want to get out of here?" The cute guy whispered in her ear.

"I can't." Lizzy continued to sway. "I'm with my friends and I'm new in town."

"I've lived here all my life. I can give you a tour of the town and then drive you home." His hands roamed over her body.

"Hey buddy." Mark poked a finger at the guy's shoulder. "Hands off. And stop grinding on her."

"Who are you, her father or something?" The guy pulled her even closer to him.

He wrapped both arms so tightly around her waist she could feel his hardened member at her backside.

"She's with me." Mark reached for her hand.

"Ugh, dude." The guy pulled Lizzy to the side like a rag doll. "You're with that other chick, not this one." The man kissed Lizzy's neck, and she giggled.

"I'm with all these chicks. So back the fuck off!" Mark gritted his teeth and shoved the guy.

"What the fuck, man!" The guy raised his arms up and walked away.

"Lizzy, are you okay?" Mark pulled her toward the table.

"Yeah, I'm good. We were just dancing." Lizzy felt a little tipsy from the beers. She wanted to keep dancing and hydrate with something other than alcohol. "I'm gonna get a glass of water."

"Stay here and stay away from that guy. He wanted more from you than just dancing." Mark grabbed her and sat her down on a stool. "I'll get it."

Right after Mark left, the cute guy from the dance floor came back with two cups, setting one in front of her.

"Hey, baby, I got you a beer."

"I'm gonna switch to water, but thanks," Lizzy smiled.

"Aww, come on. I got this just for you. I'm Neil," Neil stuck out his hand. "What's your name, beautiful?"

Lizzy shook his hand while he looked at her with puppy-dog eyes. He was so cute and sweet to get her a nice cold drink. She would take a few sips and then switch to water as soon as Mark got back. Lizzy took a tiny sip. When she tasted nothing weird, she swallowed a couple gulps.

"I'm Lizzy. It's nice to meet you." Lizzy was so hot from dancing she took a couple more gulps.

"Lizzy, what are you doing?" Maggie pulled the beer away from her lips.

"I'm talking to my friend Neil." Lizzy pointed to him. "Neil, this is my friend, Maggie."

"Uh, hi Maggie." Neil murmured and nodded toward someone behind Lizzy's shoulder.

Lizzy turned her head to see who Neil was signaling, but it must've been too fast because she lost her balance and reached for the table so she wouldn't fall. Her head felt woozy, and she saw double images of everyone around her, especially Maggie. The DJ's music sounded like it was coming from a long tunnel. She must have drunk too much at once.

"Neil, I don't feel so good." Lizzy swayed. "And I'm really tired." Neil caught her before she fell.

"I'll take you home." Neil draped her arm around his neck and pulled her toward his body.

"Oh, hell no!" Maggie blocked their path.

"What the fuck are you doing?" Mark pulled Lizzy away from Neil. "I fucking told you to leave her alone."

"Hey, Mark." Lizzy looked at Mark, but he was blurring in and out of her vision. "It's okay. Neil got me a drink because I was thirsty. Wasn't that nice of him?"

"You fucking bastard!" Maggie hollered and slapped Neil in the face. "Did you roofie her?"

"Neil wouldn't do that." Lizzy's words sounded garbled. Her mouth didn't seem to want to work. That had never happened before.

Lizzy watched Maggie face off with Neil, but then two of his friends stood next to him. Or was it one because now there were two Neils? *Did he have a twin?*

Chapter 11

Saturday Night Rescue

George

George and Sean headed to The Dragon with their lights and sirens blaring. Saturday night traffic was no joke, and by the sounds of dispatch, they needed to get there in a hurry before a fight broke out. They were the closest to the call and pulled in within five minutes.

Carmine was already waiting for him at the door.

"Hey, Deputy George. I'd say it's nice to see you, but not under these circumstances." Carmine said wryly.

"I get that." George nodded. "What happened?"

"A guy tried to roofie a girl, but he's denying it and trying to leave. The girl was with her friends, and they are not allowing him or his friend to leave the bar. I'm actually quite shocked the roofied girl's friend hasn't beat the shit out of the guy. I mean, she already slapped him once. She's fucking scary. Dave moved everyone involved by the back bar. Follow me."

George and Sean followed Carmine. As George approached the group with the bouncers, he heard Maggie's voice before he saw her.

"Is that Maggie?" Sean sounded confused.

"Yup. I knew the girls were going out, but I'd hoped Mark would handle the situation without us. Then again, drugging someone is a little different from hitting on them."

"Dude, she is all wound up." Sean smirked.

George could see Maggie screaming and pointing her finger in a man's face while Mark wrapped his arms around her, pulling her back from the guy. *Where were Angel, Frey, and Lizzy? Had they already gone home?*

"Yup, tread lightly, my friend," George murmured before they reached the group. As they weaved in and out of the crowd, they could hear the bouncers saying, 'Everything's alright. Go back to your fun. Nothing to see here. It's all under control.' Unfortunately, crowds love a good bar fight. No one was listening to the bouncers. Instead of moving away, they were pushing closer to Maggie as they sipped their drinks and waved their phones overhead, trying to record the action. Sometimes, George hated social media.

"I'll take care of the crowd. You go see what's going on." Sean stepped between the bouncers and the patrons. "Alright everybody put your phones away and go back to the dance floor or the bar. We got this."

George grinned because most of them weren't listening to Sean either. They were going to have to grab the suspect who tried to roofie the girl and take him outside if they wanted to diffuse the situation. After breaking through the bouncer defense line, because that's exactly what it looked like, George saw Dave helping Angel with a girl who could barely stand. *Was that Lizzy?* George immediately called dispatch.

"Dispatch, we need more backup and an ambulance at The Dragon ASAP."

"Backup is on the way. Ambulance is five minutes out."

"Thanks." George wanted to go help Lizzy, but he had to diffuse the situation with Maggie. Standing between Maggie and the guy she was yelling at, he said. "Maggie, calm down. What's going on?" He'd already gotten the run down from Carmine, but he wanted to hear it from the witnesses.

"That asshole, Neil." Maggie pointed over George's shoulder. "Roofied Lizzy." Maggie then pointed at Lizzy. "Look at her. She can barely stand. He put it in the cup of beer he offered her."

"No, I didn't. Step aside so I can go home." Neil looked nervous as he glanced at his friend and tried to go around Maggie.

George turned around and grabbed each of their arms. "Whoa, there guys. You're not going anywhere unless it's with me." Then he glanced at Maggie. "Where's the cup?" He could get forensics to see if there was any trace of the substance if he had the cup.

Angel lifted her hand with a napkin wrapped around the cup. "I made sure no one else touched it."

George smiled. Leave it to a lawyer to keep the evidence safe.

"Carmine, Sean," George hollered to them. "Take these two suspects and escort them outside." George shoved them toward Carmine and Sean. "Mark and Dave help Lizzy outside. The ambulance should be here shortly. Maggie, you stay with me. I don't trust you to not to kill those two idiots."

George pulled out gloves and put them on before he grabbed the beer cup. "Angel, Frey, where are the guys?"

Frey spoke up first. "I texted them when Maggie confronted the asshole. Barrett and Holt are on their way to get us."

"Great." George pointed over his head toward the door. "Let's go."

Several bouncers cleared a path for them to walk through. To George, it looked like the parting of the Red Sea except with cell phones. *Why did everyone now feel the need to record everything, even when it had nothing to do with them?* Then again, sometimes, they could get those phones for video confirmation. It was a too-way street. Social media has both advantages and disadvantages. George hurried to his car for a plastic evidence bag that could hold the cup and the liquid.

After sealing it and gently placing it in his trunk, he saw the ambulance pull up. George motioned for the paramedics to hurry because it looked like Lizzy had passed out. *Fuck!* If Dave and Mark hadn't been holding her, she'd be on the floor like a limp noodle. George rushed to her.

"I got this." George put his arm under her legs and picked her up like a passed out bride.

The paramedics wheeled the gurney toward him, and he set her down gently.

"Witnesses say she was roofied. She just recently lost consciousness." George walked with them to the ambulance.

"Got it." The paramedics were taking Lizzy's vitals, but she was unresponsive. "We gotta go, now."

"Where are you taking her?" George dropped his hand from the gurney when they quickly rolled it into the ambulance.

"Sunrise General!" one of them screamed before he slammed the door shut and the ambulance hauled ass to the hospital.

"What the hell happened?" Barrett came storming up to Mark with Alex.

"Where's Holt?" Frey looked behind him.

"We had a minor incident with some cheating, and he stayed behind." Barrett pointed to Alex. "I brought Alex."

"Tori is pissed as shit at me because I didn't let her come, but I wasn't sure if this had anything to do with the LRs." Alex turned to Maggie. "What the hell happened?"

"It wasn't the LRs." Maggie spun around and pointed to Neil. "That asshole drugged her. Go get Tori and meet us at the Sunrise General Hospital. That's where the ambulance is taking her."

"Fuck!" Alex screamed and ran his hands over his head. "How the hell did that fucker drug her?"

George heard them as he walked toward Sean, who was cuffing Neil. Maggie had it under control. They didn't need him there. What he needed to do was arrest Neil's friend and follow Sean to sally port to drop them off so he could go check on Lizzy. Both men were rambling about being innocent, accusing the crazy lady of making up stories just to get them in trouble. George ignored them. Stupid idiots needed to make smarter choices.

"I'll meet you guys at Sunrise General after we drop these two off." George hollered to his friends before he pulled Neil's friend to his car. Sean already had Neil half in and half out of the backseat of his patrol vehicle.

"What's your name?"

"Kevin."

George read him his Miranda Rights but before he could finish, Kevin interrupted him.

"I didn't do anything. I'm not sure why that crazy lady didn't let me leave."

George finished giving him his rights and pulled the back door open. "Talk to the officers in central booking."

"This sucks," Kevin grumbled. "I'm innocent!"

Suspects routinely deny the charges against them. That's nothing new. The law states everyone is innocent until proven guilty, guaranteeing a day in court to defend themselves. Kevin would get his day. George's job was to bring Kevin in, drop him off at sally port, and deliver the evidence to forensics. The detectives would take over from there.

"You better hope you boys didn't give her too much because if she dies, your charges go from a second-degree felony to a first-degree felony." George said before driving off. Disgusted with Kevin and Neil. Anyone who felt the need to overpower someone else with drugs was the scum of the earth with no morals. He couldn't wait to get this predator out of his car.

He pulled up to sally port, and an officer got Kevin out. George thanked him and drove to the sheriff's forensics lab. After handing over the evidence, he could finally drive to the hospital. He needed to check on Lizzy. She had to be okay. He still had a lot of things to say to her.

"Dispatch, I'm headed to the hospital to follow up on the victim from the date-rape drug. See if I can gather any further info for the detectives."

"10-4. SVU is on their way."

"10-4."

George was determined to find out how that moron tricked Lizzy into drinking that beer. *Why the hell was she taking a drink from a stranger? That was Bar Drinking 101 for girls. Clearly, she skipped that class.* He didn't want to interfere with the SVU detectives, but he wanted to support her.

Chapter 12

At the Hospital

Lizzy cracked her eyes open slowly. The bright light in the room intensified the pain in her head, each pulse like a hammer blow threatening to shatter her skull. The sterile smell of antiseptic filled the air as she lay in the hospital bed, surrounded by her sister and concerned friends. *Why were they talking so loud?* She wanted everyone to be quiet so she could sleep.

"You're awake." Tori ran to her bedside and grabbed her hand.

"Yes, and you guys need to stop yelling," Lizzy grumbled. "Why am I in the hospital and why is there an IV in my arm?"

"Someone put the date-rape drug in your drink."

"Yeah, Asshole Neil!" Maggie shouted.

"Easy, Nikita." Mark wrapped his arm around her waist and pulled her back against him.

"Maggie," Tori reprimanded her. "She has a headache. Can everyone keep it down?"

"Sorry," Maggie murmured.

"Hey, Lizzy." Deputy George stepped to the other side of the bed with a well-dressed couple in suits. "These are Detectives Leslie McCann and Tom Sylvester with our Special Victims Unit. They need to ask you a few questions."

Lizzy shook their hands as they introduced themselves to her.

"Let me know if you want to sue his ass." Angel stepped up to the end of Lizzy's bed. "I'll nail him to the wall."

"Okay, Tiger, let the nice detectives get all their questions answered. Then you can do your lawyering shit." Barrett draped an arm over her shoulder.

Angel humphed, "that weaselly asshole."

Lizzy's gaze was jumping around the room, settling on George before the female, Detective McCann, began her questions.

"Hi, Lizzy, you can call me Leslie." She had a kind smile. "Can you tell me what happened?"

Deputy Sylvester waited beside Leslie, poised with his notepad and pen, ready to take down her details. Lizzy glanced at George again and he nodded.

"I...I was dancing and got thirsty. Since I'd already had several beers...,"
–Leslie interrupted, "how many is several?" –Lizzy continued, "maybe two?"

"Ahem," Mark cleared his throat. "Three beers and one shot."

Maggie smacked his shoulder. "She wasn't drunk because she was dancing the entire night!"

"I never said she was." Mark held up his hands in surrender.

"Okay," Leslie ignored Maggie and Mark as they argued behind her. "Then what happened?"

"I was thirsty, and Mark," –Lizzy pointed to Mark who stopped arguing with Maggie long enough to raise his hand, "–said he would get me some water, but Neil, the cute guy I'd just met, came by after Mark left and placed a cup of beer in front of me. He said he'd just bought it for me because I looked thirsty. I felt bad not taking it since he'd spent money on it. I know I shouldn't have taken it, but I took a sip and tasted nothing strange."

Tori opened her mouth to say something, but Lizzy's eyes pleaded with her not to yell at her here in front of everyone. "I'm so stupid. But I was really thirsty, and he was so nice. I honestly didn't think he would drug me."

"You are not stupid. No one ever thinks it will happen to them." Leslie sat on the edge of her bed and held Lizzy's hand. "The men that prey on women with these drugs are cowards. You are not the first, nor will you be the last to fall for their tricks. Really, the only way to avoid getting drugged is to not drink at a bar or bring your own water that you don't let out of your sight. But no one really does that. Anyway, these drugs are colorless, odorless, and tasteless, which explains why you noticed nothing strange in your drink."

Lizzy nodded and dropped her head down as tears streamed down her face. *How had this happened to both her and her sister?*

"Hey." Leslie squeezed her hand. "Now you know, so you can be more careful. We will get these two for what they did to you. In the grand scheme of things, you are very lucky to have had your friends with you. Some girls are alone and suffer worse consequences."

Lizzy glanced at Tori and saw her body stiffen before she turned her attention back to Leslie.

"Do you remember how much you drank?" Detective Sylvester looked up from his pad. "A sip, two sips, gulps, half the beer?"

Lizzy chanced a glance at George. He was frowning at her with a piercing gaze. *Were his eyes flashing with disapproval, disgust, or disappointment?* "George, don't look at me like that. I only took a couple of big sips."

George's expression softened. "I'm not judging you. I'm worried about you, and mad as hell that they did that to you."

"I pulled the cup away from her mouth when I saw what was happening and confronted Neil," Maggie interjected.

"What happened next?" Leslie searched Lizzy's eyes for the truth.

"My vision blurred, and it sounded like I was in a tunnel. I wasn't steady on my feet and my words didn't sound right."

"She almost fell, and that asshole caught her." Maggie nodded. "That's when Mark, my fiancée, came back from the bar with her water. Neil and his buddy wanted to leave, but I wouldn't let them. No one." Maggie pointed her finger at the floor and stomped her foot. "And I mean no one...drugs my friend and gets away with it."

"You go, Punisher." Mark grinned and kissed Maggie's temple.

"Thank you, Maggie." Lizzy wiped her eyes and gave Maggie a crooked smile. If Maggie hadn't been there, she was sure Neil would have whisked her away. Then she would've been in the same boat as Tori had been with Winston. *How could she have been so stupid?* Tori would never let her out of her sight again. Oh, and her parents were going to kill her.

"You're lucky to have such a good friend looking out for you." Leslie stood.

"Lizzy, it's going to be okay." Tori placed her hand on her shoulder and squeezed.

Having her sister's support meant the world to her. Lizzy looked at her and nodded.

"Neil and his friend Kevin are at the station. Did anything else happen to you? Anything else you need to tell us? I can have everyone leave the room if you need privacy." Leslie asked softly.

"No." Lizzy shook her head. "My friends saved me and I'm okay, thanks to them. Maggie and Mark kept them there until George arrived with Sean...sorry Deputy George and Deputy Sean."

"No problem. We'll talk to George and Sean outside and then go to the station. If we need you, we'll call you." Leslie handed Lizzy her business card. "In the meantime, if you remember anything else or want to talk, call me."

Lizzy took the card. "Thank you, Leslie."

"You're welcome, Lizzy," Leslie smiled. "I'm glad you're okay."

"Yeah, me too." Lizzy placed the card on the food tray after the detectives left.

"Wow," came a woman's voice from the doorway. "Full house in here."

Lizzy leaned forward, looking around Tori and saw a nurse heading her way. "Sorry."

"No need to be sorry, honey. It just means you are well loved." The nurse walked toward the IV. "Unfortunately, I need them all to leave because you need to get dressed since you are free to go home."

"Can my sister stay with me?" Lizzy didn't want to be alone.

"Of course." The nurse glanced around. "Who's the sis?"

"I am." Tori smiled and held up her hand.

"Who is driving you ladies home?" the nurse addressed Tori, but Alex answered.

"I am."

"Perfect. If all of you can step outside, I'll tell you where you need to go. I'll bring her down to you."

"Sounds good. Thank you, ma'am." Alex nodded.

Lizzy saw George's hand move toward her hand, but then it stopped, and he pulled it back into his pocket. George cleared his throat and said, "I gotta get back to work, but call me if you need anything."

"Thank you." Lizzy nodded.

"We'll see you at home." Angel came over and gave her a side hug, then whispered, "I'll help you anyway I can."

"Mark and I are heading home too, but I'll call you tomorrow," Maggie grinned, and they left.

"You have some caring friends." The nurse disconnected the IV.

"They're actually her friends." Lizzy pointed to Tori.

"I think they're your friends, too. Stay here. I need to get a wheelchair. Every patient that leaves our hospital is required to be escorted in a wheelchair to their vehicle. It's our special form of door-to-door service. I'll be right back."

Lizzy waited until the nurse left before she spoke with Tori.

"Thank you for not yelling at me in front of everyone. I know what I did was stupid." Frustration burned in her gut, a bitter taste mirroring the careless choice that had undone all her previous efforts to drink responsibly. "I had been so careful. I can't believe I fell for a cute guy." Her shoulders slumped, the unspoken weight of her sister's disapproval pressing down like a heavy cloak. "I'm so sorry." Lizzy whispered.

"Hey." Tori lifted her chin. "It's gonna be okay. At least you were with friends, and you are safe. Just please, if you go out again, don't do that. Just cause they're cute doesn't mean they're not evil. You took several years off my life with that stunt." Tori smirked. "I'm not mad at you. How could I be? The same thing happened to me, but worse. I love you."

"Are you going to tell mom and dad?" Lizzy crossed her fingers. Please say no, please say no.

"I'm not sure yet. I know I should, but I love having you here and if I tell them, they will make you leave. So, I think for now, I'll keep it to myself. But you must promise me not to do that again. No drinks from strangers."

"Okay." Lizzy nodded. "I promise."

"All right ladies, let's do this." The nurse came in with the wheelchair.

Lizzy felt ridiculous because she was steady on her feet, but rules were rules, and she wasn't about to argue and give Tori a reason to be mad at her again. She loved her sister. Her opinion mattered. Right now, she just wanted to get to the resort and surround herself with her sister and their friends.

Chapter 13

Couple of Fuckups

Numbers

"What do you mean, the boys got caught and arrested?" Numbers yelled at Red.

"Sorry, prez." Red shrugged.

"Don't call me prez," Numbers growled at him. "Reaper is your prez, not me."

The last thing Number needed was for Red to get used to calling him prez. If Reaper found out, Numbers would be dead.

"How hard was it to give the drug to those two assholes and have them drug that sweet, young thing?" Numbers drank his beer and stared at Red.

"I didn't think it would be that hard, but they fucked up. Neil had her until Maggie blocked him from leaving. His friend Kevin panicked and stayed with him. Maggie and her crew kept them there until the police arrived.

"Fucking Maggie. She's a pain in my ass." Numbers slammed his fist on the bar. "Fuck, I need to kill that bitch!"

"Do you think Neil and Kevin will rat us out?" Red sat on the stool next to Numbers.

"I'm sure they will. Those two preppy ass boys wouldn't survive a night in jail. They'll sing like canaries."

"What should we do?"

"Stay away from those two idiots in case the police are watching them." Numbers finished his beer. "You'll need to keep spying on Maggie and Tori until we come up with another plan."

"Okay." Red nodded.

Chapter 14

Early Morning Wake Up Call

"Lizzy!"

Lizzy woke up to Tori shaking her awake. "What time is it?"

"Time to get up. I need you to go to the store and pick up some Easter themed items. They're open twenty-four hours. I meant to go last weekend or after work and totally forgot. I want to have them for today's Sunday Family Brunch."

"After last night, you're going to let me go out on my own?"

"Well, it's not like you're going to a bar, right?"

Wow, Lizzy didn't expect Tori to be so snarky that early in the morning. "No, I'm not going to a bar. I wasn't even awake." Lizzy sat up and rubbed her eyes. "How did you get in here, anyway?"

"Alex has a master key card. All the Panther's do." Tori pulled Lizzy up off the bed. "Hurry, I need it soon to decorate."

"Why don't you go?" Lizzy grumbled. It was bad enough she had to get up early, but she also had to find a store, buy stuff, and be back quick. They had flushed the drugs out of her system last night, but her body still wanted to sleep.

"I can't. I usually help Sehoy and Alex in the kitchen." Tori shoved her into the bathroom. "Please, hurry. I don't want to disappoint my mother-in-law. I need it in an hour so I can set the table."

"Fine. But for the record, you have a nice mother-in-law that would never be mad at you about that." Lizzy turned around and slapped Tori's hands off her. "I'll take a quick shower and go. How am I supposed to pay for your stuff?"

"I'll put my credit card next to your purse."

Lizzy stepped into the shower. It felt good to have a hot shower. At home, the water ran lukewarm. Out of the corner of her eye, Lizzy saw Tori's hand on the hot water knob. "Oh, shit!" Lizzy screamed when the water turned ice cold. "Tori, what the hell?"

"Stop cussing and hurry. We don't have time for you to take a leisurely shower."

"I don't know why everyone says you are the nice one." Lizzy turned the water hot again. "I was fucking drugged last night. Cut me some slack!" Lizzy wasn't sure Tori heard her, but she was pissed. She took a quick shower in case Tori returned and messed with the hot water again.

"I am nice."

"Ha!" Lizzy screamed. "Yeah, right?"

"I took care of you yesterday, didn't I?"

"Yeah, but today, you're acting like my drill sergeant. No sympathy whatsoever for what I went through yesterday." Lizzy felt relieved that she and Tori were back to their usual teasing. Their banter was better than Tori's pity or disappointment in her. Everything was going to be okay. Lizzy pushed the shower curtain aside. Tori was standing in the bathroom holding her towel, watching for any signs of distress.

"I'm good. Thank you for yesterday. You are the best sister ever."

Tori wrapped the towel around her and gave her a big hug. "No, you are the best sister ever. I love you."

"I love you too." Lizzy stepped out of the tub and cleared her throat. Time to turn this discussion back to normal. "You can leave. I'm not gonna go back to bed, especially after that cold shower." Lizzy rolled her eyes. "Thanks for that. By the way, how do I get to that store?"

"I'll text you the address. You can take Alex's truck. Oh, and when you get back, bring the decorations to Savor, the high-end restaurant in the lobby. I'll be in the kitchen. Then you can help me decorate." Tori left the bathroom.

"Bossy. I thought I left bossy when I left mom and dad's house. Guess Not," Lizzy mumbled to herself.

After Lizzy dressed, she grabbed the keys and credit card that were left by her purse on the foyer table. To avoid Tori and further shopping requests, Lizzy took the elevator and hurried out the lobby's side door.

In her hurry, she realized after she pulled out of the parking lot she had left her phone on the nightstand. *Shit! How the hell was she supposed to find a store in a town she didn't know?* She could run back in, but then Tori might see her and think she was irresponsible. No, no negative thoughts. She could do this. Lizzy assumed getting on a main road would surely lead to a store where she could buy Easter stuff. After all, today was Easter and all their merchandise would be on sale.

Shame on Tori for not getting this stuff sooner. Lizzy knew she worked hard helping Alex at the cultural center and the resort, but couldn't they separate for an hour for her to go shopping? Lizzy loved Alex but didn't think she could handle a man that was always attached to her every hour of every day. He wasn't possessive, and she knew Tori had girls' nights out, but on a day-to-day basis, since they worked together, you rarely saw one without the other.

Lizzy couldn't find the type of store she was looking for, and she'd been driving for about twenty minutes. Did she not notice a store, or was her daydreaming preventing her from paying attention to her surroundings? That happened more often than she realized. She needed to find something fast. Driving around aimlessly was not helping. Making a u-turn at the next light, she went back the way she came. She had to come up with a better plan than just driving around until she found a store that sold decorations.

The only place she knew how to get to from the resort was the cultural center. So she drove all the way back to the resort and then headed to AICC. She remembered Tori telling her that George lived upstairs above the kitchen. Since George was a cop, he would know where to go and how to get there. Besides, she needed to thank him for helping her out last night at The Dragon.

Chapter 15

George to the Rescue

Lizzy quickly parked and got out of her car. Running up to the door, she banged and hollered, "George!"

Tori had a key, but she didn't. When he didn't come, she ran to the two windows above the restaurant, cupped her hands, and screamed his name at the top of her lungs. Still no George.

"Oh, for goodness' sakes." Lizzy ran back to the door and banged some more. Finally, she saw a shirtless George with his unbuttoned jeans running to the door with a gun in his hand.

"What the hell, Lizzy?" George stepped out and looked up and down the street. "Are you okay? Was someone following you?"

"No."

"Then why are you here screaming bloody murder?" George tucked the gun in the back of his jeans and opened the door wide enough for her to walk through. "Are you ready to talk to me?"

"Not now." Lizzy pushed past him. "What took you so long?"

"I was sleeping. My shift ended at 5:00 am this morning." George locked the door and faced her with his hands on his waist. "Why are you here? I would've thought you'd be resting after everything that happened yesterday."

"Yeah, well, so did I until Tori woke me up and dragged me out of bed. I need your help."

"Now?" George ran his hands over his face. "What's going on? Did something happen after last night?"

"Yes, I need your help now and no, nothing happened after I went home. I need to get some party supplies for Tori, but I left my phone on my nightstand and don't have the address. I don't know my way around here, so please, you gotta help me. Tori will kill me if I show up at the resort without Easter stuff."

"Are you fucking serious?" George stared at her like she had two heads.

"Yes, I'm serious. I'm standing here, aren't I?"

"Fine, I'll help you, but I seriously doubt Tori will kill you," George sighed. "She is the nicest person...,"

"You know." Lizzy interrupted him. "Yeah, yeah, yeah, that's what everyone says, and she was great last night, but now that we're back to our normal sister routine, she can be mean and bossy."

"Right," George gave her a look of disbelief. "Let me shower and I'll take you. Follow me. I don't want you sitting down here by yourself."

Lizzy followed. "Thank you so much. I really appreciate this."

"How did you get here?" George started climbing the stairs.

"I have Alex's truck and Tori's credit card." Lizzy had seen that door while she was in the kitchen these past couple of days, but didn't know what was behind it. Alex told her there was a stairway that led to an apartment where George was staying, but she hadn't been up there. The door to the apartment was open. George must have been in a hurry. She followed him into a small apartment.

"Have a seat." George pointed to the table for two across from the kitchen. "I'll be quick."

"Thanks." Lizzy waited until George shut the bathroom door before she started snooping. Between the kitchen table and the bathroom was a stackable washer/dryer. She took a couple of steps into the kitchen and opened drawers and cabinets. It was simple, but had everything one would need; coffee pot, oven with stove top, microwave, sink, and fridge.

To the right of the kitchen was a nightstand and a bed, the only other place to sit. She imagined what George would do if he walked out of the bathroom and saw her naked on his bed. He wouldn't be mad at her then. Unfortunately, she needed to get back to the resort and couldn't afford to waste time. Staring at the bed, she sighed. Sex with George had been quick, but exhilarating. She would love to take her time to explore his sexy body and rock-hard abs. That thought was going to get her in trouble.

Shaking her head to release her thoughts, she glanced at the foot of the bed and saw a bookshelf with Native American artifacts. Lizzy grabbed the statue of an Indian riding a horse and pointing forward as they burst out of a mountain. A Lakota elder, Henry Standing Bear, commissioned Korczak Ziolkowski to carve a mountain depicting the Oglala warrior Crazy Horse riding a horse and pointing to his tribal land. The Crazy Horse Memorial was in the Black Hills of South Dakota. Upon completion, that memorial was going to be the largest mountain carving in the world, even larger than Mount Rushmore, and serve as a tribe to Native American history and culture. A small museum at the mountain's base offered tourists insights into the remarkable statue. Sadly, it would take years to complete.

Lizzy wasn't shocked to see the miniature version of the statue, but wondered why George had it in his apartment. Why wasn't it in the museum downstairs?

"Give me a minute to get dressed and we'll go."

George's deep voice startled her. She fumbled with it until George's hands came around her to hold her hands steady.

"Whoa, don't drop that." George was so close she could feel his minty breath on the side of her face. "I begged Thunder to buy it and bring it to me after his honeymoon when they made a trip to South Dakota."

They jointly placed it back on the shelf.

"So, it's yours?" Lizzy said breathlessly. Having George near her was making her heart race and her brain turn to mush. Lizzy turned her head and smelled his earthy scented cologne. Wow...just wow.

"That's what I just said." George chuckled and took a couple of steps back. "Are you okay? Were you sniffing me?"

"Uh, no." Lizzy straightened her back and glared at him. "I wasn't sniffing you and yes, I'm fine. Can we go now?"

George pointed to the towel riding low on his waist. "I don't think I'm dressed for a shopping expedition with you. Give me a minute."

Lizzy couldn't help but watch a drop of water that ran down his chest past his happy trail and slipped under the knot on the towel. Suddenly feeling very thirsty, she wet her lips and stared at the knot, hoping it would unravel and let her see his goods. When they had sex, it had been dark and she couldn't see him fully. She remembered his thick, smooth cock throbbing in her hand as it grew long and hard. When she tasted him, it was a mixture of explosive flavors she'd never tasted before, but she liked them. And when she eased him down into her throat, he didn't fit all the way. She knew how he felt to the touch, but wanted to see him fully aroused with her eyes.

Hearing his chuckle broke her out of her daze. She could feel her face heating in embarrassment, so she quickly averted her stare and turned toward the other sculptures on the bookshelf. The last thing she needed was to become one of his groupies.

"Okay, let's go. But we need to talk."

Lizzy spun around and saw George fully dressed in a t-shirt and sweatpants. Damn, he was fast. Or had she been daydreaming again? She loved seeing him in his uniform or in a towel.

"Not now, we don't. Are you working today? Why aren't you wearing your uniform?"

"My shift doesn't start until five. I want to get a workout in before work. The Panthers let me use their gym at the resort and I figured since I have to take you there after our shopping spree, I may as well use it then." George opened the door and motioned for her to exit.

"When do you get off work if you start at five?" Lizzy walked down the stairs and waited for George at the bottom.

"I get off at five tomorrow morning."

"You work a twelve-hour shift? Did you go back to work after you left the hospital?" Lizzy never knew officers worked such long hours.

"Yep. That's why I was sleeping when you banged on my door." George reset the alarm and locked up.

"I'm sorry. I didn't know," Lizzy winced. She felt horrible for waking him up only four hours after he got off shift.

"Let's take Alex's truck. I can always get a ride back from someone there. Give me the keys." George held his hand out.

"I don't think so." Lizzy pulled her hand back. "Tori said I could drive, not you."

"In her defense, she didn't know you would get my ass out of bed to take you to the store."

"True, but I'm driving." Lizzy headed to the driver's door.

"Fine. I'll tell you where to turn." George opened the door for her and shut it after she got in before he got in the passenger side and buckled in. "When you pull out, go to the right."

Lizzy smiled at him.

"Why are you just sitting there smiling at me?" George squinted at her.

"Because chivalry isn't dead."

"You've never had a man open a car door for you?"

"Nope."

"Then you've been dating the wrong men," George grumbled.

The trip went smooth. George was a skilled navigator and, with him being a cop, he knew many side roads which made the trip quicker. At the store, they bought all the Easter decorations they could find, which weren't much since Fourth of July stuff was already on the shelves. But Lizzy thought the tables would look cute with the items she found.

When they got back to the resort, George carried the bags to Savor for her.

"Hey." Tori ran up to her. "What took you so long? George, it's good to see you, but what are you doing here?"

"I left my phone here and got lost, so I drove to the cultural center to get George." Lizzy pointed at George, who was holding the bags out for Tori. "He helped me find the store and get some things."

Tori gave George a quick hug before grabbing the bags. "Thank you. But don't you work tonight?"

"I do." George smiled.

"I'm so sorry Lizzy woke you up." Tori glared at Lizzy before shifting her eyes to George. "Stay with us and eat brunch. Let us repay you with food."

"I can't pass that up. I'd love to," George replied.

"Lizzy, come help me put all this stuff out." Tori peeked in the bags before she carried them to the long table already set with plates, glasses, and silverware.

"How long until brunch?" George asked Tori. "I was gonna go upstairs and get a quick workout in."

"Forty-five minutes, give or take." Tori took items out of the bags.

"Sounds good. I'll be back."

George turned to leave, but Lizzy grabbed his forearm and whispered, "Thank you."

"Anytime." George smiled that panty dropping smile of his and Lizzy immediately felt the need to cross her legs from the throbbing down under. That man was gorgeous.

Chapter 16

The Boys and Their Gym

George

George stepped into the gym and saw Barrett spotting Steele on the weight bench and Holt running on the treadmill.

"Hey, man," Barrett glanced his way. "What are you doing here?"

"You said I could come work out anytime I wanted, right?" George walked to the free weights.

"I did, but you usually come later in the day or early morning when you work the night shift." Barrett helped Steele raise the weight bar off his chest and placed it in the rack.

"I helped Lizzy pick up some decorations for today's Easter Brunch and Tori invited me to stay. Figured I'd get a workout in before the food was ready. Nothing too strenuous, since I don't want to stink up the brunch table."

"I can loan you some clothes if you want to shower." Barrett added more weight and laid on the bench ready for his reps.

"If I get too sweaty, I might take you up on that." George finished his curls and got on the floor ready for push-ups, burpees, and sit-ups.

"Hey, when did you get here?" Holt got off, pulled out his earbuds, and stood over him.

"When you were sissy jogging," George grinned on his way back down for his burpee push up. These guys loved to mess with him. George called it a win when he threw the first shot. They all knew George was joking because Holt had been at a full run on the treadmill.

"Fucker," he mumbled low so Steele wouldn't hear him and dropped next to George to do burpees.

"What are you guys doing?" Steele stared at them.

"Trying to see who has the biggest di...er, ego," Barrett winced.

"You were about to say dick, weren't you?" Steele grinned at Barrett.

"Yeah," Barrett sighed. "Don't tell your mom."

George laughed. They were always trying to clean up their language in front of Steele, even though Steele had been around a motorcycle club all his life. Hell, he even lived at the clubhouse for a while not too long ago. George was sure he'd heard it all. But for Angel, they tried because she never wanted that lifestyle for Steele, even though his deceased father was a member.

"Anyway, they're doing burpees." Barrett carefully removed the extra weights from the bar.

"They look hard." Steele stared at them before glancing at Barrett. "How many can you do?"

"Yeah, Barrett, how many can you do?" Holt egged him on.

George didn't have to say a word because those two challenged each other daily.

"I can do as many as them, probably more. Burpees are hard but considered to be a full-body workout because they engage multiple muscle groups throughout the body. A burpee combines elements of a squat, jump, push-up, and stand, working the legs, hips, buttocks, abdomen, arms, chest, and shoulders. They are also effective for burning calories and improving cardiovascular fitness."

"Okay, google, get your ass down here and prove that you can do as many if not more than us," Holt taunted. "We're up to 20...you're behind."

"You want to try. I'll show you." Barrett and Steele walked to the other side of the gym for some space while Barrett showed Steele what to do.

George could see them out of the corner of his eye, but he wasn't about to stop because if he stopped, Holt would beat him, and he'd never hear the end of it.

"You're slowing down, old man." George teased Holt.

"You're younger, you little shit," Holt said through gritted teeth.

"I'll stop whenever you're ready. Don't want you to have a heart attack."

"You know, I used to like you." Holt glared at him.

"I know and now you love me like a brother." George slapped his shoulder when they were both upright. "Less talk and more action."

"Fuck! That's fifty." Holt stopped and walked around, taking deep breaths to calm his heart rate. "Are you even breathing heavy?"

"Yeah, but not as heavy as you." George did two more just to rub it in. "Fifty-two. Now for my real workout." George grabbed a towel.

"Fucker, I'm gonna go shower. Brunch will be ready soon." Holt high-fived George and left.

George was not doing more burpees. Those fucking fifty-two burpees just about killed him. But he'd be damned if he let Holt know. Steele was on his tenth one and was slowing down. Barrett was still going. George knew he would try to do at least one more than him.

"So, Barrett, I'm gonna need a shower. Whose shower can I use?" George wiped his face and draped the towel over his shoulders. "I'll be quick, I promise."

"Text Alex and let him know you're using his. They're both downstairs, anyway. Do you have your card?"

"Not on me. I left in such a hurry because Lizzy had to get back here quick with the decorations, I didn't grab it. Hell, I still gotta go home to put on my uniform before I go to work."

Steele was lying on his back, panting.

"Steele, since you're done, can you get George a t-shirt and sweatpants from my room?"

"Sure," Steele grunted and stood. "I'll get mom to find something for you, Deputy George." Steele headed toward the exit.

George stopped and turned. "What number you on?" he asked before leaving.

"Forty-five," Barrett grunted.

"Maybe you should stop before you hurt yourself."

"Fuck you, I'm going to sixty."

"Don't make me call an ambulance for you," George snickered.

"Get the fuck out. I'll see you at brunch."

"Do you guys always tease each other like that?" Steele asked when they left the gym.

"Yeah," George chuckled. "They've done it for years. I'm new to it."

"How did you meet them?"

"Remember Thunder." George waited for Steele's nod. "You know the shelter boys he helps?"

"Yeah, that's where Bryce is from."

"Yep, Holt and Frey adopted him a few months back. I wasn't so lucky. My mom and dad were high and drunk when they wrapped their car around a tree one night and died." George assumed that's why Thunder had taken him under his wing since he also lost his parents in a car accident. Although Thunder's parents weren't drunk, they had a head on collision with a drunk teen.

"Is that when you went to the shelter?" Steele stopped in front of Barrett's door..

"Nah, I wish. I was only six, like Bryce when my parents died. They tried to put me in foster care homes, but I never clicked with any of the parents. They always said I had too much energy and a smart mouth. Their way of disciplining me was to either beat or starve me. So, after the third time I ran away, they dropped me off at the shelter, and I lived there until I turned eighteen. Thunder became my mentor. He always treated me like his little brother, which I appreciated since I wasn't close to my parents. When he first moved here, his sister and her family were still in South Dakota, so we became each other's family. It's been that way ever since."

"Why didn't he adopt you?"

"By the time I met him, I was almost eighteen. Turning eighteen meant leaving the shelter, but he generously offered me a free room in his house. Then he helped me get a job. Once I'd saved enough, he helped me buy my first car and put down a deposit on my apartment. He's the best brother I could've ever had."

"You didn't have any brothers or sisters from your parents?"

"Nope, I was an only child. Which, in a way, was good because I wouldn't wish my parents on anyone."

"That sucks," Steele swiped his card.

"Shh, no cussing." George put his finger up to his lips. "Your mom won't like it."

"She's smothering me. I'm not a baby. I can take care of myself."

"Quit complaining." George placed his hand on Steele's shoulder to stop him from entering the room. "You're lucky to have a mom that loves you so much. She went through hell and back to save you from the LRs not too long ago, so cut her some slack."

Steele looked up at George and sighed. "You're right. She is cool."

"Steele? Is that you?" Angel came around the corner into the foyer and immediately pinched her nose when she reached them. "Puey, you guys stink. Hey, George. What are you doing here?"

"Sorry, I was using the gym, and I didn't bring a change of clothes. Barrett said I could shower in Alex's room, but I need to borrow a t-shirt and sweatpants." Barrett grinned.

"Sure, come in." Angel stepped back. "Steele, go to your room and shower. Tori texted and said brunch will be ready in five minutes, so don't doddle in the shower. I'll take George to Alex's room."

"Yes, ma'am," Steele grumbled and left with his head down. "See ya later, Deputy George."

"You've got a great kid there." George watched Steele walk by him and leave the room.

"Thanks. He is a great kid when he isn't being influenced by the LRs."

"Where's he going?" George was confused. He thought Steele lived with Angel and Barrett.

"Oh, he's rooming with Bryce. He said he preferred staying there, so he wouldn't have to listen to us in the bedroom. Talk about embarrassing." Angel rolled her eyes and turned toward the bedroom. "I'll be right back."

"Honey, I'm home!" Barrett hollered as he stepped in the front door.

"You hound dog." George punched Barrett in the arm. "Making sexy sounds with your girl and driving your son into another room."

"How the hell did you hear about that?" Barrett raised his eyebrow.

"Your girlfriend told me."

"Yeah, it was awkward when he caught us naked on the couch." Barrett rubbed the back of his neck.

George's eyes bulged. "Are you fucking serious? You could scar the kid for life. Why didn't you put your clothes back on or grab a blanket?"

"What? Of course we had a blanket, dumbass." Barrett shoved him.

"Hey, leave George alone." Angel glared at Barrett and handed George the clothes. "Here, you can be casino security now, too."

"Thanks." George took the clothes. "I'll text Alex and let him know I'm in his bathroom."

"No need." Angel shook her head. "I already texted Tori."

"Angel, I think you need another shower." Barrett headed toward Angel.

"Barrett Panther, do not touch me. You stink. Go shower." Angel pinched her nose again and ran behind the couch.

"I love when she plays hard to get." Barrett winked at Angel before he lunged toward her and wrapped her up in his arms, kissing her all over her face as she squirmed and complained about his body odor.

George laughed as he walked to the front door and remembered he didn't have a key card to get into Alex's room. So much for his quick exit.

"Hey, Loverboy. I need a key to get into Alex's room."

"Cock blocker." Barrett reached into his pocket, grabbed his keys, and threw them at him. "Catch."

George caught them one-handed. "Thanks, I'll return them at brunch. Gotta go, those sexy sounds are too much for my sensitive ears." George covered his ears as he headed to the door.

"Fucker!" Barrett screamed before the door shut.

Chapter 17

Memories

"I still can't believe you woke up George to help you run errands." Tori was placing the place cards at every seat.

"Leave it alone already, Tori. He's not mad at me, so why are you?" Lizzy filled the glasses with the water pitcher. "Why do we need place cards? Why can't everyone sit wherever they want?"

"I don't know." Tori shrugged. "Every time we've had brunch; I've seen place cards, so I did them. It was my turn to set up the table and décor and I didn't want to let Sehoy down."

"Oh, honey." Sehoy came up behind Tori and gave her a hug. "You could never let me down. You keep loving my son the way you do, and I'll be a happy mom for the rest of my life."

"Thank you." Tori smiled. "You don't have to worry. He's my forever."

"I'm glad to hear that." Sehoy walked around the table and pointed at a place card. "George is joining us?"

"I invited him. Is that okay?" Tori asked hesitantly.

"Of course. You can invite anyone you want to our Sunday Brunches. The more the merrier. Besides, we love George. I'm gonna go to the kitchen and start bringing out the food. Do you ladies want to help me?"

Lizzy watched their interaction and wondered why Tori was so nervous around Sehoy.

"Yes." As soon as Tori walked by Lizzy, Lizzy grabbed her arm, stopping her. Lizzy waited until Sehoy entered the kitchen before she faced Tori.

"Why are you so nervous around her?"

"I don't know," Tori exhaled loudly. "I just want to make sure I do everything right. She's Alex's mom, and I don't want to disappoint her."

"Has Alex said anything to you?"

"No," Tori's eyes widened. "He's always telling me to relax and just be myself."

"Then you should listen to your husband. Come on, let's help her carry the food out here."

"Do you think we stood out here too long?" Tori walked faster toward the kitchen.

"Really?" Lizzy followed, exasperated with Tori.

"Hey, we're here." Frey shouted from behind Lizzy.

"We're going to help your mom bring out the food. Come help us." Tori shouted over her shoulder.

"Okie, dokie." Frey put her arm around Lizzy's shoulder. "How are you feeling?"

"I'm good. Just tired."

"You're going to be even more tired after you eat all the food Alex made." Holt and Bryce skipped past them on their way to the kitchen.

"Hi, Lizzy," Bryce bellowed and waved his free hand over his head to her.

"Hey, Bryce," Lizzy grinned.

"Those two are like two peas in a pod," Frey giggled. "Come on, let's get into the kitchen and see if they need any more help."

Lizzy followed Frey but stopped in the doorway as she looked at everyone in the kitchen. Tori was helping Alex pull items from the oven. Sehoy was speaking to Bryce with her arm around him while Holt held Frey in front of him, watching the exchange. A warmth, like a gentle hug, filled the room, and she could feel the love radiating from everyone present.

She dreamed of the having a relationship filled with love like theirs. Tori knew Lizzy dated a lot back home, but she didn't know Lizzy had been a virgin before the incident with George. Lizzy always thought she would be in love when she had sex for the first time. It would be special, and the man of her dreams would gaze longingly into her eyes while he slowly made love to her. But it was quick, painful, and embarrassing.

Lizzy leaned against the doorframe and remembered the double wedding night. Everything had been going beautifully until Angel ran in and told everyone to leave because the LRs were on their way to kill everyone.

The words had barely left Angel's mouth when chaos erupted, and everyone ran for cover. Lizzy tried to get to Barrett because she had a crush on him, but he was with Angel and wasn't giving her the time of day. When Barrett noticed Lizzy, he shoved her at George and told him to take her away and keep her safe. George grabbed her hand and ran with her out of the wedding venue into the resort hallway.

"In here." George pulled her into a dark room.

"What are you doing? What if this is someone's room?" Lizzy said breathlessly while George checked the bathroom and closets.

"No one's here. Everything's empty." George walked back to her. "Stay here. I'll come back for you when everything calms down. If I can't, I'll send someone for you, but I need to go out there."

"No!" Lizzy grabbed his arm. "You can't leave me here alone."

"Lizzy, I'm needed out there." George pointed toward the door.

"Please, please, don't leave me alone?" Lizzy was trembling, tears streaming down her face.

"Hey." George set his gun on a foyer table and pulled her into his arms, running his hands over her back. "You're going to be okay in here. I wouldn't leave you if I didn't think you would be safe."

Lizzy could only think about the terrifying screams she heard after the bullets ricocheted across the wedding venue. A man who worked for the resort had just been standing at the back of the ceremony when the bullet entered the back of his head, and he dropped to the ground. The slow, dark blossoming of blood spread across the ground around his head. Then Barrett was shot, the sound echoing through the venue, and Lizzy ran to him, his white shirt blossoming crimson against his skin.

All those horrible thoughts of death were spiraling in her head. She didn't want to die at twenty-five. She hadn't gotten a chance to live her life or love her soul mate. No way was she dying a virgin. Looking up into George's beautiful eyes, *she'd spoken the four words that she never thought she would say to a stranger.*

"Make love to me."

"Uh, that is not a good idea." George shook his head.

"Why not?" Lizzy grabbed his shirt and pulled him toward her. "What if we die tonight? I don't want to die without ever having had ss...," Lizzy stopped herself. She couldn't tell him she was a virgin. "Some fun."

"What? Are you crazy? Did you hit your head?" George ran his hands over the back of her head.

Lizzy wasn't taking no for an answer. She knew what to do. She'd just never done it. Pushing the straps of her dress off her shoulders, she let the top cascade down to her waist. She hadn't worn a bra because she didn't need one for that style of dress.

"What the fuck, Lizzy?" George fumbled with the straps, attempting to put her dress back on.

Lizzy wasn't giving up. Dropping to her knees, she unbuckled his belt and slid down his zipper. Deputy George came as a guest to the wedding, not an officer, so the only barrier between his cock and her mouth were his pants and underwear.

"Lizzy, stop!" George tried to grab his pants, but Lizzy was already pushing his boxer briefs down and licking his cock. "Fuck!"

Lizzy took him fully into her mouth while one hand gripped his ass and the other his balls. She had done this with previous boyfriends, she just never went all the way.

George braced his hands on the wall behind Lizzy and groaned, "Lizzy, we should not be doing this right now. Come up here."

Lizzy heard his words, but his body was tightening with every thrust into her mouth.

"Oh, fuck me," George moaned.

"Yes, please." In one sudden move, she stood and pushed her dress to the floor. "Do it."

George's veins were throbbing in his forehead. He was staring at her like she had two heads while his chest was panting, but he wasn't moving.

Lizzy grabbed his hand and placed it on her core. "Please," Lizzy whispered before she latched onto his lips for a sensual kiss. George got with the program and took over the kiss before he slid his finger into her pussy. She felt him slide easily inside. She was so wet and ready for him. Reaching for his cock again, she stroked the head of his cock, swirling his pre-cum around.

George's mouth released hers and Lizzy saw him close his eyes and grit his teeth. She would not let him stop. Her hand pumped faster and harder until he opened his eyes. Staring into her eyes, he opened his mouth to say something, but Lizzy cut him off.

"George, I need you, please," Lizzy said breathlessly as she gazed into his eyes.

"Fuck!" George slid his finger out and slid her panties aside before he filled her with his cock.

Lizzy screamed and wrapped herself around him, holding on for dear life. He pressed her up against the wall and held her in place while he rammed himself into her, over and over again. Their frantic rhythm lasted only a few minutes until her inner walls clenched around him and they both climaxed.

"Shit, Lizzy, I shouldn't have done that. Fuck!" George said into her neck. "Please tell me you're on the pill?"

"I'm on the pill, don't worry," Lizzy mumbled.

"Okay." George stepped back and looked at her.

"I'm gonna clean up." Lizzy ducked under his arms and ran into the bathroom. She'd heard the first time you had sex; you bled. She didn't want George to turn on a light and see blood running down her leg. That was not the time to get into the 'I was a virgin' conversation.

As she was cleaning up, she heard him on his phone. Not wanting to talk to him, she snuck out of the bathroom and bolted from the room. She heard him calling out to her, but she didn't stop.

Lizzy snapped out of her daydream when Frey waved her hand in front of her face.

"Lizzy. Where did you go?"

"Sorry, it's nothing. I'm just tired."

"Hey." George stepped in front of her. "Are you okay? Your face is all flushed."

Lizzy put both hands against her cheeks. "Uh, yeah," Lizzy forced a smile. "Sorry, I just zoned out." Then she turned and headed to Tori. Grabbing the lasagna dish, she said to no one in particular, "I'll take this to the table."

Chapter 18

Jekyll and Hyde Brunch

George

George kept a close eye on Lizzy throughout the Brunch. It was easy because she was sitting next to him. She was acting weirder than usual. She kept spacing out every time anyone tried to talk to her.

"So, is anyone going to tell me what happened last night?" Sehoy looked around the table. "The children approved version."

Mark cleared his throat. "The girls wanted to go out last night, and I was their chaperone. We ran into some trouble with some rude men and George rushed in to save the day."

George was glad to see Mark and Maggie at brunch. He assumed since they moved into their new house, they would stop coming, but Maggie said she loved Alex's brunches and wanted to check on Lizzy.

"Good job, Surfer Smurf." Maggie patted his hand.

"Thanks, darlin'." Mark kissed her temple.

"Hey, I showed up to get my girl." Holt grumbled.

"You are my hero," Frey put her hands under her chin and dreamily stared at Holt as she blinked rapidly, like a true damsel in distress that was saved by her handsome knight in shining armor.

"Really?" Holt pursed his lips. "That's all you got." Holt pointed at Mark. "He got a kiss."

Frey grabbed his face and kissed his lips.

"Eww, stop!" Bryce covered his face. "That's just gross."

Everyone laughed before they continued talking about last night, but George noticed Lizzy was not eating. She just kept moving her food around her plate, scattering it so it looked like she had eaten some.

"Are you okay?" George leaned close to her ear.

"Yeah, I'm fine." Lizzy answered and scooted away from him.

"Why are you scooting away from me?" George mumbled under his breath. "This morning you were running toward me," George teased her. He tried to lighten the mood, but it had the opposite effect.

Lizzy stood abruptly. Her chair would've fallen back if George hadn't caught it.

"I...I'm sorry everybody. I'm really tired and I'd like to lie down."

"I'll walk you upstairs." Tori stood up next to her.

"No," Lizzy grinned. "You continue with brunch. I'll be fine."

"I'll walk her up." George wiped his mouth, dropped his napkin on his plate, and stood.

"You don't need to." Lizzy backed up.

"I insist." George put his hand behind her back, guiding her away from the table. "Thank you all for brunch. I'll see you later."

They said their goodbyes to George, offering Lizzy well wishes and hoping a nap would make her feel better. As they were walking away, George heard Sehoy say, "I need details later." George couldn't see who she was talking to and was glad to get away before he had to answer those questions.

Lizzy had gotten ahead of him when he was saying goodbye. "Hey, wait up." George hurried to catch up to her. She was already standing in front of the elevator.

"You don't have to come with me." Lizzy faced the elevator.

"I don't mind. Besides, I need to talk to you." George placed his hands in his pockets.

The doors opened and Lizzy entered, swiping her card for the family floor. "What do you want to talk about? I'm sorry for waking you up earlier today."

"Not that. I'll wait until we get to your room. We need privacy for this conversation."

"There's no one in the elevator."

"Uh, there's a camera."

"Where?" Lizzy looked around the elevator.

George pointed to the camera in the ceiling's corner. "Smile and say cheese because any security officer in the monitoring room is watching you right now."

"Really? Why?" Lizzy turned her head as she stared at the camera.

"They put them in after what happened to your sister."

"I guess that makes sense."

The elevator doors opened, and George followed Lizzy to her room. Lizzy stepped inside and let him shut the door.

"What do you want to talk about?" Lizzy faced him with her arms crossed.

There was only one way to say it. So George just blurted it all out. "I wanted to say I'm sorry for the 'wham bam thank you ma'am' crazy sex we had the night of the double wedding shootout. I'm not usually so inconsiderate. I guess the adrenaline rush got to me."

"The adrenaline rush? Whatever." Lizzy dropped her arms. "Just go."

"That's it?" George thought he'd have to grovel since she had ignored him for months. But she was acting like she didn't care at all about what they did. How could she not? It was hot as hell.

"I have a question for you?" Now it was George who crossed his arms and stared at her.

"What?" Lizzy put her hand across her forehead.

"Were you a virgin?"

"I don't fucking believe this." Lizzy turned around and took a couple of steps away from him before facing him again. "No."

Did her eye just twitch? Was she lying to him? George had interrogated several suspects and was getting good at spotting a lie. He would bet his life that she was lying to him, and that made him furious.

"Don't lie to me. I had blood on me."

Lizzy stormed past him to her door and opened it. "Get the fuck out of my room."

"Why can't you just talk to me?" George ran his hand over the back of his neck. She was so damn frustrating.

"Because I have nothing else to say." Lizzy shrugged. "Now, get out or I'll call the police."

"I am the fucking police!" George screamed, and Lizzy jumped. "Fuck, I'm sorry, Lizzy." George placed his hand on her shoulder, but she shrugged it off.

"Okay, fine. I'm leaving." George stepped outside her room and turned to say a few parting words.

"Stop playing games with me. One minute I'm your knight in shining armor and the next I'm your worst nightmare. We need to...," But George never finished because she slammed the door in his face.

"Motherfucker," George grumbled before he yelled loud enough for her to hear. "We're not done talking, Lizzy!"

But she never answered back. It was dead silence behind the door. To think he had left a perfectly good brunch to be told he's an asshole. This day was getting worse by the hour, and he still had to go to his apartment and change before he started his shift.

George headed downstairs and peeked into Savor. Everyone was picking up the dishes and taking them into the kitchen.

"George, is Lizzy, okay?" Sehoy spotted him and headed in his direction.

"Yeah, she said to tell you thank you, and she hoped she didn't ruin brunch for everyone." He wasn't about to tell any of them about the conversation they really had before she slammed the door in his face.

"That sweet girl." Sehoy picked up a plate. "She didn't ruin anything. I'll make her a plate for later."

Sweet girl, my ass. That sweet girl had razor-sharp claws and words that could cut right through you. But he would not tell Sehoy that. "I'm sure she would appreciate that." George smiled.

"Follow me. I'll make you a plate to take home."

George loved this family. They always took care of him as if he were one of their kids. He followed Sehoy and spoke to Alex while she grabbed a plastic container and filled it up with some of everything. When she finished, she handed it to him.

"I'm so glad you could come. You're more than welcome to join us any Sunday you want. Be safe out there."

"Thank you, Sehoy. I really appreciate this." George raised his hand and said, "see you all later."

When he got to the apartment over the cultural center, he placed his food in his fridge and took a nap before he had to get ready for work.

Chapter 19

Adrenaline Rush...My Ass

Lizzy

Lizzy didn't know what she expected George to say, but not that they had sex against a wall because of an adrenaline rush. Okay, maybe that was partially true, but couldn't he have said it was because she was so sexy, or their animal magnetism drew him to her, and he just couldn't say no. Adrenaline rush made it seem like he was so hyped he would've slept with anyone who was in that room that night.

It just made Lizzy feel even worse than she felt about that night already. She knew she had instigated the situation, but he could've at least said she was so hot, he couldn't help himself. Instead of a compliment, his words left her feeling like a mere vessel, a means to release his pent-up adrenaline. She wondered how many times he'd fucked some girl under those circumstances. His job was very stressful.

Well, she would not be one of those girls again. Goodbye and good riddance, Deputy George with the panty dropping smile and eight pack abs. The last thing she wanted to discuss with him was her sexuality, particularly the fact that he took her virginity. She was relieved he didn't transmit a disease without using a condom. Who knew how many women he slept with every night? She'd heard about how some police officers slept around and cheated on their wives and girlfriends. She would not be that girl.

Lizzy put on some pajamas and curled up in bed. Grabbing the remote, she was channel surfing when she heard a knock on her door. *Who was it now?* It better not be Deputy Jerk. She peaked through the peephole and saw her sister standing there holding a covered dish.

Lizzy opened the door and stepped aside to let her sister in. "Hey."

"Hi." Tori placed the dish on the kitchen counter. "I noticed you didn't eat much at brunch, so I brought you some leftovers. How are you feeling?"

"Exhausted." Lizzy put the covered dish in her refrigerator. The last thing she wanted right now was food. Sleep, that's what she wanted. Her bed was calling her name.

"Is something going on between you and George?"

Tori's words stopped her mid-stride. "What?" Lizzy's mouth dropped. "No, why would you think that?" How did her sister guess she had issues with George?

"Because you were both whispering at each other and none too quietly. I heard George say something about scooting away from me and running to me. What's going on? Do you want to talk about it?"

"I don't know what you're talking about." Lizzy laid under the covers and grabbed the remote.

But her sister wasn't letting it go. Tori crawled under the covers on the other side of the bed and took the remote out of her hand. She turned off the TV, rolled to her side facing Lizzy, and said, "Talk to me."

"I don't know what you want me to say." Lizzy stared at the blank TV.

"Tell me what's going on? I know something is bothering you and I want to help. You've been acting weird since the night of the shootout. You barely talked to me on the phone these past few months when I called home and you haven't been yourself since you moved here. Quite frankly, I'm a little shocked you wanted to live here."

"No weirder than you." Lizzy turned her face to Tori. "Someone tried to kill you. You're my big sister; it freaked me out."

"If you are so freaked out, then why did you move here?" Tori stared at her.

Tori always had a way of staring at her until Lizzy gave in and told her everything.

"Because I missed you and there's nothing to do on the rez. I wanted some freedom." Lizzy turned her face and stared at the ceiling. She couldn't look at her sister when she lied. Not that it was a total lie. While her answer was partially true, a significant reason was to see if George and she had that electrifying chemistry that led her to crave his touch and beg him for sex. She could've answered his calls, but a deeper curiosity held her back—the desire to see if that familiar zing would course through her body again if they met face-to-face.

Ignoring him had not been her best decision, but at first, she didn't want to talk about it. She wanted to move on as if nothing happened and see if George would chase her and beg her to move in with him and be his girlfriend. Sure, it was a stupid dream, but she'd still hoped. She'd been wrong. His only interest in wanting to talk to her was to apologize for having sex. He gave her the impression that he wasn't interested in a relationship with her. He just wanted to let her down easy since they ran in the same friend's circle.

"I believe that, but I think there's more." Tori reached out and held her hand. "Do you still have a crush on Barrett?"

"What? No!" Lizzy pulled her hand away. "How did you know about that, anyway?"

"I have eyes," Tori sighed. "I know when you set your sights on someone. I've double dated with you, remember?"

"How could I forget?" Lizzy smirked. "It's because of you that my dating went from double dates with you to mom or dad chaperoning my dates. Thanks for that."

"Sorry, but you wanted to date a hell of a lot more than I did." Tori stayed quiet for a few minutes before she asked, "so if it's not Barrett, what is it? Is it because of that asshole who spiked your drink? Talk to me. I can help."

"That's part of it." Lizzy rolled to her side and cupped her hands under her cheek on the pillow. "I feel so stupid. I was so careful and then a cute guy buys me a drink and I take it because I feel bad for him."

"Why did you feel bad for him?"

"Because those drinks are expensive, and I thought he was doing something nice for me. I'm not gonna lie. I liked the attention he gave me until I realized he'd spiked my drink. Then I just felt stupid."

Lizzy saw the sadness in her sister's eyes. "Don't look at me like that. I know I dated a lot on the rez, but it never went too far. It was nice to have a handsome city stranger look at me as if he wanted me. I mean, I would've never left with him," Lizzy mumbled the last few words. "But it was nice to feel sexy and wanted."

"Oh Lizzy." Tori pulled her into her arms and rolled onto her back so Lizzy could rest her head on her sister's chest. Lizzy remembered when they would lie like this as little girls and talk well into the night. Her older sister always keeping her safe when she had nightmares or couldn't sleep. They had been so close until Lizzy went full out boy crazy, and Tori stopped their double dating. Tori ran her hands through Lizzy's hair, and they stayed quiet for a few minutes.

"You know, it's not your fault that he did that. He's the stupid one. I'm just glad you were with your friends. When Winston took advantage of me, I was alone."

"Do you remember what happened?"

"No," Tori sighed. "Part of me is glad because I don't know where my mind would've gone. I'm so grateful to Alex. He helped me recover. If I had remembered the details of what Winston did, I might be in the same boat as Lola, Maggie's brother's girlfriend. She is just now getting around to letting José touch her. Although, to be fair, she was gang raped, much worse than what happened to me."

"That's horrible. I wish I had been here for you." Lizzy mumbled.

"I'm glad you weren't. When the LRs were still active, it was crazy around here. Everyone was always looking over their shoulder, waiting for the next attack. It's better now, calmer."

"Are they all in jail?"

"No, Numbers is still out there," Tori sighed. "But everyone is looking for him and last I heard, he left town."

"I'm glad you have Alex. I can see how much he loves you."

"One of these days you will find your soulmate and he will love you so much, he won't be able to keep his hands off you," Tori whispered with her chin on Lizzy's head. "But you have to promise me you pick someone who truly loves you before he takes your virginity."

Lizzy's body stiffened.

"It's okay." Tori stroked her hair again. "Don't be afraid of making love. It can be so beautiful with the right person." Tori's voice got softer. "Alex is so good in...,"

Lizzy shot up. "Okay, stop right there. I don't want to hear about Alex's prowess in the bedroom."

"Sorry," Tori giggled. "You're right. Let's watch something and then I'll go."

"Thanks." Lizzy settled back on her sister's chest. "I love you, Tori."

"I love you too."

Chapter 20

Friends and B-Ball

George

George woke up around noon after his shift. Between the argument with Lizzy and the crazy night shift, he'd crashed hard. Staring at the ceiling, he replayed their argument. *Why the hell had he said it was an adrenaline rush?* That sounded insulting the minute those stupid ass words left his mouth. He should've stopped talking about that night after his apology.

But he needed to know if he had been her first. That was a special gift and if he had taken that away from her, he wanted to make it up to her. What he should have said was, "I couldn't resist you. You are so beautiful and sexy." Which would've been the truth. So why the hell did he say adrenaline rush? That made him sound like a man whore. Like he slept with anyone, anywhere, anytime, which was not true.

George had dated a lot of women and when he was a bartender he'd gotten around, but since he became a deputy and he promised to protect and serve, he'd grown up and stopped his whoring days. Which was crazy because he had more women throwing themselves at him now, especially when he was in uniform.

But George didn't want anymore one-night stands. He dreamt of finding a loving partner to build a home and family with, someone who would bring joy and laughter into his life. Someone to wait for him at home after his shift and love him. He wanted to be a good father, unlike the man that created him. The only loving home George knew was Thunders and the Panthers. He wanted that. After all the shit he went through in his childhood, he deserved to be loved. And one day, he was sure he would find it.

An image of Lizzy from that night popped into his head. The way she looked at him with her pleading eyes, topless begging him to take her. She had been so sensual, he couldn't stop himself from kissing her. When she dropped to her knees and wrapped her mouth around his cock, he'd felt like he'd gone to heaven. George closed his eyes and relived the moment her mouth licked him from top to bottom before she sucked on his head.

Reaching down under the blanket, he grabbed his already hard cock and stroked it, pretending it was Lizzy's mouth and hands. She'd had just the right amount of pressure as she held him while her mouth alternated between her licking, sucking, and taking him deep down into her throat.

George's head was spinning with thoughts of Lizzy's mouth around him. His heart was racing against his chest. Sweat broke out on his forehead as his hand sped up, pumping hard and fast. Reaching his other hand down, he stroked his balls like Lizzy had done. She had made him feel so fucking good. After a few more strokes, his body went taut, and he grunted out his climax. His release rushing out like water from a hose onto his stomach.

"Fuck," George sucked in air, trying to catch his breath. He'd used his hand frequently, but his orgasms had never been as powerful as that one or the one he had with Lizzy that night. He'd wanted to hold her and kiss her, but she ducked under his arms and ran inside the bathroom. By the time his mind cleared, Barrett needed his help, and she ran out on him.

"I have to make this right," George mumbled.

Wiping himself with his sheet, he stood up and stripped his bed. He had to wash his sheets, anyway. Today was Monday, a quiet day since the cultural center was closed. He put his sheets in the washer and got in the shower to wash off. When he finished, he put on a t-shirt and shorts. Grabbing his cereal box, he poured himself a bowl.

He was antsy, his leg bouncing nervously and his fingers tapping a restless rhythm against his knee. To take his mind off Lizzy, he needed a distraction, something to occupy his mind and ease his aching heart. He called Sean while he ate his cereal.

"Hey, man. What's up?" Sean answered.

His partner had been down in the dumps since his girlfriend broke up with him because he was a cop. Some girls loved it until the relationship got serious, then they couldn't deal with not knowing if they would come home safe. Sean's ex was one of those girls. She'd chased him relentlessly, then wanted him to quit or get a desk job when they started talking about marriage. Sean wasn't ready for a desk job, and he told her he sure as hell wasn't quitting. Their relationship went downhill from there. Seeking revenge, she started cheating on him until he eventually discovered her infidelity and kicked her out.

"How about we pick up some of the shelter boys and go to the park to shoot some hoops?" George crunched his cereal. He'd forgotten to buy milk, so he ate them dry. Alex usually had milk downstairs, but he didn't want to use it. Not that Alex would mind, but if he finished it, he'd have to replace it and he'd already forgotten to get his own damn milk.

"Sounds good. I'll come get you so you can leave your patrol vehicle parked at the cultural center. Be there in ten."

"I'll be ready." George hung up and then called Tim, the oldest boy at the shelter.

"Deputy George! What's up?" Tim hollered.

George chuckled. Tim was not only the oldest, but the rowdiest of the bunch.

"You want to play some four on two ball?" Sean and George always played against the boys. Most of the time, the boys won, but Sean and George didn't care. They just wanted the boys to get out and have some fun. Since George was from that shelter and Thunder had taken him under his wings, he now mentored the boys. Thunder had such a powerful impact on his life, he wanted to pay it forward.

"Yeah, old man," Tim laughed. "We'll play you. I hope you're off tonight because you're gonna need several ice packs for your old man bones."

"Funny...not," George grinned, even though Tim couldn't see him. "Find out who wants to play. Sean and I will be by in about twenty minutes."

"Sounds good. See ya then. Oh, hey wait!" Tim hollered before George could hang up.

"Did you need something?"

"Nah, just wanted to remind you to take some ibuprofen so you don't feel the pain we're going to cause you when we slaughter you guys," Tim whooped.

"Yeah, yeah, yeah. See you soon." George hung up, washed his dish, and put on his shoes.

It would be quicker if he waited outside for Sean. The minute he locked up the cultural center and walked to the parking lot, Sean pulled in with his van. A van he bought after he sold his Corvette, hoping to convince his ex that he was ready for marriage and kids.

"Alright dad, let's go pick up the kids." George buckled in.

"Wipe that fucking smirk off your face. I'm gonna sell this van as soon as I find another sports car that I like."

"I don't know. This van looks good on you."

"Shut the fuck up, rookie." Sean smiled and pulled out of the parking lot.

George hated when he called him a rookie. He'd been with the sheriff's office almost a year now. In his mind, a rookie was a newbie fresh out of the police academy. Sean knew it pissed him off, so he called him that often.

"I called Tim. He's gathering up the troops."

"Sounds good. I got a ball in the back." Sean glanced at George. "Hey, I wanted to talk to you about something."

"Sure, what's up?"

"I'm thinking about transferring to another police department." Sean released his breath.

"What? Why?" George turned in his seat to face him.

"I gotta get out of town. After everything with Kerri, I need a change of scenery." Sean rubbed the back of his neck with one hand.

"Where are you gonna go?" George didn't want Sean to leave. Other than Thunder, he was his best friend.

"Not sure." Sean put both hands on the steering wheel. "I'd like to stay in Florida, so I'm looking around in other counties. I haven't found anything yet, but I wanted you to know. I didn't want it to come as a surprise at the last minute."

"I appreciate that. You're my favorite partner. I'll miss you."

"I'm your only partner," Sean chuckled.

"True," George nodded. "But you are my favorite."

"Smart ass," Sean grumbled.

As they pulled in front of the shelter, Tim was already standing outside with Luke, Kenny, and Jimmy. Tim was seventeen and would age out of the shelter in a couple of months. Luke was fifteen, Kenny was fourteen, and Jimmy was thirteen. They had all been close to Bryce while he was at the shelter before Frey and Holt adopted him.

"Hey, it's The Geriatric Team," Tim hollered and waved.

"I'm gonna wipe that smirk off that little shit's face on the court," Sean mumbled before he unlocked the car and waved them over.

"We'll see." George punched his arm. "They usually beat us."

The boys got in and said hello.

"Did you take your pills?" Tim grinned at George. "Better question." Tim pointed at Sean. "Did he take his. He's older than dirt."

George busted out laughing. Sean was pushing forty, but in excellent shape. Tim loved to rag on him about his age. Kind of like how George loved to tease Holt and Barrett about theirs. George saw so much of himself in Tim. He vowed to help him as much as he could as soon as he left the shelter.

"What fucking pills is he talking about?" Sean grumbled and drove to the park.

"Ibuprofen for the pain they are going to give us," George grinned.

"Yeah right," Sean humphed. "In your dreams, little whipper snappers."

"What the hell is a whipper snapper?" Jimmy snickered. "You're showing your age, old man."

"A young, inexperienced person considered to be overconfident," George answered.

"Thanks for the assist, Webster." Sean fist bumped George.

"Who's Webster?" Jimmy sounded confused.

"These old men are talking about the Webster Dictionary. It's what they used to look up words before googling was a thing." Tim spoke up.

"We're gonna school those boys today, George!" Sean pumped his fist in the air.

"We'll see, old man," Tim smiled.

George loved these days when he got to hang out with his best friend and the boys. They always had fun on the court and followed it up with food before they dropped them back off at the shelter. He would enjoy these next few days because who knew when a great job opportunity would come up for Sean and he would leave.

The boys beat them and teased them through dinner and all the way home. George and Sean didn't mind losing as long as the boys had a good day. When George got home, he showered again and went to bed. He had tomorrow off also, but it would be noisy downstairs since it was a workday.

He wondered if he'd see Lizzy. She'd been pitching in wherever she was needed. He could go downstairs and claim he was there to help Thunder. It would give him a chance to bump into her and apologize for his adrenaline rush comment.

Chapter 21

Hanging at the AICC

Lizzy didn't always have a task at the cultural center, but she went in with Tori, anyway. Most of the time, she hung out with Maggie and greeted guests as they entered. She gave tours and filed paperwork, but today she was helping Tori with inventory. They'd spent the morning in the warehouse logging in items that needed to be shipped back and items that needed to be displayed.

By lunchtime, she was starving. When her stomach grumbled, Tori stopped, and they walked through the restaurant and into the kitchen to see what Alex had cooked up. Tori went straight to Alex, but Lizzy stopped in the doorway. George was standing with Alex; they were laughing about something.

"What are you doing here?" Lizzy asked George when he turned around to give Alex and Tori a moment.

"Uh, I live here." George raised his eyebrow at her and walked toward her. "What are you doing here?"

"Helping my sister." Lizzy used her hand to push him out of her way as she walked by and heard him mumble, 'nice to see you too'.

Ignoring his comment, she strode up beside the happy couple. "What yummy dish did you make for lunch today?"

Alex's gaze bounced between George and Lizzy. "Uh, I made some Chicken Parmigiana, spaghetti, and Fry Bread."

Great, now Alex would ask Tori if anything was going on between her and George. *Ugh. Why did George have to live upstairs?* "That sounds great. Can I get a plate?"

"Why don't you and George go find a table and I'll bring your food?" Alex grabbed a plate and put a piece of chicken on it.

"You don't have to serve me. I can make my plate." Lizzy stood next to Alex with her hand out.

"Come on, Lizzy." George grabbed her hand and pulled her away. "Maybe they want a couple of minutes alone."

Of course they did. They were inseparable. But why did that mean she had to sit with George? Not wanting to make a scene, she followed George to a table, and they sat across from each other.

"So, how's your day going?" George grabbed a napkin and placed it on his lap.

"Like you care." Lizzy leaned back and crossed her arms, slouching in her seat.

"Really? I'm trying to be nice, and you want to argue?"

"It must be the adrenaline rush of seeing you that makes me want to fight with you." Lizzy smirked. She could tell she had gotten to him when he leaned forward and squinted his eyes at her.

"Well, at least my adrenaline rush was more pleasurable." George said through clenched teeth.

"Asshole," Lizzy mumbled and put her hands on the table, ready to stand up, but Tori brought all their waters.

"Water for everyone." Tori's smile dropped when she looked at both of them. "What's going on?"

"Nothing," Lizzy said is a sing-song cheerful voice.

"We're good." George's stare never wavered from Lizzy.

"O...Okay, I'll go get our food." Lizzy saw Tori scurry away out of the corner of her eye, but there was no way she was losing a stare down with George. She was tougher than that.

"Can we please be nice to each other during this meal?" George growled.

"Yes, daddy," Lizzy said sweetly.

"I told you not to call me that. I'm not that much older than you." George took a sip of water. "Call me that again and I'll take you over my knee and spank your ass red."

"Whatever you say," Lizzy paused, then whispered, "daddy."

George stood so fast his chair crashed to the floor. Everyone was now looking at him. He looked beautiful, with his blue eyes shining with lust and his nostrils flaring. His muscles bulging out of his t-shirt, barely being constrained. He opened his mouth to say something, but shut it when he heard Alex.

"Hey, did they call you in? Do you have to go?" Alex and Tori placed their lunch plates in front of them.

George took a deep breath and grabbed his chair. Setting it upright, he sat and took another drink of water. Lizzy eyed him carefully. *Was he going to oust her?* Watching him gain control over his anger was intriguing. His eyes became unemotional, and he regulated his breathing before he smiled at Alex.

"No, my phone was ringing, and I stood to get it, but then it stopped." George picked up his fork and looked at his plate, avoiding eye contact with everyone. "This looks great, thanks."

Lizzy watched George stuff his mouth with food, amused that she had gotten to him. When he looked at her, she mouthed 'daddy'. George swallowed wrong; tears sprung in his eyes as he coughed to clear his throat. Lizzy laughed. It was a mean thing to do, but he deserved it...didn't he?

"Oh, my goodness, George." Tori stood and patted his back. "Are you okay?"

George nodded, covered his mouth with his fist, and croaked, "y...yeah, w...wrong way."

Lizzy picked up her fork and began eating, complimenting Alex for his culinary skills while George glared at her. She knew her sister was picking up on what was going on, but she would never bring up the topic in public. She'd get a break until they got to the resort, then Tori would demand answers as to why she was picking on George.

Tori loved George and didn't think he could do no wrong. Little did she know he had deflowered her sister against a wall like a brute. Lizzy smiled, thinking about how Tori would feel about that. Take that Perfect Deputy George. The pedestal Tori had built for George to stand on would be decimated and Tori would see George for who he really was…a Romeo Joe, Casanova, scoundrel, asshole.

She must have had a scheming look on her face, because George raised an eyebrow at her and tilted his head as if he was asking her what she was up to. She'd never tell. Well, not to him.

They finished lunch and, like Lizzy thought, she had a reprieve until Tori followed her to her room after they got to the resort after work.

"What was that all about with George?" Tori slid in behind her.

Damn, Lizzy didn't hear her behind her. She thought she was home free.

"I don't know what you're talking about?" Lizzy put her purse on the foyer table and walked into her bedroom. She was going to put on her pajamas and fuzzy slippers.

"Lizzy, what is going on with you and George? And don't tell me nothing because when he stood up, he looked like he was going to wring your pretty little neck, then have sex with you." Tori crossed her arms, cocked out her hip, and tapped her foot. "Don't deny it. I know what sexual tension looks like."

"I bet you do," Lizzy mumbled.

"I heard that. I'm not leaving here until you tell me what happened between you and George."

"Fine!" Lizzy threw her arms up. Maybe it was time to get her sister on her side so she could put a barrier between her and George. "Remember the night of your wedding, the shootout?"

"Of course I remember. It was the best and one of the worst nights ever. Those jerks ruined my beautiful wedding to the love of my life. Were you hurt?"

"No." Lizzy shook her head and sat on the edge of the bed. "Not from a bullet."

"What does this have to do with George?" Tori sat facing her.

"Well, that night was so chaotic. I was so scared that I ran to Barrett, but he was with Angel, and he asked George to take me to safety."

"Did George leave you there?" Tori's mouth dropped; she looked shocked.

"No, let me finish." Lizzy wanted to get her story out or else she would chicken out and not tell her sister. "George took me into an unoccupied room and told me to stay there, but I was so scared I didn't want to stay there alone. I didn't know where you were. I couldn't find mom or dad. Everyone was stampeding down the hall and George was trying to get me out of the way. He said he needed to get back, but I begged him to stay with me." Lizzy's voice got low. "I lost my virginity to him that night up against the hotel room wall."

"What!" Tori bolted upright. "How could George do that? I always thought he was a gentleman." Tori paced. "I was so wrong about him. Wait until Alex finds out, he's gonna rip him a new one."

"Tori, no." Lizzy grabbed her hands and stopped her from pacing. "Please don't tell Alex. I already feel humiliated. I don't want anyone else to know. It'll be our sister's secret."

"I don't keep secrets from Alex." Tori shook her head.

"For me, please keep this one." Lizzy pleaded.

"Okay, for now." Tori hugged her. "But I reserve the right to tell him when I see fit."

"Thank you."

"It must be hard to see George," Tori whispered.

"It is because I think I have feelings for him. He didn't hurt me or do anything I didn't want him to do. I just wish it was in a more loving way."

"Did you talk to him after you went back home?" Tori stepped back and pulled Lizzy back to the bed.

"To his credit, he tried to call and text me, but I ghosted him."

"Why?"

"Because I didn't know what to do or say. I threw myself at him, and he did what any red-blooded horny male would do. He did what I asked him to do. It wasn't his fault. But in my mind, I thought he would come after me and declare his undying love, especially after I moved here. But he hasn't. He called our sex an adrenaline rush. I'm just embarrassed and I don't know how to handle it."

"Lizzy, honey." Tori stroked her hair away from her face and cupped her cheeks. "You need to talk to him. Straighten this all out."

"He's tried. He even apologized, but I can't get past the embarrassment, so I say stupid things to make him mad at me. I poke and I prod until he says stupid shit back. We can't seem to stop ourselves from egging each other on." Lizzy looked down and fidgeted with her fingers.

"Do you like him?"

"Yeah," Lizzy whispered. "I think I do. When he glares at me or I get a rise out of him, my body tingles and I want to jump his bones. What is wrong with me that even fighting with him makes me horny?"

"I think it might just be that everything about him makes you horny." Tori stood. "Please figure it out fast because George is like family and pretty soon everyone will know something is going on and I won't be able to keep my mouth shut, especially if you sexually combust."

The sound of their laughter echoed through the room as they both busted out laughing.

Lizzy gained her composure first. "Okay, we'll figure it out." Lizzy nodded. "Thanks, Tori. I love you."

"I love you too. See you tomorrow."

Lizzy spent the rest of the night trying to figure out how to smooth things out with George. Tori was right. She needed to put her big girl panties on and put everything out in the open. If only she could do that without setting George off.

Chapter 22

Feeling Restless

George

After his crazy lunch with Lizzy, Tori, and Alex, he bolted out of the cultural center to get as far away from Lizzy as possible before he pulled her into his apartment and spanked her ass like he promised. He needed to vent some of his pent-up frustration. Basketball and hanging out with the boys always did the trick. George went back to his apartment and called Sean.

"What's up?" Sean answered.

"You want to play some b-ball with the boys?" George laid on his bed.

"Wow, twice in two days. What's going on?"

"Nothing, I'm just restless." George didn't want to talk about his problems with Lizzy yet.

"Yeah, I get that. I'm feeling some of that myself."

"We'll wait for school to get out and go pick up whoever wants to play?" George placed his hand behind the back of his head.

"Sounds good. I'll come get you in a couple of hours."

"Great. See ya then." George hung up and realized he had two hours to kill. Damn, he couldn't just lie around thinking about Lizzy. He'd go crazy. A run. That sounded like a great idea. He changed into shorts, grabbed his keys, and went for a run near the cultural center. He followed the same path he sometimes took with Thunder when they ran in the mornings before work.

After his five-mile run, he had just enough time to shower and change before Sean got him. When they got to the shelter, they helped some boys with their homework and then went out to play B-Ball. They stayed at the park until dark, wearing themselves out.

He got little sleep that night. His body was exhausted, but his mind was still spinning it's wheels thinking about Lizzy. He needed to clear the air with Lizzy. This had gone on long enough. Soon Isa would have her baby, and Lizzy would be busy helping her day and night.

George was surprised that no one noticed their pointed remarks and obvious displays of rudeness, the air thick with their sarcastic banter. Everyone was probably used to Mark and Maggie and didn't give them a second thought. But it was a matter of time. He loved his friends and didn't want them to get the wrong impression of him or Lizzy. They had to reach an amicable agreement and stop going at each other's throats whenever the subject of that night came up.

After tossing and turning all night, he'd finally fallen asleep around five in the morning. George was having a pleasurable dream filled with images of Lizzy, her smile bright, her laughter echoing softly. They were walking hand in hand, strolling through the park. She smiled at him and when she opened her mouth, all he heard was a shrilling scream. His eyes snapped open. Looking around, he realized he was alone in his apartment and that obnoxious screaming sound was his ringtone for Sean. When the hell had he set up that annoying sound for his best friend?

Oh, right? He'd been playing B-Ball with Tim last night and left his phone on the bench when he used the restroom. Tim loved to mess with his ringtones. How the hell had he unlocked his phone? *Shit*, George sighed and closed his eyes. He'd called the shelter to let them know they were running late, and Tim must have picked it up before it locked. That kid was too smart for his own good. It's a good thing he was thinking about becoming a cop, because the alternative would probably land him in jail.

He grabbed his phone and checked the time. Five hours, that's all he'd slept.

"Sean," George grumbled. "What's up?"

"Your girlfriend is at the station demanding to talk to you."

"What the fuck are you talking about? I don't have a girlfriend."

"Apparently you do. She said her name was," Sean pitched his voice to sound like a girl. "Lizzy Tall Bear and her boyfriend 'Deputy George Smith' would have their heads for arresting her."

"Fuck me, no she didn't." George sat up and wiped his face with his hand.

"Uh, yeah she did," Sean chuckled. "Ray has been trying to reach you."

"Sorry, I have my phone on silent except for immediate family and friends." George checked his missed calls.

"Aww, I'm touched. I love you too, man."

"Yep, three missed calls. Shit." George stood and grabbed some clothes. "I'll call Ray now. Thanks for calling me."

"No worries. Go get your girl, prince charming," Sean laughed and hung up.

My girl, my ass. Lizzy didn't want to be his girl. She just needed him every time she was in a bind. George pulled some pants on and stopped. *Wait a minute, her calling him for help could mean she was starting to rely on him and saw him as someone she could depend on. That was a good sign. That meant she trusted him. Maybe all wasn't lost, and she didn't think he was an asshole. Or maybe she was just using him since he was a cop.* Taking a deep breath, George pulled on the rest of his clothes and drove to the station.

Chapter 23

Grocery Store Debacle

George

George made it to the police station in record time and found Lizzy was sitting in a conference room with Ray.

"Hey, sorry I missed your calls." George strode in and shut the door.

"Where have you been?" Lizzy bolted out of her chair and ran to him. Throwing herself into his arms, she murmured into his ear. "Please help me. It wasn't my fault."

George wryly whispered back, "Where have I heard that before?"

"I'll do anything. Just stop him from arresting me."

George chuckled. "Remember, you said that."

Easing Lizzy away from him, he faced Ray. "What's going on?"

"She was arguing with an old lady in the fruit section of the grocery store. Something about apples. Then she threw an apple at the lady."

"I tossed the apple back with the rest of the apples on the apple shelf thingy. She was standing next to it and when the apple landed, another one rolled off and landed on her foot. I did not throw an apple at her! Why won't they listen to me?" Lizzy threw her hands up in the air and faced George.

George placed his palm in front of her face. "Stop talking."

Lizzy grunted loudly and stomped her foot. Her face was red, seething with anger. He was not handling this well. He turned to face Ray. "Go on."

"When the lady screamed, they called the manager. The manager escorted her and the lady to his office until I arrived. When I got there, she said she was your girlfriend and to call you. I tried, but you didn't answer, so I brought her here." Ray crossed his arms.

George pinched the bridge of his nose with his fingers. He did not need this today.

"Is the old lady pressing charges?"

"No...,"

"Then why am I here?" Lizzy interrupted him.

Ray glared at her and continued. "She just wants an apology."

"Okay, do you have her address?" George would drive Lizzy over right now and have her say she was sorry.

"I am not apologizing!" Lizzy stomped her foot again. "She's lying! I never hit her."

Ray handed George a piece of paper with the info. "Thank you," George said. "Can I have a minute alone with her, please?"

"You can have all the time you want." Ray slapped his back and grumbled. "Good luck with that one."

That seemed to be everyone's mantra when having him deal with Lizzy. George glanced at Lizzy. She was just about to open her mouth and spew ugly words from the look on her face, but he stood in front of her, blocking her view of Ray. Pointing at her, he whispered, "not now. He is an officer of the law and can have you arrested."

George stared at her until he heard the door click shut behind him.

"Do you realize you could put my job in jeopardy by lying to officers about being my girlfriend to get out of a ticket or an arrest?" George braced himself and placed his fists on his hips.

"I'm sure they think you have lots of girlfriends. It'll just boost your ego."

"What the fuck is wrong with you? I can't even have a conversation with you without you getting snarky." George held her gaze.

"Yeah, well, get used to it." Lizzy shrugged and grabbed her purse.

"What is it with you and older women?"

Lizzy glared at him. "Can we go now? I still have to go back to the grocery store and get my stuff."

"We have one stop to make before I drive you to the store." George grabbed her forearm and led her out of the station.

"Quit manhandling me," Lizzy grumbled and shrugged out of his arm when they reached his car.

"Keep it down or officers will think you're not my girlfriend." George opened the door for her.

"Or they'll think you beat me." Lizzy smirked.

"Get in the fucking car, Lizzy," George growled. She really knew how to push his buttons. He should've left her at the station and denied knowing her. Shaking his head, he knew he couldn't have done that. Tori would've been so hurt, and he liked Tori.

"Why didn't you call your sister?" George put the address on his phone before setting his GPS.

"I didn't want to upset her." Lizzy mumbled as she stared out the window.

George let the subject drop until he pulled up to the address of the old lady.

"Whose house is this?" Lizzy faced him, a frown on her face.

"The old lady you yelled at."

"No." Lizzy shook her head. "I am not apologizing."

"Yes, you are. Because if you don't, I'll have you bake her an apple pie and call a truce."

Lizzy's mouth dropped open. "That's just mean."

"You have a choice. Which will it be?" George turned off the car and placed his left arm over the steering wheel, staring her down.

"Fine. I'll apologize."

"Let's go." George got out of his car and went around to open Lizzy's door. When she stepped out, he said, "be nice Lizzy. I mean it."

Lizzy nodded and followed him to the door. The old lady opened the door and glared at Lizzy.

"Hi ma'am. I'm not in uniform, but I'm Deputy George Smith. Lizzy...," –George pointed at Lizzy– "would like to say something to you."

The lady crossed her arms and smirked at Lizzy while George prayed Lizzy would be the better person, so they could leave this mess behind.

"I'm sorry about the apple falling on your foot."

"You mean you're sorry for throwing it at me?" The old lady was having too much fun watching Lizzy squirm.

"Lizzy," George grunted.

"Yes, I'm sorry." Lizzy snapped her mouth shut and didn't elaborate. George was relieved.

"Thank you," the old lady said, and George was about to grab Lizzy to leave when the lady continued, "in the future, you need to watch your temper."

Oh, fuck me. George saw Lizzy's body tighten, ready to fight the old woman. Hell no.

"Well, we need to be going. I hope you have a nice day. Come on honey," George turned Lizzy around, draped his arm around her shoulder, and as they walked away, he whispered in her ear, "let it go."

He got Lizzy in the car and waved to the old lady before getting in the driver's seat.

"Well, that went well?" He said sarcastically.

"Yeah, whatever," Lizzy mumbled.

George kept quiet and drove her to the resort.

"Why are we here? I told you I needed to get my groceries."

"We are going upstairs to talk. Then I'll take you to the grocery store and you can get your damn groceries." George turned off the car, but before he could open the door for Lizzy, she had already gotten out and slammed the door.

"I am not talking to you. I'll just get my groceries tomorrow."

George followed Lizzy as she stomped through the lobby and into the elevator.

"You live in a resort; what do you need groceries for?" George watched her staring at the numbers as they lit up past every floor they passed.

"Personal stuff."

George was trying to make conversation. "Like what?"

Lizzy turned and screamed in his face. "I fucking need Tampons, okay?" Then the elevator doors opened, and she stormed out.

George's eyes widened. Shit, he thought she was going to say toothpaste or ice cream. Hurrying behind her, he caught her room door with his foot before she slammed it.

"Go away George." Lizzy swung the door again, but it bounced off his foot.

"No, we are talking. I'm sick of this shit."

"Fine. Come in. Make yourself at home." Lizzy turned and walked to the living room. She sat on her couch, staring at him.

George shut the door and sat next to her.

"I need to know if I hurt you that night?" George didn't lift his gaze from her face.

Lizzy looked down and rubbed her hands on her thighs. "No."

"I need you to look at me when you say that." George reached his hand out and gently moved her chin to face him. "It's tearing me up inside thinking that I hurt you."

Lizzy's eyes watered. "No, you didn't hurt me. I asked you to have sex with me."

George cupped her jaw. His thumb stroking her cheek. "But I didn't have to be so rough. Please, tell me the truth. Were you a virgin?" George held his breath.

A tear fell down her face. "Yes."

"Fuck, Lizzy." George grabbed her and pulled her onto his lap, draping her legs on either side of his thighs. "I am so sorry." George held her tightly against him. One hand rubbing her back while the other stroked her hair.

Lizzy grabbed his shirt and cried on his chest. George didn't know what to do. His insides were clenching, and he felt sick to his stomach. If he'd known she was a virgin, he never would've done what he did. All he could do now was comfort her and make things right for her. After what felt like forever, she calmed down and loosened her grip on his shirt.

"Lizzy." George cupped her face and pulled her away from his shirt. Gazing into her tear-swollen eyes, he whispered, "How can I make this better? What can I do for you?" George peppered kisses on her forehead, cheeks, and nose. "I am so sorry."

"I forgive you," Lizzy's smile wobbled. "Can you make love to me? The way it's supposed to be when it's someone's first time."

She was killing him. *How could she want him when he'd done it all wrong the first time?* Her eyes pleaded with him to show her what it should have been like when two people cared about each other. Making love could be so beautiful with the right person. She deserved to know what it would feel like to be treasured and brought to the peak of an orgasm before falling into bliss.

"Are you sure?" George needed her to say the words. He wanted to make this right for her, not another wham bam thank you, ma'am.

"I'm sure," Lizzy ground herself onto him.

Overwhelmed by the feeling of possessing her, George lightly licked her lips before giving her a gentle kiss. He was going to go slow so she could feel the burn slowly building from within before he took her to the heavens.

Chapter 24

Wow, Just Wow

Lizzy

George nibbling on her lips wasn't enough. She wanted to feel his tongue inside her mouth. Lizzy opened her mouth and slid her tongue between his lips. George groaned and opened his mouth, giving her access to explore his mouth. The kiss was sweet. Her tongue tentatively darting near his. Their mouths taking their breaths away. His hand was on the back of her head, tilting it for better access, while his other hand massaged her back.

Her body undulated onto his hips, and she could feel his hardness through their clothes. Needing to breathe, she released his mouth and gasped for air. George ran kisses along her jaw to her neck. Lizzy cupped the back of his head, her fingers weaving in his hair. His open mouth kisses and licks were driving her crazy. She didn't want to go slow anymore; she needed him.

"George, please," Lizzy begged. She remembered how good he'd felt after her body adjusted to him and the pain was gone.

"I'm not rushing it this time. I'm gonna worship you like I should have done the last time." George stood up and held her ass. "Wrap your legs around me and hold on. I'm taking you to bed."

Lizzy locked her ankles behind his back and wrapped her arms around his neck. George continued to shower kisses on her neck as he walked them into the bedroom. At the foot of the bed, he unlocked her ankles and let her slide down his body. While he gazed into her eyes, he pulled her shirt off and tossed it to the floor. His eyes drifted down to her lacy bra.

"You are so beautiful," he whispered before his lips landed over hers. With a racing heart, she felt his hand on her face, drawing her in for a kiss that made her pulse quicken and her breath catch in her throat. His hands glided down her face and neck to her breasts, massaging them through the lacy bra. The roughness of the bra caused her nipples to harden and ache. Her pussy pulsed, crying for attention. Lizzy pulled her mouth away from his and let out a low moan.

George bent down and sucked her breast through her bra while the other hand tweaked her other nipple. The intense pleasure was almost unbearable, leaving her weak and trembling. George reached around her back and unhooked her bra. Her heavy breasts fell forward, happy to be free, only to be captured in George's mouth as he took turns sucking and licking each one.

"George, please," Lizzy pleaded while she held onto his shoulders.

George kissed his way to her belly. His hands undoing the button and zipper on her Capri pants. Once undone, they fell to the floor. George got down on his knees and cupped her ass, bringing her pussy to his face. Lizzy felt him smell her and lick her through her panties. Oh my God, she felt light-headed. Her pelvis moving of its own accord toward George's mouth. She needed more.

George slid his hands under her panties and slid them down. Tapping on the back of her shins, she pulled her legs out one at a time until she was standing naked in front of him.

"You take my breath away," George said as his gaze worshipped her body.

She was moving one of her hands to cover her breasts and the other to her core, but George captured her hands and held them away from her body. Slowly rising, his gaze lingered on her, drinking her in until he reached his full height and passionately kissed her.

"Don't cover yourself up." George said between kisses. "You have a beautiful body. Stand proud and own it."

"You have too many clothes on." Lizzy said after he released her mouth. His eyes were now a smoky blue, like storm clouds of lust moving in.

"Lay down for me." George grabbed the back of his shirt and pulled it off like most men could do and women wondered how they did it.

Lizzy's fingers trailed lightly down and around his chiseled abs, the warmth of his skin evident beneath her touch, as he watched her. With each caress, she felt his muscles tense beneath her touch, his breath catching in his throat. She wondered if his nipples were as sensitive as hers. She rolled one around with her finger. George moaned. His rapid heartbeat thrummed against her palm as she laid her hand over his heart, a frantic pulse that made her breath catch. Her tongue danced around his nipple, mimicking the same tantalizing movements he had used on her before enveloping it in her mouth.

"Lizzy," George mumbled. "Please get on the bed."

"Not yet." Lizzy felt powerful having this handsome man under her spell. She gave him the same open mouth kisses he had given her down her chest. She stopped at his sweatpants. Sliding her hands inside the back of his sweatpants and boxer briefs, the soft cotton felt smooth against her skin as she cupped his warm, muscular ass. Then she glided her hands down his legs, the fabric bunching up beneath her touch as she shoved his clothes down.

She watched his ab muscles tighten, his fists clenched by his side, and his cock bob toward her face as he stepped out of his pants. She ran her hands up the back of his legs until she reached his ass, then leaned in to lick him from the base of his shaft to the tip. As she tasted his salty, musky precum, she felt his cock twitch with pleasure. Squeezing his ass, she lowered her mouth onto his hard, thick cock until she could feel him nudge the back of her throat. Pulling back, she wrapped one hand around the base of his shaft, while her tongue and mouth eagerly explored every part of him.

"Lizzy," George groaned and placed his hands on the sides of her head. "Stop, this is about you, not me."

Lizzy released his engorged shaft from her mouth and looked up. Beads of sweat trickled down his forehead, and the bulging veins in his neck throbbed. "I'm enjoying this. You taste so good."

"My turn," George growled.

One minute, Lizzy was on her knees and the next she was flat on her back on the bed with her legs spread eagle while George slid his tongue between her nether lips. Her body was writhing on the bed while George used his tongue to fuck her. His hand rolled her clit, and her body jolted, trying to get away from him. The euphoria was too much.

George placed his other hand on her stomach, holding her in place while he tweaked and squeezed her clit, playing with it as if it was his new favorite toy. Lizzy couldn't hold back. Her hands gripped the sheet, her body spasmed, and she stopped breathing while her pleasure tore through her at lightning speed. Lizzy lay still, trying to catch her breath while George licked his way to her mouth.

"You taste incredible."

Lizzy tasted herself in his mouth and squirmed.

George released her mouth and looked into her eyes. "It's good for us to taste each other. Nothing we do is wrong, ugly, or bad. Okay?"

Lizzy nodded and watched George reach over to his pants and pull a condom out of his wallet. He rolled it on and laid between her legs. His cock at the entrance.

"When you're ready, guide me in." George kissed her neck.

Lizzy was ready. She wanted to feel him inside her again. Reaching between their bodies, she grabbed his cock and positioned it at her entrance. George eased in as slow as molasses. She knew he was trying to get her body to adjust to his size. When he was all the way in, he lay still and groaned.

"George, you can move. It's okay." Lizzy whispered and kissed his cheek. "I'm okay."

George went slow at first until Lizzy wrapped her legs around his hips and pushed the heels of her feet into his ass. She needed him to move quicker.

"George, please." Her body kept meeting up to his, urging him to go faster.

George chuckled. "Okay. I get the hint."

He thrust harder and faster. Lizzy gripped George tightly, eager for him to lead her to a place of heightened pleasure and ecstasy. With a subtle rotation of his hips, he ground into her; the friction igniting a fire within her, a whirlwind of pleasure that vibrated through her body, culminating in the most powerful orgasm yet. Her body clenched tight around his shaft, causing him to climax with her. He dropped on top of her, panting.

"Wow," Lizzy mumbled between breaths. "Just wow,"

"Yep." George rolled off her and pulled her into his arms. "Was that better? More like what you thought it would be?"

"Yes." Lizzy kissed his chin and laid her head to rest on his chest. "Thank you."

"You're welcome. I really am sorry."

"Stop apologizing. You made up for it. Let's move on from here, okay?"

"Okay." George ran his fingers through her hair. "I need to get cleaned up. I'll be right back."

Lizzy let him go and curled up with a pillow. Nothing had ever felt so good before. She hoped they could do it again. She wanted him to be her boyfriend, but didn't know how to ask. George came back and wiped between her legs with a warm cloth. When the cloth hit her clit, Lizzy's hips moved into his hand, and she moaned.

"I think I've created a monster," George chuckled, got them under the covers, and pulled her back into his arms.

"I think you have." Lizzy reached for his cock, which was already hard. "I thought men needed more recovery time."

"I guess I don't with you." George rolled and leaned over her. "So, no period, huh?"

"What?" Lizzy was confused. *Why was he asking about her period?*

"You said you needed tampons at the grocery store." George raised his eyebrow like an inspector quizzing his suspect.

Lizzy laughed. "Uh, I was just trying to piss you off."

"So, you lied to me, and you called me daddy the other day when I told you not to do that?" George sat up and pulled her legs over his lap.

"What are you doing?" Lizzy squirmed, trying to get off the bed, but George had a solid grip on her legs.

"Giving you the spanking I promised." George rolled her over and pulled her ass up to his thighs. But before she felt a slap, he slid his finger into her pussy.

"George," Lizzy was panting. "I like that better. Please, no spanking."

"Oh, you'll like my spanking, trust me." George spanked one ass cheek then spread her legs and lightly spanked her pussy.

When she screamed out, he thrust his finger back in. He continued this until her ass was a beautiful shade of pink and her body was ready to take him again. Putting on his last condom, he fucked her from behind. One hand held her breast while the other played with her clit until they climaxed.

"Oh my God, that was...that was," Lizzy was having trouble catching her breath. "Amazing."

"I told you, you'd like it," George said before he left her.

She could hear the water running in the bathroom sink, then felt his hands wiping her. This time, when he climbed into bed, they both curled up around each other, exhausted. Lizzy felt his chest rising and falling and could hear his steady heartbeat. She figured he'd fallen asleep.

She mumbled, "Goodnight, daddy."

"You'll pay for that," George mumbled.

"I hope so," Lizzy whispered and fell asleep with a smile on her face.

Chapter 25

A Moment of Bliss

George

George woke up from their nap with Lizzy still in his arms lightly snoring. He slowly slid out from under her, not wanting to wake her. When she grumbled, he slid pillows in her arms. Checking the time, he realized it was too late to take her to the grocery store. If he didn't leave immediately and head home to shower and change, he would be late for work.

He found his clothes, threw them on, and then, after a gentle kiss to her forehead, he quietly left the room. Although he hated leaving without saying goodbye, the peaceful, soft look on her face as she slept on the pillow eased his guilt. In the dimly lit kitchen, he found pen and paper, hastily scribbled a note, and then tiptoed into the bedroom, placing it gently on her pillow.

Smiling, he left her room and took the elevator downstairs. The doors in the resort automatically locked when they shut, but he would feel better if the chain was on. Since he couldn't magically chain the door from the outside, he called Holt.

"Hey, man. What's up?" Holt answered.

"I just left Lizzy in her room. She was asleep, so I couldn't slide the chain on her door. Can you go through your door and do that for me?"

"I can, as long as she hasn't locked our adjoining door on her side. Let me check. You do know that the doors automatically lock when you close them, right?"

George heard Frey ask Holt, who was on the phone.

"It's George. Hang on, sweetheart, I gotta check something for him. I'll be right back," Holt said to Frey.

George could hear him opening and closing doors. "Hey, her adjoining door was unlocked, so I put the chain on her front door. Anything else you want to tell me?"

George didn't want to get into it. He knew asking Holt to go in there was tricky, but he hated thinking that her door wasn't completely secure.

"Not right now," George said. "But thanks for helping me out."

"Sure, but I want that story soon."

"Okay." George mumbled and hung up.

Getting into his car, he drove to his apartment. Hopefully, the only people that would still be working at the cultural center were Mark and Maggie. Thunder should be gone by now. The dynamic duo would still ask questions, but it was easier to distract them than Tori and Alex, who might've heard about Lizzy's incident at the grocery store.

Mark and Thunder's trucks were still in the parking lot, but not Alex's. He just might catch a break. When he walked in, everyone was at the lobby desk, including Tori and Alex. *Fuck!* He hadn't seen Alex's truck, so he'd assumed Alex wasn't there. Big mistake. Of course, his truck wasn't there because Lizzy had probably used it to get to the grocery store. Yet another reason to take her back to the store.

"Hey, how's it going?" George waved at them, fully intending to walk past them and not engage in conversation.

"Good," Maggie smiled. "How are you?"

"Great, gotta hurry so I can get to work on time." George increased his pace, but stopped when Tori called out.

"George, have you seen Lizzy?"

George closed his eyes briefly and turned around with a smile on his face. "Uh, earlier today, yes." He didn't want to lie to her because Holt and Frey already knew he'd been at her apartment.

"She went to the grocery store and hasn't come back. She took Alex's truck. It's not like her to not come back. I'm worried." Tori was wringing her hands. Alex put his arm around her.

George knew he had to tell her something. He didn't want Tori thinking Lizzy could be lying in a ditch somewhere. "She had an altercation at the grocery store, and Deputy Ray took her to the police station."

"What?" Tori covered her mouth. "Is she okay? Why didn't she call me?"

"I don't know why she didn't call you, but I took care of it. Just like I did at the airport." George nodded. "Everything's fine."

"What happened at the airport?" Tori looked upset. "And why did she call you and not me?"

"Uh, she had a misunderstanding with her seatmate on the plane." George looked between Tori and Thunder. He didn't realize Lizzy hadn't told Tori about being escorted off the plane. "But I took care of it. It's all good now."

"Thunder?" Tori turned to him. "Did you know something happened to Lizzy on the plane?"

Thunder rubbed the back of his neck. George felt bad for putting him in the hot seat.

"George mentioned something to me," Thunder smirked. "But I thought it was best for it to come from Lizzy. Sorry."

"Will someone please tell me what's going on?" Tori spun around, staring at all of them with narrowed eyes, but Maggie, Mark, and Alex shrugged at her.

Sky laid her head on her paws and whined. Even she could sense the disappointment in Tori's voice. George couldn't blame Sky. He felt like shit breaking the news to Tori like this.

"Tori, I don't know what they're talking about." Maggie shook her head. "I'm just as confused as you are."

"Baby, maybe it's best you talk to Lizzy. She probably called George because he helped her before and is a police officer." Alex hugged her and glared at George over her shoulder. "Maybe she thought he could help her faster, and she didn't want to worry you."

"I'm sure that's it." George bowed his head. He hated seeing the anger in Alex's eyes.

"But why not tell me?" Tori's questions were killing him. He'd left Lizzy feeling so happy and now he wanted to wring her pretty, little neck for causing her sister distress.

"When we get home, you can talk to her. For now, let's figure out how we're getting home without my car." Alex continued to rub her back.

"Hey, on the bright side, I fixed the grocery store mishap for Lizzy at the station. Unfortunately, I took her back to the resort instead of the grocery store. Sorry, Alex. I didn't know your car was there."

"I have to pick up some stuff for Isa that she's craving," Thunder announced. "I'll drive you over there."

"What is she craving now?" George grinned, trying to take the conversation off him and Lizzy because if looks could kill Tori and Alex wanted him dead. They were going to have to wait in line until he got his hands on Lizzy.

"Cookies and Cream Ice Cream with nuts and whipped cream." Thunder smiled.

"Sounds good. At least it's not like a pickle and peanut butter sandwich." George winced.

"Bite your tongue and do not suggest something like that to her." Thunder cringed. "Come on," Thunder waved to Tori and Alex. "Let's go before my wife texts me again for the fifth time, asking me if I'm at the grocery store yet."

George knew Thunder loved every minute of being able to do something for Isa. He was overprotective of her, always making sure she was safe and cared for. His grumbling was just that, grumbling with no substance.

"Alright, well, I gotta get ready for work. See you all later." George hightailed it out of there before he got caught with more questions about Lizzy. As it was, he had less than an hour to get ready and head out on patrol.

Chapter 26

Tori aka Fierce Interrogator

Lizzy turned over and reached for George. All she felt was the bed, not George. She thought they'd had a good time, so why did he run out on her? Was he trying to get even for her running out on him last time?

Lizzy grumbled, "Ugh." Her hand, reaching for the pillow, touched a piece of paper. *Had he left her a note?*

Sitting up, she grabbed it and read.

Hey Beautiful,

I'm sorry I had to leave and didn't get to drive you to the grocery store, but I gotta work tonight. I didn't want to wake you because you looked so peaceful, even with the cute snoring noises you make...LOL. Anyway, can I see you tomorrow? I can come down and eat lunch with you or we can go somewhere. Text me.

Your boyfriend,
Deputy George

It was a really sweet note. Lizzy was glad he took the time to write it. Although, she didn't know she snored, or that it was cute. Clutching the note, Lizzy fell back onto the bed. She would love to see him tomorrow. She needed to let Tori know that she and George were on the mend. Laying in bed, she thought back over her afternoon with George. It was even more wonderful than she had imagined. The spanking was interesting, but she didn't hate it, and he didn't hurt her. She wouldn't mind calling him daddy again if that was her so-called punishment.

"Elizabeth Tall Bear, you have some explaining to do!" Lizzy heard Tori scream as she came closer to the bedroom. Shit, she didn't have time to get out of bed and put a robe on, so she held the covers up to her chest.

Tori stopped at the foot of her bed and shouted, "Why didn't you call me?"

"Uh, about what?"

"You were in jail, and you didn't think to call your sister?" Tori was pacing like a caged tiger, back and forth, back and forth. "And while you're explaining things, what the hell happened at the airport?"

"I wasn't in jail. I was waiting for George. How did you hear about the airport?"

"I just saw George at the cultural center, and he told me. You also left Alex's car at the grocery store. How were we supposed to get home?"

"Ugh!" Lizzy grumbled and dropped back into bed. *Why did George say anything?* Couldn't he have made up another story? Then again, if they hadn't had sex and fallen asleep, she would have gone back to the grocery store and gotten Alex's car. *What a mess!*

"Why are you in bed naked?" Tori walked around the bed, grabbing her clothes off the floor. "And don't you have a hamper?"

Lizzy watched Tori, waiting for it all to click in place. Suddenly, Tori stopped and looked between the bed and Lizzy's clothes in her hands.

"Did you have sex?" Tori's voice screeched. "With whom?"

"Baby," Alex stepped into the bedroom, avoiding eye contact with Lizzy. He put his arms around Tori and pulled her into the living room. "I think we need to give Lizzy some space."

"Alex, I need to talk to my sister. She's keeping too many secrets from me. I'll meet you downstairs in a few minutes." That's all Lizzy heard from their conversation before Tori walked back in.

"Take a shower and then come sit with me on the couch. I want to hear about what's been happening to you."

"Okay," Lizzy nodded.

Tori dropped the clothes and left the room. She must be furious to have tossed the clothes back on the floor rather than placing them in Lizzy's hamper. Lizzy was going to have to tell Tori the truth. Which was okay. The cat would be out of the bag soon about her and George now that they were dating. *Were they dating? Was he her boyfriend or just being sarcastic since that's what she'd called him at the station?*

Lizzy finished her shower and got dressed. Tori was sitting on the couch on her phone.

"I'm sorry I didn't call you," Lizzy started first before she sat next to Tori. "I thought George could help me quicker, since he's an officer."

Tori put her phone down. "That's what Alex said, but I still don't know why you didn't call me after George helped you. You had Alex's car. How did you expect us to get home?"

"I'm sorry, okay." Lizzy sat back on the couch and closed her eyes. "I wasn't thinking straight. Besides, you work with your friends. I'm sure any of them would drive you to the grocery store."

"That's not the point. What you did was irresponsible."

"I know." Lizzy opened her eyes and turned her head to look at her. "You're right."

Tori leaned against the arm of the couch and crossed her arms. "Tell me everything. About the airport, the grocery store, and George, because somehow George is involved in all of your mishaps."

"Fine."

Knock, knock

"Hang on. Let me get that." Lizzy got up and headed to her front door. She wasn't expecting anyone. Looking through the peephole, she saw Angel. Unlocking the door, it stopped short. The chain was hooked. *How did George get the chain on her door?* She'd have to ask him later. Sliding the chain, she opened the door for Angel and stepped back.

Angel barreled in. "Oh my God, Alex just told Barrett that you were at the police station today. What can I do to help you?"

"Hi Angel," Lizzy rolled her eyes. "Have a seat and I'll explain everything to you and my sister."

Angel worked in the prosecutor's office but had been a defense attorney for years. She was Reaper's daughter, the president of Lucifer's Renegades MC, and after the wedding shootout fiasco had stopped defending the men in the MC and worked with the state to put them away.

"Hey, Tori. It's good to see you." Angel sat on the couch, leaving a space between her and Tori.

"Good to see you too, Angel."

It amazed Lizzy that Tori and Angel were such good friends, given that Reaper had tried to kidnap Tori and Winston had assaulted her. Sitting between them on the couch, Lizzy recounted how a fight with Karen resulted in her removal from the flight, and George forcing her to apologize to the lady at the grocery store.

"That's crazy," Angel humphed. "I could've helped you with either of those issues. Next time, call me."

Tori frowned at Angel before looking at Lizzy. "I'm glad George had some sense and made you go over there to apologize. What if she'd pressed charges?"

"I would've dealt with it." Lizzy rolled her eyes. "I can't believe you think I don't have any sense."

"Listen to what you just told me." Tori raised her arms and dropped them, exasperated with Lizzy. "You don't listen to what anyone says, and you pick fights. Sometimes it's best to say nothing, even when you know the other person is wrong."

"That's what George said," Lizzy sighed.

"Or you could press charges against them?" Angel shrugged.

"You are not helping." Tori pointed at Angel. "Do you not remember Barrett coming to your aid when you punched that lady in the casino? She could've pressed charges against you."

"Yes, I do. But I could've pressed charges against her too."

"Yeah, but wasn't it easier to just apologize and get on with your night?" Tori said, exasperated with them both.

"Maybe," Angel shrugged.

"I'm not like you Tori." Lizzy sat up and shook her head. "I don't shy away from my opinions. Why should I? Everyone is entitled to their beliefs, and I don't understand why I have to be the one to back off. It's not fair."

"Life isn't fair." Tori scooted closer to Lizzy and rubbed her back. "I'm not saying you are wrong about what you said to those people, but you need to know when to agree to disagree, so you don't get in trouble. George has kept you out of jail twice now. How many more times is he gonna have to save you? He can only do so much before you land behind bars."

"You are so dramatic," Lizzy sighed.

"No, I'm not. Lizzy this isn't like the rez. The people who live in this city are incredibly diverse, representing a wide range of cultures and beliefs. You need to learn to read the room and stop an argument before it gets out of hand. "Please, promise me you'll at least attempt to be less confrontational with people," Tori pleaded, her eyes filled with worry.

"Or you can call..." Angel commented, but stopped when Tori glared at her.

Lizzy looked at her sister. She loved her and didn't want to cause her any unnecessary heartache.

"Okay," Lizzy nodded. "I'll try to stop before I go too far. I'm sorry I didn't tell you. The thought of you being disappointed in me hurts, and I didn't want to see that in your eyes. I'll be more careful."

"Thank you," Tori side hugged her. "Now, tell me what is going on with George. Last time we talked, you weren't too happy with him, but now you've called him in as your knight in shining armor three times that I know of."

"Three times?" Lizzy quirked her eyebrow.

"Wow, Deputy George, is your knight in shining armor?" Angel smiled.

"Yeah, three." Tori raised her fingers as she counted the times. "Once, at the airport. Second time was when you got him to take you shopping for our brunch decorations, and now you called him after the grocery store argument that landed you in the police station. And let's not forget when he went to The Dragon after you were roofied."

"That night sucked." Angel sat back and huffed.

Lizzy winced. All of those incidents made her sound like an insolent child. "We made up."

"Is he the one that was in your room today?" Tori questioned her.

"George was in your room. Ooh, do tell." Angel sat up and stared at Lizzy.

"Yes, he was." Lizzy answered, short and sweet, hoping Tori didn't ask for any intimate details.

"I don't want to know the details only if it was more of what you expected your first time." Tori placed her hand on Lizzy's chin and turned her face toward her. "Did he hurt you?" Tori whispered.

"You were a virgin?" Angel looked appalled.

"Maybe you should go." Tori stared at Angel. "This is a private conversation."

"Oh, I'm sorry." Angel's body drooped before she placed her hands on the couch to stand.

"No, Angel. You can stay. You're family." Lizzy pat her knee.

"Okay. If you're sure?" Angel glanced between Lizzy and Tori.

Tori sighed, "It's fine. I didn't mean to snap at you, Angel. I'm sorry. Lizzy's right. You are my soon to be sister-in-law and I'm sure Lizzy could use your opinion."

"Thank you, Tori." Angel smiled.

"To answer your previous question, no." Lizzy shook her head. "Making love to George was beautiful and perfect. I think we're dating."

"You said making love, not fucking," Angel grinned. "This must be serious."

"What do you mean, you think you're dating?" Tori tilted her head.

"Well, he left me a note asking me to have lunch with him tomorrow and asked me to text him."

"I want to see this note." Tori stood and pulled Lizzy up with her.

"Me too." Angel stood with them.

"Okay, hang on. I'll get it." Lizzy ran into the room and brought them the note.

"Aww, that is so sweet and funny. Go, George!" Angel punched her arm in the air.

Tori smirked at Angel and handed the note back to Lizzy. "That was nice. So have lunch with him and see where this all goes. But be nice to him Lizzy, he's a good guy."

"We love Deputy George." Angel nodded. Lizzy and Tori both stared at her. "And... we love you too. You make a cute couple. Group hug!"

"Hey, what's going on?" Frey asked from the adjoining door to her room. "Why did Holt have to come in here today and put the chain on your door? Are you okay?" Frey's gaze bounced between them. "Why are we hugging? I want a hug." Frey ran to them and wrapped her arms around them. "I love group hugs."

Frey's comment finally explained the mystery of the chain on the door. She'd have to talk to George about involving Holt.

"So, who's gonna tell me what's going on?" Frey plopped on the couch and stared at them, one by one.

A groan escaped Lizzy's lips as she prepared to recount her story to Frey. She knew Tori and Angel would have plenty to add to her story. That's okay. It was comforting to have a close-knit group of girlfriends she could confide in and seek advice from, their laughter echoing in her ears.

Chapter 27

Warnings

George

Exhausted from his shift, George stumbled through the door and collapsed into his bed. The good thing about his job was that no two days were the same. The bad thing was that he was bone-tired. He needed to sleep for a few hours before he went downstairs and joined Lizzy for lunch. She had texted okay to their lunch date but never said if she wanted to stay in the cultural center or go out to eat. A wide grin stretched across his face because he didn't care if they stayed in or went out. He just wanted to spend some quality time with her outside the bedroom, focusing on their relationship instead of constantly keeping her out of jail. George loved her adventurous spirit and confidence, and didn't mind rescuing her, but did she really need to pick a fight with everyone? Granted, The Dragon incident wasn't her fault, that guy preyed on a pretty girl. George set his alarm for noon and went to bed.

When his alarm woke him up, he texted Lizzy that he was going to shower and then come downstairs for lunch. On one hand, he wished she would've come upstairs when she got to work and crawled into bed with him, but on the other, he knew they needed to get to know each other better so their relationship could grow into something other than sex.

He felt a powerful pull towards her and a deep desire to learn more about her life and experiences. He was intensely curious about her, wanting to know everything from her favorite foods and colors to her hobbies, movies, and songs. She intrigued him with her comments and her sass.

George showered and changed into jeans and a t-shirt. He would come up later and put on his uniform. With a smile on his face, he entered the kitchen and saw Alex at the stove.

"Hey Alex, how's it going?"

Alex pointed at him. "You better not hurt her."

"Whoa," George put up his hands. "If you mean Lizzy, I like her a lot. I'm not planning on hurting her. Hell, what if she hurts me?"

"Yeah, right, Romeo Joe." Alex smirked.

"Hey." George walked closer to Alex. The last thing he needed was for the guests at the center to overhear their conversation. "I haven't slept around in a while."

"What, like a couple of days?"

"No, more like since your wedding."

George didn't like the way Alex was looking at him. Like he didn't believe him. But it was true. Since he'd thought he'd deflowered a virgin, he hadn't had the impulse to have sex with anyone else until he talked to Lizzy. He wasn't an asshole, and he always tried to protect the girl and himself.

"Right?" Alex turned back to the stove.

"It's true!" George raised his arms, pleading for Alex to believe him, but he may as well have been preaching to the choir because Alex wasn't looking at him.

"What's true?" Thunder said behind him.

George turned around and saw Thunder, Lizzy, and Tori standing inside the doorway to the restaurant.

"Hey, George." Lizzy was the first to acknowledge him.

"Hi," George grinned at her and held up his hand, stopping anyone else from speaking. Deciding to clear the air and tell everyone his intentions, he blurted, "I was just telling Alex that I care about you and we're dating."

Lizzy's face beamed. She strolled to George and hugged him. George hugged her back and then looked around the room, ready for any further questions. Alex coughed. Thunder had a puzzled look on his face, and Tori frowned. Okay, then.

"Can I talk to you a minute, George?" Thunder pointed out the door.

"Sure," George glanced down at Lizzy. "Can we eat when I'm done?"

"I'm kinda hungry, but I'll wait for you."

"No need, I have things I can work on while you two eat your lunch." Thunder came up to George and slapped him on the back. "Come see me when you finish."

"Okay." George nodded, not sure what Thunder wanted to talk to him about, but he would find him.

"I can get you a plate if you want to grab a table?" Lizzy grabbed two plates.

"Is it busy out there?"

"It's not too bad." Tori stared at him and crossed her arms.

He'd never seen Tori act anything but sweet to him. She was acting like a mama bear, with Lizzy being her cub.

"Then I'll get my food, and we'll walk out there together." George grinned at Lizzy and took the plate she handed him.

"Okay." Lizzy blushed and quickly removed her hand from his plate when their hands touched.

They served themselves and left the kitchen while Alex and Tori stared daggers at him. On his way out, Tori lightly grabbed his elbow and whispered, "Don't hurt her." George nodded. As if he hadn't heard that before. *Why did everyone think he would be the villain in this story?*

George followed Lizzy to a table in the corner near the outside window.

"I'll go get us some waters. I'll be right back," Lizzy said after placing her plate on the table.

"No, you sit." George rubbed her shoulder. "I'll get them."

George braced himself before entering the kitchen again. Alex and Tori were standing together, talking about Lizzy and him.

"Guys, listen." George walked up to them. "I care about Lizzy. Tori, I already promised Alex I wouldn't do anything to hurt her, and I meant it."

"Maybe you guys shouldn't date," Tori mumbled.

"That's not fair." George ran his hand over his head. "You guys know me. I would never do anything to purposely hurt her."

"What if you hurt her unknowingly?" Tori cocked her eyebrow.

"Well, hell, Tori!" George threw up his arms and spun around.

"Hey, watch your tone." Alex pointed at him.

"Sorry." George leaned against the counter. "Look in a relationship anyone can get hurt, intentionally or unintentionally, but we won't know if this can work between us if we don't try."

"George is right." Lizzy came over and wove her arm around his arm. "I know you both love me and want to protect my heart, but it's mine to give. I want to date George and see where things go. I'm going into this with my eyes wide open. Please honor my wishes and stop giving George a hard time."

"Okay," Tori sighed. "I'm sorry George. I worry about you getting hurt just as much as I worry about Lizzy. We love you both. Just be careful with each other's hearts." Alex nodded at his wife's words.

"We will." George and Lizzy walked over and hugged both Tori and Alex. "Thank you."

George grabbed two water bottles out of the refrigerator and followed Lizzy back to their table.

"Well, that went better than I thought." Lizzy sat and picked up her fork. "I'm sorry they were giving you a hard time."

"It's okay. They love you. I get that." George grinned and reached for her hand.

Lizzy placed her hand in his.

"How about we talk about something else? Like, what's your favorite color?" Lizzy squeezed his hand.

George laughed, "I like blue. What's yours?"

Lizzy smiled back. "I like red."

"Figures you'd like a hot, passionate color." George winked at her.

They continued sharing each other's likes and dislikes until George saw the time and realized he still had to talk to Thunder. He helped her take their dishes to the kitchen, gave her a hug and a kiss on her forehead in front of Alex and Tori, then headed for Thunder's office. As he passed Maggie and Mark at the lobby desk, they both grinned at him and winked. Great, now they also knew he and Lizzy were dating.

Thunder sat behind his L-shaped desk, facing his computer on his right side. George lightly knocked, not wanting to enter until Thunder saw him. Thunder spun his chair around and waved him in.

"What's up?" George sat in the chair in front of Thunder's desk. "You wanted to see me?"

"I want to make sure you are okay." Thunder quirked his eyebrow. "After the airport and The Dragon incidents, I didn't realize Lizzy had been in more trouble. I know we've both been busy, but I'm always here for you and I haven't spoken to you in a few days. I just wanted to check in."

George always went to Thunder for advice, except when he'd had sex with Lizzy. He should've talked to Thunder about it months ago when it happened, but he didn't know how to approach the subject because Lizzy was Tori's sister and a childhood friend of the family in South Dakota.

George knew Thunder was already worried about Isa and the baby following the terrifying ordeal with the motorcycle club and he didn't want to burden him with any more stress. It had been a mistake, because Thunder could've helped him sort everything out. Better late than never. George stood and closed Thunder's office door. He didn't want to be overheard.

"I'm doing okay...now." George sat down and faced Thunder. "I...Lizzy and I had sex the night of the shooting."

Thunder's eyebrows raised so high they almost reached his hairline, but he stayed quiet.

"That was a crazy night. Barrett asked me to get her out of the area, and I did. She was so freaked out about dying, she begged me to stay with her. I knew I had to go, but she was very persuasive. I'll leave it at that, and we ended up together. She ran out on me and then I went to help Barrett. Later on, I thought she might've been a virgin and wanted to talk to her about it, but every time I called her in South Dakota, she wouldn't answer my texts or calls."

George sighed. "Imagine my surprise when you asked me to pick her up at the airport. I finally had my chance to talk to her, but she refused to talk to me about that night." George looked down at his hands and fidgeted with his fingers. "I'm not proud of the way I handled the situation. Yesterday, we finally talked about it and sorted it out. We both like each other a lot and want to give dating a go."

Thunder was still silent. George glanced up, ready to face Thunder's anger. But Thunder wasn't angry. He was nodding and placed his arms on his desk before he said, "I see. This all makes so much sense now."

"Are you mad at me?" George sat up straight, waiting to be disciplined by his mentor, brother. Thunder's opinion of him meant the world to him.

"No," Thunder sighed. "I can see that you tried to rectify your actions. All I ask now is that you be careful with her heart. I will support you any way I can, but you need to know I will support her, too. Just be careful with each other. Be the kind and responsible man I know you to be. Everything will work out in due time."

George's shoulders slumped, the tension draining from his body like water from a leaking bucket, leaving him feeling lighter than air. Only then did he understand how important Thunder's opinion was to him.

"Thank you," George whispered and stood.

"I love you, George." Thunder went around his desk and wrapped his arms around him. "You are the little brother I never had."

"I love you too, big bro." George hugged him back.

Chapter 28

Amateur Night

Lizzy

Lizzy saw George when he left Thunder's office, but left shortly after with Tori and Alex. At the resort, Tori was helping Alex, Frey picked up a shift helping her fellow Blackjack dealers, and Angel was working late finishing up a case. That left Lizzy all alone and bored. She changed into a cute dress and went looking for Tori and Alex. She told them she wanted to go shopping. Alex gave her the keys to his truck, with the promise of bringing it back.

She went to the mall, but soon realized shopping wasn't fun without some girl friends. Leaving the mall, she decided she wanted to dance. She would've asked Maggie to go with her, but after the fiasco at The Dragon, she went by herself. Lizzy just wanted to dance. She was not accepting drinks from anyone, even if they were cute. It felt like she had driven all over town looking for a fun place when she saw a building ahead on the right with purple shining lights. That looked like a fun place.

Pulling into the parking lot, she noticed a lot of guys going in, but not too many girls. Maybe it was girls' night, and the women were already inside. She noticed that was a thing in Ft. Lauderdale. Some places even had a male revue for women and opened their doors to men after the show was over. Lots of men went later so they could get lucky with women that were already primed and ready for them. She loved this town—so full of life.

Lizzy paid the cover and entered. As soon as she walked in, she knew she had stepped into a strip club. It wasn't dingy like she'd seen in movies. There was a purple glow and there were bouncers by every door, bars, runways, and stages. She had never seen so many runways and stages in one room. Each runway and stage had at least one pole and multiple women in various levels of undress. None were nude, but several were topless, and all had beautiful bodies.

Lizzy strolled up to the bar and ordered a beer in a bottle. She watched the bartenders' every move. She would not get roofied again. Fool her once, but not twice. The bartender looked at her with a frown but placed the beer bottle in front of her. Grabbing her beer, she turned to face the crowd and watched the girl's dance.

One guy, fueled by bravado, attempted to leap onto the stage and grope the dancer, but two enormous bodyguards, swift as hawks, tackled him before he could even lift his leg. Lizzy could hear the guy apologizing as they walked by her, but the bodyguards didn't care. They just kept repeating, 'you don't touch our girls', before they threw him out.

A waitress wearing a skimpy bathing suit that left little to the imagination, far more revealing than anything Lizzy had ever seen, approached the bar.

"Max, I need two Bud Lights, a whiskey, and a tequila shot." She hollered to the bartender before looking at Lizzy. "You're new." She eyed Lizzy from head to her toe. "Are you dancing tonight at amateur hour?"

"No," Lizzy smiled. "I just stopped in for some fun, but I didn't realize this was a strip club."

"Best one in town." The waitress winked at her. "My name's Amy."

"I'm Lizzy."

"So, first time in here, huh?" Amy nodded toward the crowd.

"Yeah, I'm new in town."

"Well, if you ever want to let loose and dance like those ladies..." Amy pointed to the stage. "This is the place to do it. The guys will keep you safe. You should think about it. You look like you're in good shape and the tips are incredible."

"Do you dance?"

"Sometimes on amateur night, but mostly I'm a server."

"Here you go, Amy." The bartender put the drinks on her tray.

"Thanks, Max." Amy smiled at him. Picking up her tray, she left Lizzy with interesting parting words. "Think about dancing. It's very freeing."

Lizzy had never danced at a club like this before, but after Amy left and she watched a few more girls strip and dance, she wanted to try. Amy saying it was a freeing experience taunted her every thought. Lizzy longed to break free from her parents' suffocating rules, her sister's constant judgment, and the stifling weight of societal expectations. For just a few minutes, she yearned to experience the sweet freedom of having no burdens. She knew Tori and her parents would kill her if they found out what she did, but they would never know. Hell, no one she knew was here. What could go wrong?

Amy came back and placed another order with Max.

"Have you thought about dancing?" Amy smiled. "I can see the wheels spinning in your head."

"Yes. I want to do it. Who do I need to talk to?" Lizzy's mind was made up. She was not turning back. Every time a patron got handsy or tried to grab a girl, she'd seen the bouncers react instantly, protecting the dancer. Up on that stage, with the music thumping, she could lose herself in the dance and forget her troubles.

"Max, I'll be right back for that order. Lizzy, come with me."

Amy grabbed her hand and pulled her to a booth at the back of the club. A man sat hunched over a glowing computer screen, a young girl perched beside him, her gaze fixed on something else entirely.

"Carl." Amy pushed Lizzy forward. "Lizzy here wants to dance tonight for amateur night."

Carl looked up from his computer. "Have you danced before?" His eyes scanned her body.

"No, sir." Lizzy shook her head. "But I've watched them and know I can do it." A proud feeling swelled in Lizzy as she spoke with confidence, though a cold sweat slicked her palms, betraying her inner fear. *Was she really going to do this?*

"I gotta go back to my tables. Good luck Lizzy." Amy waved behind her back as she walked away.

"Okay." Carl's gaze never wavered from her body. "What are you wearing under there?" He pointed at her clothes. "The men will want to see you either topless or down to bra and panties."

"They'll like what I'm wearing, but I can borrow pasties if you have an extra pair."

"Kendra, help her out." Carl motioned to the girl next to him. "You'll get tips, I keep half."

Chapter 29

I Just Wanted to Dance

Lizzy followed Kendra closely, listening intently to her instructions.

"The most important thing to remember is to smile and look sexually at the men. The more you do that, the better the tips. Regulars like the new girls since they've seen us before, but you have to engage with them, or they'll ignore you. Got it."

"Got it."

Kendra led her to a changing room that had girls dressed in sexy outfits as they applied makeup.

"Mama Lush," Kendra called out to one dancer. "This is Lizzy. She wants to dance during amateur hour. It's her first time. Do you have an extra set of pasties she can borrow?" Kendra faced Lizzy. "Mama Lush has been here since we opened and had danced for years. She can help you with anything you might need."

"Thank you," Lizzy said before Kendra left her with Mama Lush, who was the epitome of her name. She looked to be in her forties with a voluptuous, hourglass body. Her boobs didn't look real, but who was she to judge?

"Hi, honey." Mama Lush opened a drawer in her station and pulled out a box filled with pasties. "Pick whichever one you want.."

Lizzy rummaged through the pasties until she found a turquoise beaded pair with tassels dangling from the center. "These are beautiful, thank you."

"Great choice. They will go perfectly with your Native American coloring. Now, follow me. I think we have a headband with feathers you can use." Mama Lush stood and walked to another door. "If you can help the men wrap their heads around a theme, they'll create their own fantasies and you will have them eating out of your hands. And believe me, girl, you want that, so you get good tips."

Mama Lush sashayed to a shelf on the far wall which displayed hair pieces. Anything from wigs to hats. She grabbed a beaded headband, the tiny beads clicking softly as she revealed the bright, iridescent feathers. Lizzy noticed two leather ties on the headband, used to fasten it at the back of her head. It was the perfect compliment to her turquoise pasties.

"Take off your clothes and let me see your panties." Mama lush held the headband while she watched Lizzy.

Lizzy hesitated.

"Don't be shy. If you're uncomfortable stripping in front of me, you have no place stripping out there." Mama Lush pointed over her shoulder.

Point taken. Lizzy gathered up all her courage and took off her dress. Despite the odd situation, a bright smile adorned her face as she twirled in her bra and panties, feeling liberated and carefree under Mama Lush's curious gaze.

"You have a great ass in your thong, but I have something else with a little more pizzazz that you can wear when you go out there."

Mama Lush grabbed a blingy, turquoise scrap of clothing from a box and handed it to her. As Lizzy examined the undies, they sparkled under the lights. Turning them around, she noticed they were also thongs. Thank goodness the bling was on the front panel and not on the thong part. The last thing she wanted was to have blingy things in her coochie.

Then she noticed there were no price tags on them. *Were they used?* She didn't want to wear someone else's underwear. That would be weird and unsanitary. Lizzy's head jolted up, and she stared at Mama Lush with her mouth hanging open. She must've looked crazy, because Mama Lush busted out laughing.

"Honey, don't look at me like that. Anything in that box is new. When the girls wear them, they don't return them. I would never give you skanky undies."

"Now, change your undies and put these pasties under your bra while I bag up your dress and thong."

Lizzy did as she was told, while Mama Lush continued to give her instructions.

"They'll see the turquoise pasties shimmering under the bra since it's lacy and they'll be salivating in their seats, waiting for you to take it off. Are you okay not getting that bra back? Because when you toss it, it's a fifty-fifty shot that whoever catches it will keep it."

"No, I don't think I'd want it back if it lands on a man's face and he licks it or something." Lizzy curled her lip in disgust.

Mama Lush busted out laughing. "Are you sure you've never done this before because so far, you're a natural, well, except for when you hesitated when I first asked you to get naked? Why are you doing this, anyway?"

"All the girls were smiling with such confidence, and it seemed like pure freedom." Lizzy was grateful for her front clasp bra. She opened it and attached the pasties to her breasts. She noticed Mama Lush going through clothes on a rack.

"Ah, here it is." Mama Lush was holding up a simple Indian girl costume. "This will fit you. The girl who used to wear it was about your size."

"It's pretty, but how do I strip out of it without struggling to get it over my head?" Lizzy was turning the dress, looking for a way to put it on and take it off.

"I like you. You don't have it on yet, but here you are thinking about how you will take it off." Mama Lush chuckled. "The girl who made it hid the Velcro seam down the front to the waist. Let me show you how she took it off, then you add your own thing."

Mama Lush set the bag with her clothes inside on a chair and pretended to pull the top open and shimmy the dress down her hips, turning around and shoving her ass out when the dress got to her hips.

"I can do that." Lizzy smiled. If she thought of this as performance art, she could so do this.

"Great, now put it on. Amateur hour starts in ten minutes, and there are only a couple of girls going on stage. If you're ready, you go first. If not, you go last."

Lizzy loved a challenge. Thanks to Mama Lush, she was dressed and ready in record time. Though the thrill of the moment was exhilarating and she couldn't wait to dance beneath the flashing lights on stage, a nervous flutter beat inside, causing a queasy feeling. Lizzy pressed her hand against her stomach and took several deep breaths.

"Drink this." Mama Lush handed her a shot.

"Is there anything else in that shot?" Lizzy squinted at her. "Because a guy tried to roofie me a few days ago."

"Nope, just straight tequila from the bottle in my drawer. No drugs, I promise."

Mama Lush had been so nice, she took her chances and drank the shot. Liquid courage. Wasn't that what they called drinking? The liquid burned down Lizzy's throat, causing her eyes to water. After a few seconds, she felt heat in her belly, but she wasn't seeing double. Lizzy gave the empty glass back to Mama Lush while she clutched her chest. She'd tasted nothing that strong before. She usually drank fruity drinks like Strawberry Margaritas or Piña Coladas.

Mama Lush guided her to the side of the stage. The thumping bass vibrated through Lizzy's chest as she listened to the sexy music pouring from the stage. She closed her eyes. The music swelled in her mind, and she imagined herself dancing in her room, completely free.

When they called her name, Lizzy stepped out onto the runway, the bright lights reflecting off her shimmering Native American dress as she seductively walked to the end of the stage. All the men were hooting and hollering, calling her a squaw. Lizzy froze. The word squaw was considered offensive and disrespectful. She was just a dancer, not a prostitute. *Why were they calling her that?*

Mama Lush screamed from the side of the stage. "Dance honey, don't just stand there!"

Hearing Mama Lush's voice snapped her out of her thoughts. Mama Lush was giving her two thumbs up and beaming from ear to ear. Lizzy smiled, tuned out the men's voices and began her routine.

She swayed her body and kept her gaze pinned to the back wall, smiling the entire time. After a few hip rolls, she pulled open the dress and slid it slowly down her body. She repeated the moves Mama Lush had taught her and the men went crazy when she bent over and showed them her ass in the thong.

They were no longer calling her a squaw. Their energy was invigorating and giving her the confidence to turn around and toss the dress to the back of the stage for future use. She stayed in the bright red fuck me pumps that Mama Lush had lent her and wrapped her arms and legs around the pole. Spinning around, she tried several moves she had seen the previous dancers do. She was grateful that she wasn't too heavy and her core was semi-tight because spinning on a pole was harder than it looked.

When the men began chanting for her to take it off. She got off the pole and whipped off her bra, her breasts flying free, with only the tasseled pasties covering her nipples. Her natural C cup breasts swayed as she moved her body in time to the rhythm of the music. Now was the time Mama Lush had told her to crawl to the edge of the stage and let the men stuff her panties with bills.

As soon as she got to the edge and sat on her knees with her hands, lifting her hair off her neck, she could feel their rough hands pushing bills down the sides of her panties. The bouncers got closer to the stage and watched the men, but not before one man pulled at one of her pasties, causing her pain. Another cupped her pussy, and a third grabbed her arm and pulled her face first onto the stage.

Lizzy was shaking as she pulled away with all her might, trying to break the grip the third guy had on her arm. The bouncers jumped in and ended up having to punch the man because he wouldn't release her. That caused a full out fight. Fists were flying between the bouncers and the patrons. Another bouncer came out of nowhere and pulled her behind him, attempting to keep the men away from her and keep her safe.

Lizzy gripped the bouncer's shirt. She was terrified someone was going to pull her away from him. It felt like forever before she heard sirens in the background. Some patrons fled the bar, but burly bouncers roughly grabbed and held most back.

Lizzy dropped her head on the bouncers back and said, "thank you."
"No problem."

Chapter 30

Lizzy?

George

George's night had been slow. He'd had a couple of traffic stops and helped Sean with a DUI before a call came in about a disturbance at The Purple Palace. *Shit!* That was the upscale strip club across the street from the skanky strip club. The Purple Palace was where business executives went with their customers to show them a good time.

George had never been into strip clubs. He'd gone when he was younger, but they weren't his thing. As an officer, he'd talked to several of the girls whenever there was a disturbance and most of the young ones were saving money to leave town and go to college in another state where no one knew their name. The more experienced dancers loved the protection the bouncers offered and couldn't pass up the money the men gave them.

As far as strip clubs went, The Purple Palace was the nicest one in town and usually safe. He wondered what the hell had happened that the bouncers called the cops. With his lights and sirens blaring, he joined Sean and several other cops in the parking lot.

Upon entering, it was like all hell had broken loose. Men and women were fighting all over the place. Bottles were flying across the room while some pushed tables over to hide from the fight. The girls were trying to run to the back of the stage while men were pulling them toward them.

Lieutenant Harris screamed instructions. "Sean, the backdoor. Ray, get them to turn on the lights. George, get to the stage area. Everyone else with me."

When the house lights came on, everyone froze and blinked. That's when everyone noticed the cops and it got even more chaotic.

Lieutenant Harris screamed, "Police, freeze!"

A wave of shouting patrons surged toward the front and back exits as they shoved each other to escape the police. The officers and bouncers roared, their voices a thunderous wave echoing through the club as they pushed the patrons away from the exit doors, but some still surged toward the stage, desperately seeking another way out; the smell of sweat and fear hung heavy in the air. It was a clusterfuck of epic proportion.

George was at the stage and noticed a man fighting with a bouncer who had a dancer behind his back. Her head was bent, and she was gripping his shirt. He couldn't see her face, but he knew that body all too well. With a grunt, George hustled the man roughly against the stage, the cold metal of the handcuffs clicking shut.

"Thanks, Deputy," the bouncer was panting.

"Yeah, sure." George pointed behind his back. "Who's behind you?"

"One of our amateur dancers. That fucker." The bouncer pointed at the cuffed man. "Tried to pull her off stage and started this mess."

George looked around and noticed the men were being arrested and the chaos had died down.

"Let me talk to her." George crossed his arms and braced his legs apart. Oh, he wanted to talk to her alright. But first he wanted her to see his anger.

"Honey?" The bouncer turned around and grabbed her arms. "It's okay. The police are here to help you. This officer wants to talk to you."

He eased her toward George. She was trembling uncontrollably, her face wet with tears as she looked up at George. The rage that had consumed George moments before evaporated, leaving behind an icy knot of worry in his stomach.

"Lizzy, come here." George opened his arms and Lizzy walked into them.

"You know her?" The bouncer tilted his head.

"Yeah, she's my girlfriend," George mumbled and held her tight against his chest.

"Shit man, she's too beautiful to be dancing in front of these scumbags."

"No shit." George kept shushing her while he used his hands to massage the back of her head and stroke her back, trying to calm her down. "Thanks for looking out for her. Any chance you could find a blanket or something to wrap her in?"

"Yeah, give me a second." The bouncer turned, jumped on the stage, and disappeared behind the curtain.

"Fuck," George heard Sean whisper. "I'll take this guy. You take care of your girlfriend."

"Thanks," George nodded.

"Here you go." The bouncer returned with a black blanket with fringes.

George carefully wrapped it around Lizzy. She grabbed the ends but stayed pressed against his chest.

"We're going to have to talk about your adventures," George murmured before he kissed her forehead.

"I'm sorry," Lizzy whispered. "Please get me out of here."

"Where are your clothes?" George bent down to look at her.

"Backstage with Mama Lush."

"Of course they are," George sighed. "Come on, I'll take you home."

"No!" Lizzy grabbed his arm. "You can't take me to the resort like this. Too many people will ask too many questions, please."

"Okay, I'll take you to my place. But I can't be there until my shift is over. Will you be okay there by yourself?"

Lizzy nodded. "Yes, thank you."

"Deputy Smith, everyone is saying all this trouble is because of this young lady." Lieutenant Harris looked at Lizzy. "Young lady, we need a statement from you about what happened."

Lizzy shook her head, pressed herself against George again, and began crying. George hated seeing her like this.

"Sir, this is my girlfriend, Lizzy. Can I calm her down, get her some clothes, and I'll bring her to the station?" George pleaded with his lieutenant.

"Your girlfriend, huh?" Lieutenant Harris cocked his eyebrow at George.

"Yes, sir." George was going to stand behind Lizzy. She needed his support right now, and he wasn't about to let her down. Even though when they got to his place, he wanted to know what the fuck had happened for her to be almost naked in a strip club. The bouncer had said something about her being a dancer. Had she stripped on stage? What the hell was wrong with her? Was she fearless or reckless? Didn't Lizzy realize she could've gotten badly hurt? Had she not learned her lesson after she got roofied?

"Okay, but I want to question her in an hour. Got it."

"Yes, sir. Thank you." George walked away with Lizzy still attached to him. He could hear the lieutenant say to another cop. "Why the hell is his girlfriend stripping?"

George wondered the same fucking thing. After he got the answers from Lizzy, he would explain everything to his lieutenant. But first he had to take Lizzy to his apartment and get her a pair of his sweatpants and t-shirt. The last thing he wanted was for his fellow officers to see her nearly naked body again. It was bad enough he had to walk her out of that place while they watched. Some were grinning, a few shook their heads, and other were in shock. Yeah, he'd be the talk of the squad room for weeks to come.

Chapter 31

Another Foiled Plan

Numbers

Motherfucking shit! How the hell did she escape again? Numbers was livid. When he saw Tori's sister stripping on stage, he knew he had her this time. He could take her and use her as leverage to get Tori, Maggie, and Angel to come to him instead of him having to chase them all over the fucking town.

He'd paid that idiot business man and his friends' good money to do whatever necessary to get her ass off the stage and out the back door into his car. When he left, they were doing a good job of getting to her, so what the hell had happened?

Numbers had waited with Red as long as they could until they heard the police. Leaving the parking lot, they watched the back door, expecting the fool to reappear. The man, apparently an idiot, emerged in handcuffs, a police officer escorting him into the back of a squad car. Numbers then saw Tori's sister, wrapped in a blanket, leaving with their police officer friend, George.

Fuck! She'd escaped him twice now. Lucky bitch. He needed a plan, and he had to do it himself because clearly everyone else was too stupid to follow orders. Sending a boy to do a man's job was a mistake he wouldn't make again. Getting into Reaper's good graces required killing Tori, Maggie, and Angel. If he couldn't get to them with this girl, then he had to come up with another way. But it would have to be quick. He had a feeling his days were numbered.

If something happened and they found and arrested him, he wouldn't survive in jail. He was sure Reaper and his other brothers would kill him for not being able to make Steele one of them. Reaper could forgive the botched kill order on Angel, but losing Steele as his grandson and the future president of the LRs was an unforgivable mistake. Steele meant everything to Reaper. He wanted to keep the LRs presidency in the family. He had to kill Tori, Maggie, and Angel; otherwise, he'd be signing his own death warrant.

Fucking up the shootout at the wedding was bad enough, but when Numbers fucked up the human trafficking shipment that got most of his brothers either killed or arrested, he knew Reaper would kill him. Hell, there were no LRs left that he knew of except him and Red. And they still had to lie low or risk being arrested. They were fugitives. With their faces plastered across every news channel, the police sought information that would lead to their arrest.

"Red, let's get out of here. Go to the clubhouse."

"You got it, boss."

Numbers never corrected Red from calling him boss. Right now, he was his boss.

"We need a new plan," Numbers mumbled. "This one has to fucking work because if Reaper finds out we're back, he'll find someone to take us out."

Chapter 32

Huge Mistake

Lizzy

Lizzy followed George up to his room and locked herself in his bathroom to put on the clothes he gave her. They were a little big on her, but better than the blanket she had draped over her pasties and undies. During the drive, she remained quiet, stealing quick glances at George, her heart pounding a nervous rhythm against her ribs. The way his hands were clenched on the steering wheel, the furious set of his jaw, and the way his teeth were grinding made it obvious he was fuming. She had really fucked up this time. What had initially sounded like a fun adventure had morphed into a big mistake.

What she thought was going to feel freeing ended up feeling frightening. When the first man pulled her pasties, the suction hurt so bad she leaned into him, not expecting the other guy to grab her pussy. The feel of his hand on her privates had caused her to withdraw, but not before a third man grabbed her arm and pulled her face toward the floor. She'd used her other hand to stop herself from face planting into the stage and attempting to pull away from him.

She was so grateful for the bouncer who showed up just as the man was getting ready to jump on stage and pull her away. Her mind wrestled with her horrible predicament. She owed that bouncer her life. He continued to protect her until George cuffed the man and held her.

Tori was going to kill her. That reckless stunt was incredibly stupid. She'd promised her sister she wouldn't do anything that would get her into trouble, but she'd done it again. Granted, she promised not to say anything stupid, but her actions in this case had worse consequences than her words.

"Are you okay in there?" George knocked on the door. Lizzy jumped; her thoughts interrupted by the noise.

"I...I'm fine. I'll be out in a minute."

"Hurry up! We need to get to the station, or my lieutenant will have my ass."

"Okay." Lizzy washed her face and braced herself against the bathroom counter. Looking up at herself, she took a couple of deep breaths and calmed down. She was safe. She was with George, and he would never let anything happen to her. Unfortunately, he was furious with her.

Lizzy opened the door and stepped out. George was leaning against the counter with his arms and ankles crossed. Sliding her gaze to his face, she saw the lingering anger etched in his features, his jaw tight, eyes narrowed.

"George, I'm...," Lizzy began, but George held up his hand to stop her.

"We'll talk later. Let's get to the station so you can give your statement." George pushed away from the counter and grabbed his keys.

"But George." Lizzy held her hand out to touch his shoulder as he walked past her. George froze, but didn't look at her.

"Not now Lizzy. I'm too pissed at you to have a calm conversation. Let's get this done and then we'll come back here and talk."

"Okay," Lizzy whispered and followed George to the car.

The ride to the station was also quiet. Lizzy sat with her hands between her thighs, head turned, watching the passing scenery. There wasn't much to see since it was well past midnight, but it was better than looking at the disappointment and anger on George's face. She knew that relying on George any further could jeopardize his position and she couldn't expect him to keep risking his job for her. The thought of him losing his job because of her reckless decisions filled her with guilt.

"We're almost at the station lieutenant, where do you want Lizzy Tall Bear?" George said into his radio, startling Lizzy from her thoughts.

"Interrogation room three."

"10-4. I'll let you know when she's in there. May I stay in the room with her?"

Lizzy waited, hoping the lieutenant would allow George to stay with her. He might be mad at her, but she needed to have a comforting person in the room.

"Sure, let me know when you get there," the lieutenant said, and she heard a click.

"Thank you for staying with me during my statement," Lizzy whispered.

"Sure."

George didn't add anything else; silence hung heavy in the air. She wasn't sure if he wanted to be there or felt like he had to be for Tori and the rest of their friends and family. When they arrived at the station, Lizzy kept her head down and followed George into the room assigned to them. There was a table with three chairs. Two chairs faced the one. Lizzy sat on the side of the two chairs, hoping George would choose the chair next to her and not make her sit alone on one side.

George radioed his lieutenant and told him they were ready for him. He sat back in the chair next to hers and they both waited quietly until the door opened.

"Hello, Lizzy. I'm Lieutenant Johnson." Lieutenant Johnson held his hand out to shake Lizzy's before he sat down in front of her. "I need you to tell me what happened tonight."

"Okay." Lizzy glanced at George, who nodded to her. "I didn't know it was a strip club when I paid the cover, but realized it as soon as I walked in. I wanted a beer and went to the bar to ask for a bottle. I watched the bartender closely since I had been roofied at another club last week." Lizzy noticed George's body tense.

Lieutenant Johnson was writing on his pad. When Lizzy stopped, he looked up and said, "go on."

"While I was at the bar, a waitress came up to me and asked if I was there for amateur night. I wasn't." Lizzy looked at George. "I swear I didn't know it was amateur night." George just looked at her with a blank expression on his face.

"Anyway." Lizzy turned back to the lieutenant. "She made it sound like fun, so I said yes. Then Mama Lush," –"who's Mama Lush," the lieutenant interrupted– "she's a regular who's been there a long time. She's really nice. She helped me come up with a theme and find the perfect outfit to get me the most tips."

"I bet she did," George mumbled.

The Lieutenant glanced at George and shook his head, clearly telling George, not now. "Please, go on."

"I was first up, and it was going well until I bent down for tips like Mama Lush showed me and a man pulled one of my pasties." Lizzy folded her hands on the table and looked down as she fidgeted with her fingernails. "It really hurt, and I leaned forward to relieve the pain. That's when another guy grabbed my female front part." Lizzy trembled and closed her eyes.

George scooted closer to her and stroked her back. The warmth of his hand was a welcome change from the silence that had fallen between them.

"Whenever you're ready, Miss Tall Bear. I know this is difficult, but we need to know what charges to press on each individual." Lieutenant Johnson whispered.

"Sorry." Lizzy wiped the tears from her cheeks and looked up at the lieutenant. She couldn't look at George as she continued. If he judged her, she wouldn't be able to finish.

"No need to be sorry. You have done nothing wrong. Take your time." Lieutenant Johnson nodded.

"It's okay. I'm here." George whispered and kissed her temple. "It's going to be fine."

Lizzy cleared her throat and nodded. "When I tried to scoot back, the third man in the group grabbed my arm and pulled me toward him. I used my other hand to stop myself from hitting the stage and to pull away with all my might. The man was getting ready to jump on the stage when the bouncer punched him. Then I hid behind another bouncer until I saw George."

Lizzy wanted to say my boyfriend George, but after this he might not be her boyfriend any longer.

"Okay. I'm going to show you three pages of photos. Each of the men who we think assaulted you are on these pages. Please point them out if you remember their faces, even though it was dark, and you were scared. If you can ID them, we can arrest them. I'll go get the folder; would you like some water?"

"Yes, please." Lizzy looked at the lieutenant. "Thank you."

"You're welcome." Lieutenant Johnson stood. "I'll be right back."

Lizzy watched him leave, then looked back down at her hands. She didn't know what to say to George.

"Are you okay?" George murmured. After he kissed her temple, he'd turned sideways and draped his arm on the back of her chair. His hand was under her hair, massaging her neck.

"I'm nervous about seeing those photos. Those men terrified me." Lizzy rested her elbows on the table and dropped her face into her hands.

"I know. I'm sorry you had to go through that. Just a few more minutes and it will all be over."

Lizzy pulled her face away from her hands and looked at George. "It'll never be over. I'll never forget how quickly that impulsive decision spiraled into a terrifying nightmare, the chilling fear still vividly etched in my mind. I was terrified of what they would do to me if they caught me."

George took a deep breath and pulled Lizzy into his arms. "It wasn't your best idea, but I'm glad you are okay." Kissing the top of her head, he held her like that until the lieutenant came back with a bottle of water for her and a folder.

He dropped the folder on the desk and placed the water in front of her. Lizzy pulled away from George and uncapped her water to take a drink. She was glad it was an unopened cold water bottle. At least she was smarter about whatever was placed in front of her to drink, even if she was in a police station. The lieutenant placed a stack of papers in front of her.

"Please, look through these," –the lieutenant placed a stack of papers in front of her– "and let me know if you recognize anyone."

Lizzy flipped through the pages. She thought she recognized one man on the first page, but she wanted to look through all the pages first. There were three pages, and the three men were on pages one and two. She placed the two pages side by side and then pointed to the men who assaulted her.

"It's these three."

After identifying them, she looked at George. He smiled and nodded.

"Thank you." Lieutenant Johnson placed the pages back in the folder, closed it, and stood. "George, you can take her home now. It's close to the end of your shift. Stay with her. I'm guessing you both have a lot to talk about."

"Yes, sir. Thank you." George stood.

Lizzy waited until the lieutenant left before she stood and faced George.

"I'm sorry," her voice faltered.

George hugged her. "Come on, let's get out of here. Do you want to go to my place or the resort? I'm off tomorrow night, so I'll take you wherever you want to go."

"I need to go back to the strip club and get Alex's truck."

"I already had an officer drive it to the resort after we left." George placed his hand on Lizzy's lower back, guiding her out of the room.

"Thank you."

"So, where do you want me to take you?"

"The resort, please. It's early enough that I don't think I'll see anyone that I know in the lobby."

"The resort it is."

Lizzy saw several deputies heading their way.

"I'm glad you're okay, Lizzy." Sean stopped in the hallway to give her a hug.

"Thank you, Deputy Sean. I appreciate your help."

"Anytime, but hey next time, tell them I'm your boyfriend so I can get off my shift earlier," Sean grinned at her and George.

"Fucker." George gave him the middle finger.

Lizzy smiled for the first time in the past several hours. "I might have to do that. I'm not sure he will be my boyfriend for long."

Sean dropped his grin and smiled. "I wouldn't be too sure about that. Go on, you crazy kids, get out of here. We need to book some suspects."

"Thanks," George nodded and continued to guide Lizzy to his car.

Again, their ride was quiet, but Lizzy assumed he wanted to wait until they got to her room. Then he would let her have it and break up with her because when she suggested it to Sean, George didn't deny it. Her nerves were so tight, she felt like they might snap. With a sinking heart, she prayed he would listen to her side of the story. Although now that she'd had time to think about it, her decision to strip down and dance in front of strangers felt reckless and foolish, not freeing.

*** Sean ***

"So, Jeffrey," Sean sighed and sat in the chair across the table from the man who tried to pull Lizzy off the stage. "You want to tell me your side of the story?"

"Man, some guy paid me and my friends to get that girl and take her out the back door to him. We just did what he told us to do." Jeffrey crossed his arms and leaned back in his chair.

"Didn't you think that assaulting that girl and giving her to some man was a bad idea?"

"No, he said he was her boyfriend, and he needed to talk to her, but she was mad at him. We didn't think we were doing anything wrong." Jeffrey insisted.

"So, pulling her pastie and grabbing her crotch was not a wrong thing to do?" Sean quirked his eyebrow at him.

"She's a dancer, probably a fucking prostitute. I'm sure men do that to her all the time." Jeffrey shrugged his shoulders.

"She was not a prostitute. It was an amateur night. But even if she was a lady of the night, none of you had a right to touch her like you did. She wasn't soliciting you for sex, she was dancing. Have you been to the Purple Palace before?"

"Sure, many times."

"Then you know not to touch the girls dancing or the bouncers will toss your ass out. Was the money that good?" Sean crossed his arms and leaned back, imitating Jeffrey's pose.

"Not enough to be arrested, if that's what you're asking. What are you charging me with, anyway? I never took her anywhere."

"You are being charged with assault, disturbing the peace, and attempted kidnapping. However, if you tell me who hired you to do what you and your boys did, we might reduce the sentence."

Those guys didn't have a previous record. If anything, they were guilty of being drunken idiots. He would love to put them behind bars for a long ass time, but he was more interested in whoever hired them. While they'd still face a fine and jail time, cooperating and revealing the kidnapping plot's mastermind could reduce the charges to a misdemeanor.

Sean knew the Purple Palace had banned them from ever entering their establishment. And once the Purple Palace owners talked to other club owners in the area, they would be persona non grata.

"The guy was bald and skinny. He was about my height and was hanging around with a black-haired man. The two of them were thick as thieves and enjoyed asking us to get the girl. They paid us two hundred bucks each and promised more once we took her out to them. That's all I know. Can I go now?"

"In a minute. Hang tight."

Sean left the room and asked another deputy if they got the footage of the inside of the strip club before the fight. The deputy nodded, and they walked into a room where an IT officer had it cued up and ready to roll. They fast forwarded and rewound several times until they could get a better image of the man talking to Jeffrey. *Holy Shit, it was Numbers and behind him was Red. Fuck! He had to tell George.* Numbers had changed his appearance, but not enough to not be able to identify him. Now that they knew what he looked like, they could send out a current photo of him to all the deputies in the area.

"Isn't that Numbers, the last remaining Lucifer's Renegade member who left town after the shooting?" One deputy pointed at the screen.

"Yup, print out that image. I'm gonna show it to Jeffrey and verify that's the man who gave him money to kidnap Lizzy."

Sean tossed the picture on the desk in front of Jeffrey as soon as he entered. "Is that the man that paid you?"

"Yeah, yeah, that's him."

"Great." Sean nodded. "Someone will be here to take you to jail."

"Wait, I cooperated. I've learned my lesson. I won't ever do that again, you promised!" The man stood.

"I promised to help you, but you still have to face some charges. You'll receive a court-appointed lawyer if you don't have one when you appear before the judge for sentencing." Sean grabbed the photo and left Jeffrey staring at him.

Douchebag actually thought he was going to go free with no repercussions after what he did. Sean nodded to several officers who waited outside the interrogation room. "He's all yours, boys."

Sean went into the squad room and called George. He didn't answer. So, he texted.

Call me for an update on the arrests.

Then he put away his phone and got to work on getting an arrest warrant for Numbers and Red.

Chapter 33

Making Better Choices

Lizzy

Lizzy was right. None of the Panther family was in the lobby, which made it easier for them to get to her room. The first thing George did once they entered was lock her adjoining door to Frey and Holt's room. Lizzy waited anxiously in the living room, wringing her hands. George grabbed her hand and pulled her with him into the bedroom. He closed that door too. It was obvious he wanted as much privacy as he could get.

George stripped off his uniform.

"What are you doing? I thought you wanted to talk?" Lizzy stepped back when he went around her to place his firearm on the nightstand.

"Take off your clothes. We're going to take a shower and wash off the night." George cupped her face and kissed her. "It's going to be okay."

Lizzy wasn't ready to mess around. She still had the thoughts and feelings of when those men were touching her.

"Hey, we're just going to shower. I promise." George sighed and pulled her tightly against his chest. "I'll get the water nice and hot."

Lizzy watched George finish taking off his clothes and walk into the bathroom. She heard the shower turn on. A hot shower sounded good. Suddenly, she couldn't wait to wash off their touch. Stripping, she tossed her panties into the trashcan, never wanting to see them again. Using warm water from the sink, she gently removed the pasties. She felt bad throwing them out. Maybe she should give them back to Mama Lush. No, she would find out how much they cost and send her the money.

George watched her quietly. Tossing the pasties into the trash, she stood straight and turned to him. George stepped into the shower. He held the curtain open, offering her his other hand. Lizzy took his hand and stepped inside the hot, steamy shower.

George turned them around so she could have the showerhead shooting water at her back. Lizzy leaned back and let the water run over her head. When her hair was totally soaked. George turned her around and slowly massaged shampoo into her hair. Lizzy covered her breasts with her hands from the burst of water hitting her chest. Her one breast was still tender from when the man pulled on her pastie. After he shampooed her hair, he rinsed and conditioned it. Leaving the conditioner in her hair, he shifted them, so his back was under the showerhead.

George soaped up his hands and held them up as he gazed into her eyes. "May I?" He choked out.

"Yes, please." Lizzy closed her eyes and cried out, taking a step back from him when he touched her tender breast.

George stopped immediately. "Lizzy, open your eyes and look at me. It's me. I won't hurt you. But if you prefer, I'll wash up quickly and leave you in here alone."

"No." Lizzy grabbed his hands and placed them on her breasts. "I need to feel something other than pain. As long as it's you, I'm okay."

George nodded. "If it gets to be too much, let me know? I want to help you, not hurt you."

Lizzy lifted the side of her mouth into a partial smile. "I know."

George stared into her eyes as he gently washed her breasts before moving on to her stomach and her legs. Stepping closer to her, with his eyes never leaving her face, he washed her backside and then her core. He touched her body with slow, gentle strokes not meant to excite, but to comfort. Every pass of his hands got her body ready for him, even though her mind wasn't quite there yet. When he finished soaping her up, he placed her under the water, and she rinsed off.

"Get in bed. I'll be there after I wash off." George kissed her forehead and stepped behind her toward the showerhead.

Lizzy got out and dried off. She wanted to be skin on skin with George, even though she wasn't ready to have sex. Towel drying her hair, she slipped under the covers and waited for him. When she closed her eyes, the images of the lascivious looks on the men's faces flashed in her mind. She must've made a sound because George was getting in bed behind her, spooning her.

"Shh, it's okay," George whispered in her ear and kissed her shoulder. "They're in jail and can't hurt you."

Lizzy rolled over and wrapped herself around George. George kissed the crown of her head and stroked her hair.

"I'm sorry I did that." Lizzy mumbled into his chest. "It was a bad idea. I just wanted to feel free. I've always felt so caged in, and I thought that would help. But it didn't. All it showed me was that there are horrible men out there who can't stop themselves from hurting women."

George sighed, "Aw, Lizzy. I wish that wasn't a lesson you had to learn...twice. You are going to be the death of me."

"Are you breaking up with me?" Lizzy held her breath, praying he would answer quickly and say no.

"No, I'm not."

Lizzy's breath whooshed out. "You were so mad at me. I thought you never wanted to see me again."

"I'm not gonna deny I was mad. You need to promise me you won't do that ever again, but I care about you and I'm falling for you, even though you drive me crazy. You definitely keep me on my toes, that's for sure." George chuckled.

Lizzy lifted her head and stared at George. "I'm falling for you too," she whispered.

"Please come to me when you get an idea and we'll figure something out together," George gazed into her eyes.

"I promise."

George slid his mouth over hers, slowly licking and nipping at her lips. Opening her mouth, she let him inside, taking his breath along with anything else he offered. Firmly holding her head in place, he devoured her mouth and sparred with her tongue. Not only was Lizzy's heart racing with a glorious speed, but her nipples hardened, and her core clenched. She wanted him desperately, but George slowed down the kiss before he gave her a couple pecks on the lips and pulled away.

"I just want to hold you. Let you feel safe. In the morning, if you are ready, reach for me. I'll give you anything you want." George rolled to his back and placed her head in the crook of his shoulder, holding her tightly against him. Lizzy draped her legs over his thighs and wrapped her arms around his waist.

"Goodnight, George," Lizzy whispered.

"Goodnight, babe." George kissed the crown of her head one last time before sleep took over for both of them.

Chapter 34

Spread the Word

George

L ast night after his shower, he heard Lizzy whimpering in bed. He knew
he needed to keep his focus on her and not any phone messages, so he'd
silenced his phone and crawled into bed.

Now it was morning, and he'd woken up before Lizzy. George knew Sean
was in charge of booking the suspects and he wanted an update. If something
important had happened while they questioned the three men, Sean would've
sent him a message.

Reaching over to grab his phone from the nightstand, he unlocked his screen
and saw Sean's text. He knew it was early, but knowing Sean, he'd only slept
a few hours anyway after his shift. George slowly slid out from under Lizzy's
arms, grabbed his boxer briefs off the floor, and stepped out of the bedroom
into the living room before he called Sean.

"Hey," Sean grumbled.

"Sorry, I thought you'd be up by now." George had the phone on his shoulder
while he put on his boxer briefs and tried not to fall.

"I'm up, just lying here debating whether to get up or roll over and catch
more z's."

"What did you find out?" George began pacing.

"Those guys were paid off by none other than Numbers and Red."

"Are you shitting me?" George stopped and rubbed his face.

"I wish I was."

"Fuck! That's twice that he's tried to get to Lizzy." George put his hand on
his waist.

"Before my shift was over, I sent out a BOLO to all agencies. They've both
changed their looks, so I included their new photo that we got from a camera
at the Purple Palace. I'll text you the photo now."

George pulled the phone away from his face and checked his text. Yep, they
looked different. He would have to show Thunder and the rest of the guys so
they knew who they were looking for. "Thanks, I'll let everyone know at the
AICC and the Rock 'n' Roll Resort & Casino."

"How's Lizzy?"

"She's asleep. I'm gonna spend the day with her. Maybe do something fun. Not sure what yet."

"Okay, call if you need me."

"Will do." George hung up and turned to head back into the bedroom.

Lizzy was standing in the bedroom doorway wrapped up in the bedsheets.

"Hey." George tossed his phone on the living room end table. "I thought you were still asleep."

"I woke up, and you weren't there," Lizzy whispered.

"Sorry." George wrapped his arms around her and held her. "I was talking to Sean."

Lizzy stepped back. "What happened? You look tense?"

"Sean told me someone paid those three guys off to take you out the back door."

Lizzy looked so lost and scared as she gripped the sheets and stared at George. "Who paid them?"

"Numbers and Red." George didn't want to sugarcoat it. He needed her to be aware of her surroundings when he couldn't be there to watch her.

"I...I'm not sure I know who they are. I mean, I've heard their names mentioned, but I don't know what they look like. Why do they want me?" Lizzy sat on the edge of the bed.

George left the bedroom and grabbed his phone from the end table in the living room. He needed to show her their photos.

"Here is a photo of them. Do you remember seeing them last night? Before those men grabbed you?" George pulled up the photo and turned his phone toward her.

"Yes, I remember seeing them. The bald man's glare was intense, burning into me as I danced, making me feel uneasy. His eyes, blazing with fury, took me by surprise, leaving me utterly confused because I'd never met him before." Lizzy shivered and pushed George's phone away from her face. "I don't remember the other one."

"Okay. Numbers is the one you remember seeing?"

Lizzy nodded.

"He's one of the few LRs left who miraculously escaped arrest during the deadly shootout at your sister's wedding and the harrowing night at the docks when we saved Steele. I'm not sure how much Tori told you about that night, but the LRs were at your sister's wedding to kill her and Maggie. It seems now you are one of his targets too." George sat on the bed next to her. "He blames Tori for his friend Reaper being in jail."

"I remember Tori telling me about Reaper and Winston, but why does he want Maggie?"

"It's a long story, but Maggie's brother José shot him and killed some of his LR brothers. He also wants to kill Angel and turn Steele against her, so Steele can run the LRs as president until Reaper gets out of jail."

"Wow, he has a lot of anger." Lizzy raised her head to look at George. "And it's all directed toward me now?"

"I'm sure he's angry at everyone. He wants to get into the good graces of Reaper since he botched up the shootout at the wedding and got the rest of

the LRs arrested or shot during the human trafficking transport at the docks."
George sighed.

"But Reaper's in jail. How can he get to Numbers?"

"Reaper is a dangerous man with a lot of contacts in and out of prison.
Numbers is running scared with his sidekick Red, one of their prospects before
the club fell apart."

"Okay." Lizzy dropped her head and nodded. "I'm a little overwhelmed."

"It's a lot. I know." George slid to his knees in front of Lizzy and held her
hands. "That's why I need you to stay close to me, Thunder, Alex, Holt, Barrett,
or Mark. We will protect you, but you can't wander off by yourself. At least until
we arrest Numbers and Red. Will you do that for me?"

Lizzy stared at George. "Yes. I can do that."

"Okay." George released a breath, not even realizing he was holding it. "I
have an idea about what you can do that gives you a freeing feeling." George
smiled and stood, pulling her up with him.

"What is it?" Lizzy squinted at him.

"Roller skating." George beamed at her.

"What?"

"You know, you put on these shoes with four wheels and glide around."
George released one hand and made a circular motion.

"I've never skated."

"I'll teach you." George squeezed her other hand. "It'll be fun. What do you
say?"

"Okay, but don't let me fall."

"If you do, I'll rub your ass or any other part of your body that hurts until you
feel better."

"Okay," Lizzy laughed.

George felt like he could breathe again when Lizzy laughed. He loved putting
a smile on her face and hoped to keep it there for as long as possible. If she
was happy with him, and they shared exciting adventures, maybe she wouldn't
concoct reckless schemes that would lead her into danger. He hoped the feel of
his hand in hers and the thrill of their shared laughter might keep her grounded.

"I gotta make some calls. Go shower and get ready. Afterwards, I'll change at
my house before we go skating." George winked teasingly. "If I'm in my uniform,
you might get jealous of all the female attention I get while I'm teaching you to
skate."

"You are so full of yourself." Lizzy pushed him and her sheet dropped.

George groaned and licked his lips as his gaze devoured her from head to
toe.

"I think it might be the other way around. You might be fighting men off me,"
Lizzy chuckled.

"Damn right I would." George took one more look and closed his eyes.
"You're testing my patience. Go shower and change so we can go on a skating
date."

"Okay." Lizzy rubbed her body against his and kissed him before strolling
into the bathroom and turning on the shower.

George counted to ten and begged his dick to calm the fuck down. Putting
on his pants, he stepped into the living room and called Thunder's cell.

"Hey, George, what's up? Where are you? I didn't see your car when I came in."

"I had a rough night. I'm with Lizzy in her room at the resort. Are you alone?" George wanted to tell Thunder so he could tell Tori and Alex in person about what happened to Lizzy last night.

"Yeah, let me shut the door." George heard the click. "Okay, what's going on?"

George told Thunder everything that had happened with Lizzy. He informed him that Numbers and Red had contracted three men who were now under arrest.

"Their appearance has changed, but they are still identifiable. I'm texting you the photo now." George sent it. "Lizzy is in the shower. I'm gonna head to the cultural center when she's done so Tori and Alex can see her. I'm taking her roller skating and I need to change my clothes. Can you talk to Tori and Alex?"

"Absolutely. I'll talk to them as soon as we hang up. Is Lizzy okay? She does realize that what she did wasn't in her best interest?"

"Yeah, she does. She also knows to be with one of us until we catch Numbers and Red."

"Agreed. I'll send this photo to all the guys and tell Maggie to send it to all the girls. I'd ask Tori to send it out, but I think she will freak out as soon as she hears about what happened to Lizzy. Everyone needs to be on the lookout."

"Thanks, Thunder." George didn't hear the shower, so he walked into the bedroom.

"Okay. See you then. Be careful."

"Will do...you too." George hung up and finished putting on his uniform. To avoid the temptation of pulling Lizzy into bed, he made sure he was fully dressed. While easily removed, his clothes provided a flimsy barrier, better than nothing at all.

George's eyes followed Lizzy as she sauntered out of the bathroom, wrapped in a towel, toward her closet. Dropping the towel in the doorway with a flick of her wrist, she glanced at him over her shoulder, a sassy smile playing on her lips giving him a magnificent view of her delicious ass. *Fuck me!* He had just gotten his cock to calm down and now he was hard as a rock again. Shit, she was going to kill him. George put on his belt and inserted the gun. He was better off waiting for her in the living room.

Chapter 35

Skate Date

Lizzy should've known when George was in the living room, he was calling either Thunder or Tori and telling them what happened. As soon as she entered the AICC behind George, Tori was running to her and wrapping her up in her arms.

"I'm okay." Lizzy rubbed her back.

"I'm so glad." Tori stepped back. "Why would you do what you did? Are you crazy?"

"I just wanted a little freedom," Lizzy smirked. "But I will agree it was a bad idea."

"Lizzy." George placed his hand on her lower back. "I'm gonna change before our date. Please stay with everyone. I'll be back in a few minutes."

Lizzy turned to him and nodded.

"Come into Thunder's office and talk to me." Tori grabbed her hand and dragged her.

"I gotta hear this." Maggie bolted out of her seat and followed them.

"I'm gonna do a perimeter check," Mark hollered. "Come on, Sky."

"You ladies can talk privately in there." Thunder said as they passed him. "I'll sit out at the lobby desk. Take as long as you need."

Tori pulled Lizzy to the couch while Maggie shut the door and pulled a chair to face them.

"Tell me everything." Tori sat sideways on the couch, staring at Lizzy intently.

Lizzy hated reliving her worst night. It was even worse than the night she'd been roofied. She started at the beginning and left nothing out. Even the information about Numbers and Red.

"I'm so sorry." Tori dropped her head into her hands. "This revenge war started when I caught Winston selling drugs."

"Hey, don't beat yourself up." Maggie grabbed one of her hands and one of Lizzy's. "We're all in this together. After all, it was my brother who sought revenge for my parents' death and injured Numbers. We are all victims of those stupid ass men. I can't tell you how happy I am that my brother is no longer involved in a one-percenter MC."

"I wish they had arrested Numbers after the shootout or at the docks when they arrested everyone else for human trafficking." Tori sighed.

"Me too." Maggie squeezed their hands. "But we are strong women, and we will beat him. We must stay vigilant and make sure we don't go anywhere alone." Maggie looked at Lizzy. "Tori and I have learned some self-defense moves from Mark and Alex. I think you should ask George to teach you some pressure points or moves. If he's too busy, I'm sure Mark and Alex would help you."

"That sounds like a good idea. I'll ask George."

Maggie raised her arms, making Tori and Lizzy's arms to go up too. "Okay, ladies. Repeat after me. We are strong and we will not be victims again!"

Lizzy and Tori repeated their mantra before they released their hands. Lizzy felt more empowered by Tori and Maggie's support. They had both been through so much worse than her and they were stronger for it. She wanted to stand tall and confident like them.

"The only other question I have is why did you feel the need to strip?" Tori faced Lizzy again.

"The waitress said it was a freeing feeling. And I must admit it was at first, but then when I looked out into the audience and saw the men's faces, I got scared. They were looking at me like a thing they wanted to possess and hurt, but I didn't want to run offstage. I didn't want them to know they scared me. But when those men grabbed me and caused me pain, I was terrified and realized the mistake I made. I won't be doing that again, I promise." Lizzy saw a blurry Tori and wiped her eyes.

"We all make mistakes; hell, I dated a rapist," Tori sighed.

"And I got so drunk that I got kidnapped by the LRs." Maggie winced.

"I think we all need a group hug." Tori scooted next to Lizzy on the couch.

Putting one arm around Lizzy, Tori extending the other for Maggie to join their group hug. Maggie leaned over and fell on them as they hugged each other and laughed.

"So, I guess everything is okay now?" George chuckled from the doorway.

The ladies stood and pulled George into their group hug.

"Hey, what about me? I saved Lizzy and Maggie." Mark joined in the hug behind Maggie.

"Surfer Smurf, I can feel this is turning you on," Maggie laughed.

"Being behind you always turns me on," Mark murmured.

"Okay, okay, break it up." Alex's voice boomed into the room. "Who's hungry?"

Lizzy didn't know who pulled Alex into the group hug, but next thing she knew, he was between her and Tori.

"Uh, are you all done?" Thunder laughed. "You too Sky?"

Lizzy heard Sky barking and then she was in the middle, jumping up and down, licking anybody's body parts she could find, causing them all to laugh even harder before they all broke apart. Lizzy needed that. George grabbed her hand and pulled her toward him.

"Lizzy and I are going roller skating. We'll see you all later," George smiled at everyone and pulled her out of the room.

Everyone waved goodbye and headed back to work. George opened the passenger door for her, waited until she buckled in, shut it, and went around the front to get in.

"Thank you for calling ahead." Lizzy squeezed his shoulder. "I don't know what you said, but it made it easier for me when I got here."

George grabbed her hand and raised it to his mouth for a kiss. "I'm glad it helped." Then he placed their intertwined hands on her lap.

He drove like that, using only his left hand on the steering wheel, all the way to the rink. Lizzy glanced his way several times. He looked so sexy and manly as he drove one handed. If he played his cards right, he might just get lucky tonight.

They had to rent skates because neither of them owned a pair. George skated backwards, showing her how to move her feet and stay balanced. Although she stumbled a few times, George offered his hand each time. They completed several laps together. Lizzy quickly learned, and soon she was skating alongside him. With their hands intertwined, she danced to the music, the wind a cool rush against her face as they moved swiftly. The only issues she still had were crossing her feet on the turns and stopping.

Not that she stopped much. George got behind her and held her waist, while Lizzy held her arms out to the sides. The rush of air and the upbeat tempo of the songs filled Lizzy's ears as she skated around and around, giving her a sense of flying. It was just the free feeling she'd been looking for and she owed it all to George.

George whispered in her ear, "I think you've done this before."

Lizzy giggled. They didn't have skating rinks on the reservation, but she had tried her friends' skates one time outside her house. The bumpy uneven concrete was so bad, she fell on her ass and took them off. Technically, she didn't lie to George. She had never gone skating.

The DJ announced they were going to play some games. Lizzy preferred skating with George to playing games on skates. She wasn't that comfortable with her balance. Excusing herself, she left George at the concession stand. He was going to get them some waters and a snack.

Going to the bathroom with skates was difficult, but she held the railings, doors, walls, or any other solid object available on her way to the stall. Each step was precarious on the dangerously slippery bathroom tile; she moved with agonizing slowness, wishing she'd worn socks instead of skates. Then again, the floors looked like they hadn't been cleaned in years. After doing her business and washing her hands, she skated out to find George.

He was sitting at a booth with water bottles and nachos. A girl was standing next to him, twirling her hair. *Was that skanky girl flirting with her man?* George fidgeted, his eyes darting around the room, avoiding the girl's gaze. When he spotted Lizzy, he waved her over.

When she approached their table, she smiled at George, ignoring the girl. The girl slid her foot out, tripping Lizzy. George bolted out of his seat and grabbed Lizzy's arm while her other hand grabbed the table. She knew the girl had done it on purpose. Girls could be so damn catty, especially when a hot guy was involved.

"I'm sorry." The girl covered her mouth. "I didn't see you."

Lizzy stood upright, ready to give the girl a piece of her mind, when she felt George wrap his arm around her and whisper her name in her ear. She'd promised not to lose her temper and cause trouble.

"It's okay," Lizzy smiled at the girl. "I'm new at this. No worries."

"Here babe, let me help you," George said, holding her arm until she sat. "I got us some drinks and nachos." He sat back down across from her.

Lizzy was impressed with George; he didn't even glance at the girl, who shifted awkwardly by their table, still waiting. He only had eyes for her. But Lizzy noticed the way the girl glared at her.

"Did you need something?" Lizzy said sweetly. She'd always heard the saying 'kill them with kindness' but had never actually done it. The girl huffed and skated away.

"Babe." George reached for her hand and brought it to his mouth for a kiss. "I am so proud of you. I thought for sure you were going to go off on that girl, but you held it together and acted like the bigger person. Thank you."

"I was nice, right?" Lizzy smiled and took a drink of water.

"You were." George nodded and grabbed a nacho.

"I wanted to rip every follicle of hair off her head when I saw her flirting with you." Lizzy said, barely suppressing her rage. George cocked his eyebrow. Lizzy snatched a nacho and continued. "But when I saw that you weren't interested, I calmed down. Thank you for ignoring her and getting us nachos. I love nachos."

"I remember you telling me you liked them." George smirked. "Are you having a good time?"

"I am. I can't believe I've never done this before. It's a lot of fun."

"Really? Cause you took to it pretty damn fast." George glared at her with his interrogation look.

"Okay." Lizzy threw her arms up. "Don't look at me with such suspicion, as if I were a criminal you're trying to intimidate into confessing. I tried on my friend's skates once, but it wasn't in a skating rink and I busted my ass on the concrete. It hurt so bad I never did it again."

George laughed. "No wonder you picked it up so fast. Anyway, I thought you might like the speed and the music."

"I did. I do. You make it so much easier since you hold my hand and help me." Lizzy winked at him.

They continued to watch the games and comment on the kids who were playing. Before long, they finished their nachos, and the lights dimmed because the games were over. A slow song came over the speakers.

"May I have this dance?" George stood next to the booth with his hand out.

"Absolutely, but let's clean up on our way."

"You read my mind."

George carried most of the trash so Lizzy could concentrate on skating. After dumping it, George reached the skating floor first and held his hand out to help her step in. He skated backwards, holding her while she concentrated on staying upright as she skated forward. A hard task, especially when his loving gaze made her heart flutter. For another two hours, the rhythmic pulse of the music filled her soul, a vibrant beat that matched her own racing heart, until Lizzy's burning legs forced them to stop. They returned their skates and got in the car.

Chapter 36

Great Date Night

George

"Do you want to go to the resort?" Lizzy turned in her seat to face George. "We can eat dinner and then watch a movie."

George had loved every minute of their date and didn't want it to end. "Sure, I'd like that." George drove them to the resort and parked. "Do you want to eat at Savor or Rush?"

"Let's grab something from Rush and take it to go. I'd rather eat in my room."

"Sounds good to me." George held her hand as they walked through the lobby and to the bar at Rush.

Alex came out. "Hey, how was skating?"

"Exhilarating," Lizzy beamed.

"That's good. I guess Skater Boy here is an excellent teacher," Alex laughed. "What can I get you?"

"Can we get a couple sandwiches, chips, and drinks to go?" George looked at Lizzy to make sure she also wanted a sandwich.

"Sure, what kind?" Alex leaned against the counter.

"I'll have a turkey and provolone." Lizzy sat on the bar stool.

"Just like your sister and Frey, huh?" Alex grinned. "And you, Skater Boy?"

"You're not funny," George smirked. "I'll have an Italian sub."

"You got it. Come around back." Alex waved them over. "Pick out your chips and drink."

George waited for Lizzy to slide off the bar stool. Placing his hand on her lower back, he followed her to the kitchen, where Alex was putting their sandwiches together.

"Lizzy, let me guess, you just want mayo?" Alex asked after he sliced the sub roll.

"Yes, please."

"You girls could ask for something more complicated, you know. I am a gourmet chef," Alex sighed.

"We could, but we really like your turkey and provolone."

Lizzy and George grabbed their favorite chips.

"How about you, Skater Boy?" Alex had already finished Lizzy's sandwich and wrapped it up.

"Is this going to be a thing?" George pulled open the refrigerator and held it open for Lizzy to get her drink.

"Is what going to be a thing?" Alex sliced his bread.

"You know what I'm talking about." George pulled out a drink for himself. "The Skater Boy thing."

"Ha," Alex hollered. "If the shoe, or should I say skate, fits."

"You're not funny," George said again.

"What toppings do you want on your sandwich?" Alex pointed the knife at him. He'd already put all the meat on the bottom half of the bread.

George frowned. "You've made them for me before. Add whatever you usually add."

"You got it, Skater...," Alex never finished because he ducked as George threw his chips at his head. "Hey, no food throwing in my kitchen."

"Then shut the fuck up and finish my sandwich so I can take my beautiful girlfriend upstairs to watch a movie." George grunted and caught the bag of chips that Alex threw back at him.

"Geesh, touchy, touchy." Alex finished and wrapped up George's sandwich. He placed them both into a brown bag and handed them to George. "Have fun, you too. Well, not too much fun, if you know what I mean. Make smart choices."

Alex kept screaming crazy sayings as Lizzy and George left his kitchen. Lizzy was laughing, but George left him with a flying bird. When they got upstairs, they ate at the table while Lizzy flipped channels, looking for something they could watch.

After they ate, they moved to the couch. George laid down with Lizzy in his arms, a blanket pulled over them. Lizzy found a romantic comedy but promised to play an action movie after. George didn't really care what they watched as long as he could hold her in his arms. He thought it was a sweet movie and was glad the guy got the girl. Happy endings always made girls happy, and if Lizzy was happy, then he was happy.

The next movie had action-packed suspense. Lizzy's breathing grew soft and even as she slept soundly in his arms, long before the movie ended. The warmth of her body pressed against his, and the intoxicating scent of her hair brought him such peace that he avoided the slightest movement that might disturb her. When the credits rolled, he reached for the remote and turned off the television.

He maneuvered around Lizzy, sliding off the couch. With one arm behind her back and the other under her legs, he picked her up and carried her into her bedroom. Lizzy mumbled something and tightened her arms around his neck. Using the hand behind her back, he bent down and pulled her comforter and sheet back. Slowly, he placed her on the bed and tucked her in.

Turning to leave, he heard her say, "Where are you going?"

"I was going home." George's fingers stroked her hair off her face.

"Please stay." Lizzy scooted back and pulled the covers back. "I don't want to be alone."

"Okay." George slipped off his shoes and crawled into bed next to her.

"Are you okay sleeping in your clothes?" Lizzy mumbled.

"You're in your clothes," George mentioned.

"Yeah, and I'm uncomfortable." Lizzy was moving around under the covers.

George chuckled. "Are you taking off your clothes?"

"Yep, and so should you, so we can both be comfortable." Lizzy tossed her pants out from under the covers.

"Okay." George unbuckled his jeans and tossed them out. He would be more comfortable in his boxer briefs. Deciding to keep his shirt on if Lizzy kept hers on. He wanted her to feel safe. They had done nothing sexual since the strip club. George turned toward Lizzy just as her shirt and bra went flying.

"Your turn." She pointed at him. A devious look on her face.

George took off his shirt and sent it flying before he laid down on his back.

"Much better." Lizzy wrapped herself around him, stroking his chest and abs.

If she kept that up, they weren't going to get much sleep.

"I had a great time today." Lizzy kissed his chest. "That was the best date ever."

"I'm so glad you enjoyed it." George kissed the crown of her head.

"George?" Lizzy continued to kiss his chest.

"Yeah." George's abs tightened, and he closed his eyes. She was weaving her magic around him and if she continued, she would decimate him into a bundle of need.

"Are you tired?" Lizzy swirled her tongue around his nipple.

George sucked in his breath and grumbled. "No, you were the one that was asleep on the couch."

"I'm awake now." Lizzy continued to suck his nipple while her other hand wandered down over his abs.

The slow descent was killing him. Would she stop before she got to his dick or continue until she grasped it and stroked him?

"I can see that." George shifted his body. He was trying to stay still and let her have her way, but his body yearned for her.

"George?"

"Um, hm," George groaned when he felt her hand slide into his boxer briefs and grip his cock.

"Can you take these off, please?"

"Mm, hm," George sat up and watched as Lizzy licked her lips when his cock popped out as he dragged his boxer briefs off. *Motherfucker!* He was going to go off just from the way she was looking at him. Tossing his briefs over the side of the bed, Lizzy pushed him down and slid between his legs. One hand gripped the bottom of his cock while the other massaged his balls. His stomach muscles clenched when he felt her tongue lick him from the bottom to the head before she sucked him into her mouth. He thought he had died and gone to heaven.

"Fuck, Lizzy." He hesitated, not wanting to force his way into her mouth. He wanted her to set the pace, but the urge to run his fingers through her silken hair was too strong to resist. His heart hammered against his ribs, a frantic drumbeat against the soaring pleasure that filled his soul. As she brought him to the back of her throat, he could feel his body shaking in anticipation, yearning for release.

George clenched his jaw and took a deep breath. "Lizzy," George growled and tilted her face to look at her. "You have to stop before I come in your mouth."

"What if I want you to?" She stared at him as her tongue darted across the top of his head.

"Fuck me," George moaned and dropped his head back onto the bed. The lust in her eyes floored him. In this moment, he would give her anything she wanted. He would gladly be her boy toy.

Lizzy began to suck and lick in earnest. George held out as long as he could before his body tightened and he screamed out, filling her mouth with his orgasm. Lizzy licked her way up to his neck while George calmed his breathing. It was his turn now, and he couldn't wait to taste her again.

George placed his hands under her arms and pulled her up before rolling on top of her.

"Can I have a turn now?" George watched her carefully. If she showed any signs of distress or hesitation, he would hold her, and they could sleep.

Lizzy pulled his head down to her lips and mumbled against his lips. "Please. I need you."

George wasn't about to make her wait. If his girl needed him, he was more than happy to please her. Releasing her mouth, he trailed kisses down her jaw to her neck. Sucking passionately, he located the sensitive area where her neck and shoulders connected. He'd learned about that spot the first time they were together. Her body was so responsive it always told him what she liked.

His hands massaged her breasts slowly, not wanting to cause her any pain. He wanted her to feel only pleasure. Gently rubbing one of her nipples, his mouth latched onto the other breast, and he swirled his tongue around the tight bud. Her body was now writhing under him. Releasing his hand off of her breast, he slowly glided it down her body into her panties and mumbled against her breast. "Take your panties off."

Lizzy bucked against his hand, allowing him to slip his finger inside her while she struggled to pull off her panties. George leisurely ran his tongue from her breast to her belly. Giving her a couple of kisses before he sat up and used both of his hands to help her pull down her panties.

Spread out before him, Lizzy was a vision of beauty, her flushed pink skin contrasting with the stark white sheets. He could see all his love marks marring her beautiful, flawless skin. Grabbing her thighs, he opened them wide and drove his tongue into her core. Lizzy cried out and grabbed the sheets. Her hips pumped into his face so hard he had to release her thighs and hold her down with one hand while the other played with her clit. Her thighs clamped around his head, holding him in place. He didn't care if she suffocated him, he would die a lucky man with her body holding him and her taste in his mouth.

"George, please," Lizzy moaned.

George knew what she wanted. She needed help to release the tension that coiled around her body. He used his thumb to massage her clit while he inserted two fingers inside and reached the spot that drove her crazy. Between his fingers and tongue, Lizzy exploded her sweet cream into his mouth. He gladly lapped it up before releasing her legs and kissing his way up her body to her mouth.

Kissing her, he tasted their union. Nothing had ever tasted so sweet and good. But it wasn't enough. He had to be inside her now.

"Lizzy," he whispered, his voice raspy with urgency. "I need you. Are you okay with that?"

"Yes, please, I need you too." Lizzy's hips undulated against his.

George reached for his pants and pulled out a condom. Ripping it open with his teeth, Lizzy reached out her hand.

"Can I do it?"

"Sure." George took the condom out of the packaging and handed it to her.

Lizzy sat up and used both hands to roll it on. George closed his eyes and groaned. She stroked him twice before he kissed her tenderly as he guided her down to the mattress. When he laid on her, she slid her hand between their bodies and guided him into her. George pushed in and held himself in place while he caught his breath. Every time with Lizzy was better than the last, if that was even possible.

When she clenched her muscles around his dick, George sunk into her as far as he could. Needing to claim her for his own, George set the pace. Lizzy wrapped her arms around his waist and dug her heels into his ass. Needing to give her everything he had; he released her mouth and ground into her. Swirling his hips with every thrust.

Lizzy was panting and so fucking wet. He could feel her muscles tighten around him. Sliding his hand between them, he found her clit and played with it until his cock continued to hit her special spot. Lizzy screamed and dug her nails into his back as her orgasm shook her body. With both hands he lifted her hips, giving her a different angle as he pounded into her, prolonging her orgasm long enough for him to release his.

George's heart was racing like he'd run a fucking marathon, but he felt like the king of the world with his queen in his arms. Dropping to his elbows, he cupped Lizzy's face and kissed her. Showing her all the love he had in his heart for her. But showing wasn't enough. He had to tell her.

Lifting his face but staying close enough to kiss her, he gazed into her eyes. When she opened them, George smiled.

"I love you, Lizzy," George whispered.

"I love you, too." Lizzy responded and kissed him back.

George felt utterly drained, but those four words jolted him back to life, and ready for round two. They got little sleep that night.

Chapter 37

Annihilation Plan

Numbers

Numbers had a close call last night. When Red and he were leaving a fast-food joint, three guys approached them. Two of them held Red while the big guy beat the shit out of Numbers with his fists and a pipe. Numbers was lying on the ground when the big guy pulled him up by his shirt and whispered in his ear.

"Reaper says finish the job or we'll be back and neither of you will survive the next beating."

Releasing Numbers shirt, he collapsed to the ground. Numbers ribs were killing him, and he was having trouble catching his breath. They must've broken one or more of his ribs. He could barely see the big guy out of his right eye.

"Don't make us come back here. You won't like it." The big guy motioned for his goons. One of them punched Red in the gut before they all left.

Red held his stomach before he stumbled to Numbers.

"Are you okay, boss?" Red croaked.

"No asshole. My right eye is fucking swollen shut and throbbing," Numbers said, frustration clear in his voice. "I think that fucker broke some of my ribs. Help me up. We gotta get out of here before someone sees us." Numbers reached his arm out for Red.

Red put Numbers' arm around his shoulder and straightened as best he could. Numbers was limping, but with Red holding him up, they made it to their white stolen van and drove to their hideout—a rundown old motel. Following the chaotic scene at the Purple Palace, police arrived at the clubhouse with an arrest warrant for him and Red, forcing them to find a new, less-than-ideal location—hence, the dilapidated motel.

Shit! That meant Reaper knew about his two failed attempts. Damn, that motherfucker had a lot of contacts in and out of jail.

At the motel Red helped Numbers lay down on a nasty mattress. The mattress was filthy as hell with not much cushion left, but better than lying on the floor.

"Red, we gotta come up with a plan," Numbers groaned.

"Here, drink this water and let's throw some ideas around." Red handed Numbers a bottle of water.

Numbers didn't know where he got it from, and he didn't care. The cool water eased his throat enough for them to discuss the annihilation of Maggie, Tori, Angel, and Lizzy.

"We could blow up the cultural center?" Red grinned.

"Although I would love to blow that place up, we don't have any bombs."

"We could run in there and shoot them all. You know, the element of surprise would be on our side."

"I like your idea, but instead of running in, how about if we shoot them as they come out?" Numbers laid down. His ribs were throbbing.

"How do we get them to come out?"

"We can pick them off one by one as they come out at the end of their workday," Numbers sighed.

"They don't come out at the same time."

"They do on Saturdays," Numbers grinned wickedly before he took another sip.

"Let's say we get Maggie, Tori, and Lizzy. How do we get Angel? She's not at the cultural center." Red sat on a rickety chair.

"I'll call Angel with a threatening call about an hour before the center closes. You know she can't resist warning them. Then, as they leave, we pick them off."

"Okay, but Saturday is tomorrow, unless you want to wait a week?"

"I'm not waiting a fucking week." Numbers pointed at Red. "I need you to get us some guns and ammo."

"Where am I supposed to get guns from?"

"Fuck Red! Figure it out. Sneak into the clubhouse, see if you can find any, or go steal some from a pawnshop. I don't give a fuck where you find them. Just go get them." Why couldn't Red stop questioning him and do what he was told to do? Fuck, didn't he know that prospects didn't question brothers?

"Fine! I'll be back as soon as I can. Anything else?

"Yeah, get me any type of pain pills you can find. My face and ribs are killing me."

Numbers heard Red leave and prayed he'd be back soon.

Chapter 38

Not Again

After declaring their love, George and Lizzy made love well into the night. They couldn't keep their hands off each other. When they got up, Lizzy told George she wanted to help Tori today at the cultural center. George agreed to take her because he needed to do laundry, anyway. After a little more kissing and pleasuring in the shower, they got dressed and went to the cultural center.

"Good morning," Lizzy sing-songed to Maggie at the lobby desk.

"Hey, what are you doing here?" Maggie came around the desk for a hug.

"Hey, Lizzy, George." Mark waved hello from behind the desk.

Sky went over to them for a quick pet before she went back to Mark and laid down next to him, facing the front windows.

"Hey guys." George waved back. "Lizzy, I'm heading upstairs. See you for lunch?"

"Sounds good." Lizzy smiled and kissed his cheek before he left.

"Well, well, well, I see someone is getting cozy with Deputy George." Maggie winked and went back to her seat.

"He's great," Lizzy sighed.

"Is he as great as his abs?" Maggie inquired before Mark grumbled.

"What, he does have great abs?" Maggie smiled at Lizzy. "Doesn't he Lizzy?"

"He sure does." Lizzy nodded.

"Lizzy can admire George's abs as much as she wants." Mark spun around in his chair and pointed at her. "But you, ball buster, can't."

"Fine, take away all my fun. Why don't you?" Maggie began typing something on her keyboard.

"You don't remember how much fun I can be?" Mark raised his eyebrow at her. "Cause I can show you."

Maggie laughed and blew him a kiss.

Lizzy knew they were sharing an inside joke, their eyes lingering on each other with a knowing smirk that suggested something risque and sexual. That was her cue to leave them alone and go find her sister.

Lizzy pointed toward the kitchen. "I'm gonna go find my sister."

"She's in the warehouse with Thunder logging in new inventory," Maggie shouted.

Lizzy pivoted from the direction of the kitchen to the warehouse. She loved doing inventory. It was easy, and she'd helped Tori do it before. She knocked on the door before entering.

"Hey, put me to work. I'm here to help today." Lizzy said as she walked in.

"Hey." Tori stood up from behind a table with a clipboard. "Sounds good, because Thunder has to leave."

"I'll be back. I just gotta pick up more ice cream for Isa." Thunder grinned. "She wants Rocky Road now."

"Her cravings are really kicking in, huh? Do you need me to go get it or hang out with her?" Lizzy walked to the table and picked up one of the beautiful sculptures.

"Nah, she's bingeing movies with Sarah and Lilly. I'll be back quick. I'm glad you're doing better." Thunder gave her a quick hug and left.

"Here." Tori handed her the clipboard. "I'll tell you what the items are, and you can write them down for me.

"Sounds good." Lizzy took the clipboard and followed Tori around the tables.

Thunder came back before lunch and George came down to eat with them. Since it was a slow day, they all sat in the restaurant to eat. Lizzy noticed Maggie and Mark sat facing the front door in case someone entered. Lunch was delicious per usual because everything Alex cooked was delicious.

After lunch Lizzy went back to helping Tori and George went upstairs to finish his laundry and clean his apartment. Lizzy told him she would check it before she left and make sure it was spotless. George rolled his eyes and left.

Lizzy was just finishing up with Tori when Alex came in and told them it was time to go.

Lizzy texted George.

> Hey, I'm leaving. Will I see you tonight?

> I hope so. You want to catch a movie?

> At a movie theatre or my room.

> Whichever you want.

> My room.

> I'm craving Chinese food. I'll pick some up and be at your place around 6?

> Sounds good.

What do you want from the restaurant?

Sweet and Sour Chicken with Fried Rice

Done. See you at 6

"What are you smiling at?" Tori tried to glance at her phone.

Lizzy moved it away from her. "I'm seeing George tonight."

"You just saw George." Tori grabbed all their inventory sheets and headed out of the warehouse.

"I'm excited about seeing him again. Don't you get excited every time you see Alex?" Lizzy rolled her eyes.

"Valid point. Let me put these sheets in Thunder's office and I'll log them in on Tuesday."

Lizzy walked to the lobby desk just as Maggie and Mark were shutting down.

"I'm not sure if I'll come in on Tuesday. I might check in on Isa," Lizzy said as she leaned against the counter.

"We'll miss seeing you, but I'm sure Isa will appreciate it." Maggie organized her desk.

"Are we ready?" Alex stood next to Lizzy.

"Yep," Tori answered on her way to Alex.

The three of them waved goodbye to Mark and Maggie, then turned and Lizzy collided with Angel, who was standing at the front door. Gasping for air, Angel's hand pressed against her ribs. Her breath hitched in her throat.

"You guys need to leave. I just got a call from Numbers. He set a bomb here at the cultural center. You need to get out. Hurry!"

Chapter 39

Saturday Shitshow

That was the second time that Angel came running into a room to warn them about the LRs. Lizzy looked around, seeing everyone's mouth drop. Thunder was the first to respond.

"Quick." Thunder pointed to the front doors. "Everyone, get out of here. Your lives are more important than this building. I'll call the police."

"George is upstairs. He doesn't know what's going on. I need to get him." Lizzy frantically took a few steps, but Thunder stopped her.

"I'll get George, you go outside with Alex."

"I'll do a perimeter check after I let Sky run inside. Sky, search." Mark gave Sky her command, and she bolted into the museum. Sky, now a fully trained dual-purpose dog, was ready for anything. Her keen nose could detect not only the faintest trace of narcotics, but also the unsettling scent of explosives hidden within suspicious packages.

"I'm staying with you." Maggie ran after Mark, who followed Sky.

Alex was at the door when he turned and said, "Lizzy, Tori, Angel, let's go." Lizzy followed them even though she really wanted to get George. Turning before she left the lobby; she saw Thunder run into the kitchen.

Angel was between Alex and Tori, but a couple of steps behind. Lizzy was next to Angel, to the right of Alex.

"Let's run to my truck. I'll park it as far away from the building as I can," Alex huffed as they ran to his blue truck parked to the left of Mark's. They always parked in the order in which they came in. So, the first two spots were usually Mark and Thunder because Alex and Tori always started work after them.

Lizzy was glad they didn't have far to run. Then shots rang out and Tori screamed, grabbing her arm.

"Fuck!" Alex hollered and pressed Tori against the front grill of Thunder's truck. It was the closest one to them.

Angel grabbed Lizzy and pushed her next to Tori. Lizzy saw Angel pull a gun from the back of her skirt. Lizzy was impressed. Not only was Angel dressed like a professional lawyer in her business suit and heels, but now she was a badass with a gun. Bullets pinged the truck all around them. As soon as they stopped,

Angel popped out and shot toward the shooter. Lizzy couldn't see where the shooter was, but she knew they were behind Alex's truck. She wished she had a gun so she could help Angel.

Alex didn't carry a gun because they scared Tori. Guns didn't scare Lizzy; she would love to have the extra protection. Lizzy kept watching the volley between Angel and the shooter.

"I think there's two of them!" Angel shouted over the noise of the bullets hitting the truck. "We need to get a few trucks over, so when the others come out, they can use this truck for cover." Angel pointed toward Alex's truck, which was parked to the right of Mark's truck. "Stay here. Once I'm in front of the truck, I'll shoot in their direction to give you guys time to follow me. Then we'll do the same thing again one more time." As soon as the bullets stopped, Angel kept her gun pointed at the shooters and scooted to the front of Mark's truck.

Alex had pulled his belt off, wrapping it multiple times around Tori's arm to stop the bleeding. Lizzy turned to Tori and held her hand. She looked pale from the loss of blood.

"Lizzy, are you hurt?" Alex ran his hands over her arms and legs.

"N...No." Lizzy answered Alex, but stared at Angel, awaiting her cue.

Alex wrapped his arm around Tori's waist and as soon as Angel stood, Alex and Lizzy helped Tori get behind Mark's truck.

"Are there two shooters?" Lizzy stared at Alex, wide-eyed.

Alex was crouched in front of them. "It looks that way. I can't see them, but the shots are coming at the same time from two different directions."

Just then, Lizzy saw Mark, Maggie, and Sky sprinting toward them, their faces flushed and hair flying. Before Lizzy could scream, a gunshot rang out, and Maggie crumpled to the ground, clutching her leg. Seeing her struggle, Mark immediately dropped to his knees to help. But Maggie was no shrinking violet. With a gasp, Lizzy watched Maggie's face twist in agony as she pushed herself up; the searing pain in her leg was evident in her clenched jaw and the sweat beading on her forehead.

"Motherfucker!" Maggie screamed, her voice sharp and shrill, yanking Mark's gun from its holster. She shoved him roughly backward, her leg dragged behind her as she cursed loudly, rushing toward the sound of the gunshot.

Mark hit the ground, a surprised gasp escaping his lips, his jaw slack with shock as he watched Maggie limping toward the gunmen. "Killer, get the fuck down." Mark sprang up and tackled her from behind, the force of his body pushing her hard against the truck's side as another shot zipped past, dangerously close.

With a sharp yank, Mark ripped the gun from Maggie's grasp and returned fire. "Sky, attack!"

With a burst of energy, Sky shot off like a speeding train, a blur of fur and legs against the black paved parking lot.

"While Sky is distracting them, we need to move to the next truck. Thunder and George should come out soon." Angel pointed to Alex's truck.

Alex and Lizzy moved Tori. Lizzy, peeking between the two trucks, saw a black-haired man, whom she assumed was Red, drop his gun, eyes wide with shock, as Sky launched into the air, the man's thud echoing as Sky landed heavily on his chest with a low growl, her teeth bared inches from his face.

A guttural howl ripped from the man's throat as he frantically begged them to remove the dog, tears streaming down his face.

Lizzy turned her head, looking for Mark, but he wasn't in front of Thunder's truck. Maggie sat in front of the truck alone, her hand pressed to the wound as blood ran down her leg. Her eyes blazed, her mouth a snarling line, as her head slammed against the truck's grill, her face contorted in a mask of pure rage. Her lips moved, and Lizzy knew Maggie was probably letting loose a string of curses, but the sound of gunfire drowned out her words. Mark must've left her to follow Sky, who was pinning Red to the ground, her slobber landing on his face as she continued to growl.

Lizzy gasped and covered her mouth as she saw movement behind a white van. A gun poking out toward Sky. Angel must've seen it too, because she ran to Maggie, checked on her and then went around the truck, probably near Mark.

"Police freeze!" Lizzy jumped at the sound of George's voice. She was so focused on the shooters and worried about Sky that she forgot George and Thunder were still in the building. Terror seized her when she saw George and Thunder running toward them.

As they reached the blood-soaked spot where someone shot Maggie, Lizzy screamed, her voice trembling, "George, watch out!" Then she crouched behind the truck, the metallic ping of bullets echoing around her.

George pinned his back to the wall, but not Thunder. He kept running toward the shooter as he screamed their Lakota battle cry. In horror, Lizzy watched a bullet graze Thunder's temple. He stopped, touching his head and pulling his hand away, blood coating his fingers as he stared at the crimson stain against his skin. Lizzy had never seen such hatred in Thunder's face as he glanced up and screamed. Ready to launch himself forward again, but George pushed him from behind to the front of Thunder's truck, next to Maggie. Lizzy was relieved that Thunder didn't keep running toward the bullets. He didn't have a gun. How the hell was he supposed to fight the shooter without a gun? If anything happened to him, Isa would be devastated.

Thunder ripped a strip of his t-shirt and created a tourniquet above Maggie's wound. With a sharp rip, he tore another strip and secured it around his head, the cloth now a makeshift bandana. The blood soaked into the cloth at his temple, turning it a crimson red that mirrored the color of their blood-stained hands. Thunder cupped Maggie's head, yelling at her to stay awake. The high-pitched wail of police sirens mixed with the deeper, more resonant clang of firetruck sirens rang out louder and louder as they got closer. *Hurry, hurry, before someone dies.*

"Numbers, put the gun down. Your partner is already down. Don't make me shoot you." George yelled. Lizzy peeled her eyes off Thunder and Maggie to watch George. His legs were apart, both hands held his gun firmly as he leaned on the hood of Mark's truck.

"I ain't goin' to jail. Reaper will kill me if I haven't gotten rid of Tori, Maggie, and Angel."

"He's not going to kill you!" George yelled back. "We can keep you separated. You've already shot Tori and Maggie. That has to count for something to Reaper. Just put the gun down before someone else gets hurt."

Lizzy couldn't believe it when George stepped away from the truck and walked between the trucks toward Numbers. *Why was he making himself a bigger target?* Lizzy left Tori and Alex and crept along the side of Alex's truck. She wanted a better look at what was happening. Grabbing Mark's back fender, she peaked around the side and saw Numbers standing out in the open. Looking past him, she saw Sky's mouth now clamped around the man's neck. He was still whimpering and screaming, "Get it off!"

Mark was standing behind Numbers, but in front of the man on the ground, his gun aimed at Numbers back. She also saw Angel to the right of Numbers with her gun pointed at him. Her face fuming with anger.

"You're gonna have to kill me. Cause I ain't dropping my gun!"

"Doesn't matter. You're dead either way!" Angel shouted. "If you wind up in jail, my father will never let you live to see tomorrow. You are such a fuckup!"

What the hell was Angel doing antagonizing him? He was already a loose cannon.

Numbers swung his gun at Angel. "Shut up, bitch! You should've died the first time we kicked your ass."

The sirens were getting louder. They had drawn a crowd. You would think with shots being fired, people would scatter, but no, these spectators, they were fearless. Some were talking on the phone while others held their phones out, recording everything. Lizzy couldn't believe they weren't afraid of getting hit by a stray bullet. She was terrified hiding behind a car, but they were standing on the sidewalk like this was a rehearsed scene of a movie.

"Don't do this, Numbers!" George shouted. "Put the gun down and get on the ground."

"Not gonna happen before I kill this bitch." Numbers' hand twitched before he pulled the trigger.

Then it all seemed to happen in slow motion for Lizzy. Several shots rang out at the same time. Gravel exploded around Angel's feet, sending tiny stones skittering across the ground as she dove right, and fired at Numbers. George fired at Numbers', the crimson stain blooming across his arm as the gun clattered to the pavement, a metallic thud echoing in the sudden silence. He howled in pain like an injured animal while he held his injured arm. Several police cars pulled into the lot at different angles. Officers jumped out of their cars and screamed orders. George approached him and kicked the gun away. Mark commanded Sky to release the black-haired man.

The police kept yelling at everyone to freeze as they surrounded them with their guns raised.

Lizzy stood and raised her hands.

"We need an ambulance!" Alex yelled.

Chapter 40

Another Hospital Visit...A Reoccurring Theme

George raised his arms up and held his gun out, his finger away from the trigger while he shouted. "I'm an off-duty police officer. My name is Deputy George Smith. I fired one shot from my service revolver. These two men were shooting at us. We need an ambulance. We have five injured people."

Lizzy watched as two officers grabbed George. One took his gun, while the other pushed him against the car with his hands behind his back. George didn't struggle. A couple of other officers grabbed Numbers and several approached Mark, Sky, and Red. Mark held his hands up like George while one officer took his gun and the other checked him for more weapons. Sky sat staring at the officers near Mark. Red was being cuffed.

"Hey, hey, wait." Lizzy turned and saw Deputy Ray in full uniform running toward them. "He's an officer. Don't arrest him."

"Sorry." The officer that held George's wrists released him. "We weren't sure if you were telling us the truth."

"It's fine." George held up his hands. "You would've run my ID and found out soon enough. Thanks for the assist, Ray."

Lizzy went to George, wrapping her arms tightly around his waist; he gently kissed her forehead.

"Sure. You want to tell us what the hell happened?" Deputy Ray looked around at all the chaos. "Hey!" he screamed to the officers near Mark. "Let that man go, too. He's a security officer here, and that K9 is a police officer. Just arrest the scumbag on the ground."

Lizzy ignored the conversation going on around her between George and the officers. Her focus was on the four ambulances that pulled up around them. Glancing between them, she watched Tori as they carefully placed her on a gurney and wheeled her into one ambulance. Alex was talking to Thunder, pointing to Tori's ambulance. Thunder nodded and jumped in before it took off. Lizzy saw Mark holding Maggie's hand in the second ambulance before the door shut. Sky sat behind the ambulance barking, but as soon as the door shut, she turned and ran to George. George laid his hand on her head, and she sat next to him.

A paramedic and an officer gently guided Red toward the back of the third ambulance, the wail of the sirens a constant background hum, as another paramedic and a stern-faced officer carefully placed Numbers, his hands bound to the gurney, into the last ambulance. The ambulances departed in quick succession, their red lights flashing rhythmically, the wail of their sirens echoing in the street. With a knot in her stomach, she hoped Numbers and Red wouldn't end up at the same hospital as Tori, Maggie, and Thunder.

Alex looked lost as he stared at Tori's ambulance as it drove away. Lizzy wanted to check on him.

"I'll be right back." Lizzy interrupted George in the middle of his statement to Deputy Ray. "I need to talk to Alex." George nodded.

Lizzy stood next to Alex and put her arm around his waist. He put his arm around her shoulder and sighed.

"Where are they taking them?" Lizzy watched the red taillights fade into the distance.

"Sunrise General," Alex murmured.

"Is that where they're taking the bad guys?" Lizzy watched those ambulances to see if they followed Tori and Maggie's.

"I don't know, but I hope not." Alex was speaking, but his voice sounded disjointed from his body.

"Alex." Lizzy squeezed his waist, trying to snap him out of it. "You need to go. Tori needs you."

"Thunder is with her." Alex blinked when the ambulance turned. "I'll go as soon as George comes over. Tori would want me to stay here with you."

"Okay." Lizzy followed Alex to the back of his truck.

He pulled down the tailgate, and they sat side by side, silently watching everyone. The forensics team took photos of all the evidence. George, with Sky by his side, was still talking to Deputy Ray while a female officer spoke to Angel. Deputy Ray must've asked about her or Alex, because George pointed to them, and they headed their way. When George was an arm's length away, Alex jumped off the tailgate.

"I'm gonna head to the hospital now that you're here with Lizzy," Alex said to George.

George put his hands on Lizzy's waist, she placed her hands on his shoulders, and he lifted her off the tailgate, setting her down next to him. Alex closed the tailgate.

"Can I get your statement before you go?" Deputy Ray interjected, his pad and pen ready to take notes.

"Can you get it at the hospital? My wife was shot, and I need to go check on her."

"Sure, of course." Deputy Ray nodded. "I have other statements to get there, so I'll find you for yours." Deputy Ray wrote something down on his notepad.

"Thanks." Alex nodded and opened his car door.

"Mr. Panther, wait!" Deputy Ray hollered and hurried over to Alex, grabbing the driver's side door before Alex could close it. "I'm sorry, but you can't take your car. It has to be processed since it was at the scene of a crime, but an officer will drive you to the hospital."

Alex got out of the car. Deputy Ray shut the door before screaming, "Carlos! Take Mr. Panther to Sunrise General, lights and sirens please, his wife was shot."

"Will do." Carlos waved Alex over and they ran to his patrol vehicle.

"Can I get your statement now, Lizzy?" Deputy Ray faced her.

"Will it take long? Alex's wife is my sister, and I'd like to be at the hospital, too." Lizzy looked between Deputy Ray and George.

"It's best to get it over with." George pulled her in for a hug and kissed her temple. "The events of what happened will be clearer in your mind now."

"George is right." Deputy Ray cleared this throat. "But if you remember anything else later, you can always call me and let me know."

"Okay," Lizzy sighed. "Can I sit, please?"

George opened Alex's tailgate again and helped Lizzy get comfortable. He sat her near the end so he could stand next to her but still wrap his arm around her. Sky immediately jumped up and laid next to Lizzy, resting her head in Lizzy's lap. With Sky and George's support, Lizzy felt a sense of relief and calm wash over her. She lazily stroked Sky's head while she recanted everything she witnessed. When she finished, Deputy Ray shut his notebook and addressed George.

"We'll keep the service revolver used today for the pending investigation. You'll be placed on administrative leave, pending a full investigation to determine your innocence. We can provide you with another revolver until you are cleared, but you need to stop by the station to pick it up. Any questions?"

"No." George shook his head.

"Then you guys are free to go. I'm sure I'll see you at the hospital at some point."

"Thanks, Ray. Can you stay with Lizzy for a minute while I go get my keys and lock up the cultural center?"

"Sure, not a problem." Ray sat on the other side of Sky.

"Well, this was quite the shitshow, huh?" Ray stroked Sky's back.

"Yeah," Lizzy agreed. "I'm just glad it's over. Deputy Ray, Can I ask you a question?"

"Sure, you can ask me anything." Deputy Ray's eyes softened.

"Are the bad guys going to the same hospital as my sister?" Lizzy blurted.

"No." Deputy Ray shook his head. "They'll go to another hospital that's closer to the jail."

Lizzy sighed in relief and nodded.

"Lizzy, are you okay?" Angel walked toward her.

"Yeah, just waiting for George to lock up. Then we're heading to the hospital. Are you coming?"

"I'm gonna get Barrett. Alex must've already called him, because I'm getting angry texts flooding my phone from Barrett asking me why the hell I provoked Numbers.

Deputy Ray chuckled. "Good luck with that. I've seen Barrett mad, and I'd hate to be on the receiving end of that."

"Yeah, me too." Angel smirked. "But I have my ways of calming him down."

"I'll bet you do." Deputy Ray laughed.

"See you at the hospital." Angel waved and headed to her car.

George returned and helped Lizzy off the tailgate again. Holding her hand while Sky trailed behind them, they walked to his car. Luckily, his police vehicle was parked far enough away from the chaotic shootout that he could drive it out of the lot.

"Sky, upfront with Lizzy." George waved her over after he opened the door for Lizzy.

With a satisfying click of the seatbelt, Lizzy settled in, feeling Sky's warm fur against her legs as the dog rested contentedly, paws wrapped around her waist, and head on Lizzy's thigh. George got in and drove off, turning on his lights and sirens.

"I need to call Grayhorse," George broke the silence. "I gotta tell him Thunder is at the hospital. He needs to get Isa there. Thunder was only grazed, but she's gonna freak out."

Lizzy held out her hand. "Give me your phone. I'll dial it for you." George scooted to the side and slid his phone out of his back pocket, handing it to her. Lizzy dialed and connected the call through the car speakers. Sky whimpered while Lizzy stroked her head, comforting her.

"George, what's up?"

"There was a shootout in front of the AICC. A bullet grazed Thunder's temple, so they took him to the hospital. Isa doesn't know yet. Can you please tell her and drive her to the hospital so she can see he's okay?"

"Fuck!" Grayhorse screamed. "I'll tell her. Was anyone else hurt?"

"Tori was shot in the arm, and Maggie in the leg. They're all at the hospital with Mark and Alex, who were unharmed. I'm heading over there now with Lizzy and Sky."

Thank goodness George had his lights and sirens on because he was breaking many speed limits. Lizzy was gripping the 'oh shit bar' tightly with her right hand. It was like driving with an Indy 500 driver as he cut corners sharply but never lost control of his vehicle. *They must have taught him that at the police academy.*

"Shit, Maggie is Isa's best friend. I'm gonna have to get her in the car and lie about where we're going so I can tell her at the last minute." Lizzy heard Grayhorse's heavy breathing as if he was running.

"I can drop off Lizzy and come get you guys with a police escort and all that." George turned into the hospital.

"No, you stay with Lizzy. I got this. See you soon." Grayhorse hung up.

George parked his car in the police parking spot closest to the emergency room. Lizzy waited for Sky to get out before she bolted out of the car and ran to the desk with Sky next to her.

"Tori Tall Bear," Lizzy took a deep breath. "She's my sister. The paramedics brought her in by ambulance. She has a gunshot wound to the arm. Do you know where she is? How she is?"

The nurse glanced down at Sky. Luckily, Sky was wearing her K9 Officer vest and the nurse wouldn't deny her entry into the hospital. Lizzy was glad Mark kept that vest on her when she worked alongside him at the cultural center.

"She's in surgery right now. You can head to the 3rd floor. When you get off the elevator, make a left. There's a waiting room for the family of surgical patients. Her husband is there as well."

"Thank you, thank you so much." Lizzy grabbed George's hand and ran to the elevators. Once they reached the waiting room, they saw Alex and Mark. Sky made a beeline for Mark and jumped. Mark caught her mid-air and clung tightly before he sat with Sky in his lap. His head bowed while Sky licked his face.

Lizzy rushed toward them and hugged Alex. "How are they?"

"Still in surgery." Alex mumbled, released Lizzy, and sat in a nearby chair.

"I'll go get us some coffee." George helped Lizzy sit next to Alex.

"I need to call my mom," Lizzy whispered. "What do I say?" Tears blurred her vision.

"I already called your mom and my mom," Alex squeezed her thigh. "They are all on their way. " Alex nodded to George. "I'll watch after her while you get the coffee. Can you get Mark and I two black coffees, please?"

"Of course." George answered.

They all looked at Mark, who now sat hunched over with his elbows on his knees and his face in his hands. Sky sat beside him, her head resting on his thigh, nestled between his waist and elbow. His body shook occasionally. *He must be crying.* Lizzy's heart ached for him, a dull, heavy pain in her chest. Maggie's injury had looked worse than Tori's.

George came back with the coffees, and they all drank in silence, except Mark. He still hadn't touched the cup George placed on the small table next to his chair.

Lizzy jolted in her seat, her hand flying to her heart as a bloodcurdling scream, like nails on a chalkboard, echoed down the hallway. Lizzy watched wide-eyed as Sarah and Grayhorse held each of Isa's biceps, holding her up as they entered the waiting room.

Chapter 41

Labor Pains, Devastated Men, Surgical Update...Oh My!

Lizzy

"Where is he?" Isa held her belly, stopped, looked around, and took several breaths. "What the hell happened, George? Tell me everything." Isa was doing Lamaze breathing in between her plethora of questions. Lizzy had worked in a nursery and been around pregnant women. She knew what Lamaze breathing meant. And apparently, so did George.

"Are you in labor?" George ran to her.

"Yes, she's in labor, but the stubborn woman won't sit in a fucking wheelchair and let me take her to the maternity ward." Grayhorse glared at Isa. "So please give her an update on Thunder because then I'm carrying her ass to that floor, whether she likes it or not."

"I don't have an update." George shrugged. "They haven't come out yet, but now that you're here, his wife, I'm sure we'll find something out."

"Okay, that's it." Grayhorse bent down and picked Isa up, cradling her in his arms. "You saw, you heard. Let's get you checked in."

A nurse came rushing toward Isa with a wheelchair. "I heard your breathing and saw that you could barely walk on your own from the pain. Please sit in the chair so we can call your doctor."

Isa pointed at the chair and screeched. "I am not sitting in that chair until I see my husband!"

"Ma'am, I'll go check on your husband, please." The nurse nodded to Grayhorse to put her in the chair.

As soon as Grayhorse set her in the chair, Isa grabbed the armrests and tried to stand up.

"Isa honey, why are you causing so much trouble?"

Lizzy had been so focused on Isa; she didn't see or hear Thunder coming into the waiting room.

"Thunder, oh my god, are you okay?" Isa reached out to him.

Thunder squatted in front of her and cupped her face. Tears were streaming down her face as she ran her fingers lightly over the bandage on the side of his temple.

"Honey, I'm fine. The bullet just grazed me. But you," –Thunder kissed her– "need to see a doctor. You will not deliver our baby in a waiting room. Please, let's go."

"Okay." Isa nodded. "Okay, let's go. I'm ready now that you're here."

"Thank fuck," Grayhorse murmured before he pointed at George. "Text me as soon as you hear any updates about Maggie or Tori. Sarah and I are gonna go with them. Aurora and Matteo are on their way."

"Will do." George nodded. "Let us know how the delivery goes."

"You got it." Grayhorse patted George's back and looked at Mark. "If you need me," –Grayhorse whispered to George– "let me know. He's not looking too good."

"He's been like that since I showed up. I brought him coffee, but he hasn't paid any attention to the cup on the table next to him."

Thunder stood and held Isa's hand while the nurse wheeled her out. Grayhorse and Sarah followed them. Lizzy, with her limited knowledge of childbirth, worried that Isa's distress over Thunder's shooting and giving birth a week early might have hurt the baby. The sounds of Isa's pained breaths filled the air. Lizzy couldn't do anything for Isa, but she could go comfort Mark.

"I'm gonna sit with Mark." Lizzy got up and sat in the chair next to him. Rubbing his back, she felt his body trembling. A silent shudder ran through him. "It's gonna be okay. She's a strong woman in great shape."

"I know," Mark mumbled into his hands. "If anything happens to her...if there are any complications...I'm gonna lose my shit. She is our entire world."

Lizzy knew Mark meant him and Sky. "Is there anything I can do for you?" Lizzy scooted closer and pet Sky with her other hand.

"No." Mark shook his head. Lizzy could barely hear his words. He was speaking so quietly. "I just need her to get better. I need to see her beautiful eyes so I can tell her I love her. We have plans to get married and fill our house with kids. She can't leave me now when I found my soulmate." Mark's words came out choked and full of pain. "I need her. I can't breathe without her. I can't wait for her to come out of surgery and give me shit. Hell, I just need her to call me Surfer Smurf with her special sassiness that I love so much."

Lizzy's heart was breaking. With her arm draped over Mark's shoulders, she laid against Mark's back as he cried into his hands. Even she had tears streaming down her face. The world would be a sad place without Maggie. Her infectious laughter and sharp, funny sarcasm brightened even the darkest days and touched everyone around her.

A doctor walked in. "Which one of you is Alex Panther?"

"I am." Alex lurched out of his chair and walked to the doctor.

"I'm Dr. Halstad, your wife is getting set up in a room. As soon as she wakes up, we'll take you to her. The bullet went through and hit nothing major. A little more to the right and it wouldn't have hit her at all."

"Thank you." Alex shook his hand and released several breaths.

The doctor walked over to Mark. "Are you Mr. Holmes?"

Mark stood and wiped the tears from his face. "Yes, sir."

Lizzy watched his body jerk to attention; he was bracing himself for bad news. Meanwhile, Lizzy was praying for good news.

"I wasn't in your wife's surgery, but I asked a nurse for an update for you. She said Dr. Winthrop will be out in a few minutes to talk to you."

"Thank you." Mark nodded.

Dr. Halstad turned around and stopped when he saw the other doctor.

"Mr. Holmes, here he is now," Dr. Halstad motioned to the incoming doctor. "Dr. Winthrop this is Mr. Holmes." Then he turned to Alex. "I'll check on Tori in the morning."

Alex nodded.

"Hello, Mr. Holmes, I'm Dr. Winthrop. Your wife is in stable condition. The bullet hit her femur, the bone in her thigh, breaking it, but luckily it didn't shatter. It then bounced off and embedded itself into a nerve. It is best to leave the bullet in because if it is removed, it could cause more damage. The body will surround the bullet and hold it safely in place. We have secured her femur with a plate that runs up and down her thigh secured by a couple of compression screws. However, she will still need to be in a leg cast and wheelchair for several weeks. We want to keep her leg immobilized and make sure the bone heals properly. After we take the cast off, she will need some therapy. We expect her to have a full recovery. We'll keep her in the hospital at least overnight and treat her with anti-infection drugs because bullets usually carry debris. They are placing the cast on her leg as we speak. A nurse will come get you as soon as she is in a room."

"Can you place both ladies in the same room?" Alex interjected. "They will want to check on each other, and I really don't want either of them to leave their beds."

"I don't want them leaving their beds either," Dr. Winthrop smiled. "I will talk to the nurses and get that set up. Do you have any questions for me, Mr. Holmes?"

"Not at the moment. I'm still processing what you said. I'm shocked as hell that she is going to be okay and grateful to you for taking such good care of her." Tears streamed down Mark's face. Placing his hands on his hips, he looked down. His body swayed. Alex grabbed his arm in case he passed out.

"I'm glad I could give you good news. Barring any complications, I'll check on her in the morning." Dr. Winthrop left.

"Mark, have a seat before you fall down." George helped Alex guide Mark back into the chair he was sitting in. "She's gonna be okay."

"Thank god." Sky jumped on Mark's lap the minute his butt hit the chair. He held her tightly and kissed her muzzle before looking around the waiting room.

Lizzy grabbed his cold coffee from the table and handed it to him. "Drink some coffee."

Mark took a sip. "It's cold."

"Duh." George lightly punched his shoulder. "I bought it for you hours ago."

"Sorry, I didn't notice."

"No worries, man. I'll go get you a fresh hot cup." George winked at Lizzy and left.

"Alex!" Sehoy ran into the room with Osceola following behind. "We just talked to Angel at the resort before we left. She, Barrett, and Steele will be by later. Are Tori, Maggie, and Thunder, okay?"

Chapter 42

Family

Lizzy

Alex gave his parents a rundown on what the doctors had said about Tori and Maggie. He explained that Thunder was fine, but Isa was in labor.

"I'm so glad you asked for them to be in the same room," Sehoy sighed with relief. "When can we see them? Oh, and then we must see Isa. Is Aurora here? Do I need to call her?"

"*Chatski*, take a breath." Alex placed his hands on his mom's shoulders, holding her in place as he stared at her. "The doctor said a nurse would come find us. Grayhorse will update us on Isa. Aurora and Matteo are on their way. Why don't you have a seat?" Alex turned his mom toward a chair, but Sehoy stepped away and headed for Lizzy.

"Lizzy, are you okay?" Sehoy pulled her in for a hug.

Lizzy had learned early on that Sehoy had a mind of her own. She considered all of them her kids.

"I'm okay." Lizzy stepped back and smiled. "I just want to see my sister and Maggie."

"George," Sehoy reached her hand out for him. "Are you good?"

"Yes, ma'am." Sehoy glared at him. "Sorry, yes Sehoy, I'm good."

Sehoy continued to check on all of them like a crazed mom until she reached Mark. Sehoy hugged him tight and whispered in his ear. Lizzy couldn't make out what she said to him, but Mark smiled and kissed her cheek.

The police showed up and took down Mark and Alex's statements. They were going to wait until Tori and Maggie were in their room, but George asked them to wait until tomorrow. They hesitated, but agreed.

"Mark!" Lizzy watched three people rush into the waiting room straight for Mark. She assumed it was his mom, dad, and brother. Mark stood and clung to his mom. His father and brother joined in the group hug.

"How did you get here so fast?" Mark said after they all broke apart.

"Uh, our plane." His brother smirked at him. "We called Chris, and he was more than happy to fly us down."

"We couldn't stay at home when Maggie was in the hospital." His mom kissed his cheek.

"Thanks, mom."

Mark walked them over to the rest of the crew. "Everyone, I'd like you to meet my parents and my little brother. This is my mom, Janice." Mark motioned to each one. "My dad, Frank, and my little brother, Steve." Then Mark pointed to the rest of them. "Mom, dad, and Steve, you've heard me talk about everyone. You would've met them at our wedding, but now you can finally put the face to the names. That's Deputy George with Lizzy, Tori's sister. Alex, a talented chef, and Tori's husband. And last but not least are Sehoy and Osceola, Alex's parents, who always treat us like family."

"It is such a pleasure to meet all of you." Janice was the first to shake hands and give hugs. "I've heard so much about you all."

Lizzy and George stepped back after all the hugs.

"Mark has a personal plane?" Lizzy quirked her eyebrow at George.

"Yeah," George chuckled. "Apparently he's loaded, but doesn't want to be a rancher, so he moved here and has worked for Thunder since he met him."

"Wow, I never would've guessed." Lizzy was dumbfounded. Mark never acted like a spoiled rich man.

"None of us did." George sat down and pulled Lizzy into his lap.

"What does administrative leave mean?" Lizzy had been dying to ask George, but hadn't found the right moment.

"It means I get to stay at home and hang out with you." George smiled.

"For how long?"

"As long as the investigation takes. It could be days, weeks, or months." George leaned back against the wall, pulling Lizzy against his chest.

"Do they pay you?" Lizzy rested her cheek and hand on his chest.

"Yep. I don't lose benefits or pay until they either clear me or fire me," George mumbled.

"What?" Lizzy pulled away and stared at George.

"Lay back down," George chuckled. "It'll be fine." George pulled her head back to his chest. "I did nothing wrong. Not only will they figure that out from all the witness statements, but they'll see it on the video's that all those people took while they watched our drama unfold."

"That was weird, right? I mean, if there was a shootout, I wouldn't be standing on the sidewalk videotaping it." Lizzy snorted. "I'd be getting the hell out of there."

"Good to know," George mumbled.

Lizzy burrowed into him and closed her eyes. George was a thousand times more comfortable than any chair in the room.

Another hour passed before the nurse came in and said it was okay to see Maggie and Tori. Each patient was allowed two visitors at a time. Alex and Lizzy went in for Tori. Mark and George went in for Maggie. Sehoy and Osceola agreed to stay in the waiting room with Mark's family.

Alex and Lizzy each took up a side of Tori's bed. Lizzy was between Tori and Maggie's bed. George stood at the foot of Maggie's bed while Mark sat on the other side and leaned gently against Maggie. Lizzy let Alex talk to Tori first while she watched Mark pepper kisses all over Maggie's face as he continued to tell her how much he loved her. It was so sweet.

Lizzy glanced at George, but he was also staring at Mark with a grin on his face.

"Lizzy, are you okay?" Tori touched Lizzy's hand.

Turning to face her, Lizzy nodded as tears welled up in her eyes. She was all choked up seeing her sister lying in a hospital bed with a bandage around her arm.

"Hey, I'm okay." Tori squeezed her hand. "They're only keeping me overnight in case of infection."

"I was so scared when I saw the blood dripping from your arm." Lizzy carefully hugged her sister. "I love you, Tori. I was afraid I'd never get to say that again."

"I love you, too." Tori stroked her hair with her good hand.

"Alex took good care of me." Lizzy wiped her tears and straightened.

"As he should. I mean, you are the love of his life's sister." Tori winked at her and smiled at Alex.

"You are so right." Alex leaned down and gave her a brief kiss on her lips.

Lizzy walked to George to give Tori and Alex some time alone.

George stood behind Lizzy. Resting his chin on the top of her head, with his arms wrapped around her. Lizzy let out a long, slow sigh of contentment as she leaned back into his warm embrace, feeling completely safe.

"They're gonna be okay," George mumbled. "I texted Grayhorse. He said Isa hasn't dilated enough to start pushing and Thunder was pacing the room, about to lose his mind every time a contraction hits."

"I'm sure he would gladly take on her contraction pains if he could," Lizzy murmured.

George chuckled. "You're right about that, babe. He hates seeing her in pain."

Mark looked calmer now that he sat on the bed next to Maggie with his arm around her as she laid her head on his chest.

Maggie looked at George. "Mark said Isa is in labor. Do you have any news? I need to go see her."

"You need to stay in bed and rest, Energizer Bunny." Mark grumbled and held her back.

"What?" Tori looked from Lizzy and George to glare at Alex. "You didn't tell me Isa was in labor? Is Thunder okay? How far along is she?"

"Thunder is fine. The bullet just grazed his temple. He was bleeding like a stuck pig because the head always bleeds a lot," George smiled. "And Isa needs to dilate more before she can start pushing."

"She knows I'm okay, right?" Maggie took a sip of the water from the cup Mark offered her.

"Yup, I texted Grayhorse as soon as we came into the room." George winked at Maggie. "You were just too busy with Mark's blubbering to notice me."

Maggie laughed, but Mark gave him the finger and said, "You're just a regular comedian today, aren't you?"

George shrugged. "I try."

Lizzy chuckled because George's comments were easing the tension in the room.

"Can we come in now?" Sehoy said from the doorway.

"Who's we?" Alex raised his eyebrow at his mom.

"Frey, Holt, and me. We'll only stay a few minutes, then Mark's parents would like to see Maggie."

"Your parents are here?" Maggie stared at Mark.

"Yep. Chris flew them out here just for you." Mark kissed her temple.

"Aw, that is so sweet. I can't wait to see them." Maggie held out her hand. "Not that I don't want to see you guys," she smiled at Sehoy.

"We understand, dear." Sehoy smiled back.

"You guys can come in," Alex nodded. "George and Lizzy, will you step out with me so they can come in? We'll go check on Thunder and Isa."

"Tell Isa I love her and I'm fine!" Maggie hollered as they left the room.

It was like Grand Central Station in the hallway. Alex, Lizzy, and George hugged it out with Frey and Holt before they walked to the elevator.

"Lizzy." Alex stood behind Lizzy and George as they waited for the elevator. "I hope it's okay that I asked you to leave. I know Tori is your sister, but Mark's hanging on by a thread and I didn't want to ask him to leave Maggie."

Lizzy turned and smiled at Alex. "It's fine. I'm not mad. I totally understand." Then stepped in first when the doors dinged open.

"I'll text Frey and ask her to let me know when they leave." Alex pulled out his phone.

"In the meantime, let's try to calm Thunder down," George grinned. "Grayhorse said he's out of control."

Chapter 43

The Dawn of a New Day

George

As soon as George opened the door to Isa's room, he froze, causing Lizzy and Alex to bump into him. Thunder stood like a sentry unmoving with his arms crossed and his legs braced hip width apart while Grayhorse stood in the corner smirking.

"What do you mean she's not there yet?" Thunder screamed at the nurse. "Help her. She's in a lot of pain. Isn't there something you can do?"

"Thunder, calm down or I'll have the nurse throw you out!" Isa hollered between breaths while Sarah held her hand.

"How can you throw me out...throw her out? She's the one not helping you!" Thunder pointed at the nurse.

"You went to classes with me. You know how this works. Your yelling is not helping." Isa said through gritted teeth before she turned to Aurora and said, *"¡Mami, por favor, sácalo de aquí!"*

"¡Ay, niño, para afuera, dale!" From the little Spanish George knew, it sounded like Isa wanted her mother to remove Thunder from the room. Aurora was pushing her entire body weight, which wasn't much, against Thunder's chest. It was like watching a leaf trying to move a tree. His body never budged.

"I can't calm down when I see you in pain!" Thunder threw up his hands and spun around to face Grayhorse angrily when he laughed. "Why the fuck are you laughing? I didn't laugh at you when Sarah was popping out my nephew and niece."

"I wasn't freaking out like you are." Grayhorse waved his arm in his direction.

"Okay." George gently pulled Aurora off Thunder. "How about I take Thunder outside for some fresh air?" George looked at the nurse. "Do you know how much longer before she's ready?"

"It could be ten minutes or an hour," the nurse shrugged. "Who knows? Every birth is different."

"Well, you're a wealth of knowledge," Thunder mumbled.

"George, please get him out of here before I take your gun and shoot him myself," Isa glared at Thunder.

"On it." George grabbed his arm.

"Don't you fucking touch me. If I want to be in here with my wife, I'll be here." Thunder pulled his arm away.

"Grayhorse, a little help?" Sarah scowled at her husband. "Lizzy, you can stay here with us."

"Oh, she can stay, but the father of the baby is being kicked out?" Thunder cocked out his hip, crossed his arms, and shot daggers at Isa.

"She is not the one arguing with the nurse or making your wife upset! Grayhorse, take him outside, now!" Isa continued to take a few short shallow breaths, followed by a long exhale.

Grayhorse raised his hands. "Alright, alright." Grayhorse approached Thunder. "Let's go, brother, before these women castrate us."

Between Alex, Grayhorse, and George, they pushed Thunder out of the room and into the elevator.

"I'm gonna get you all back for this." Thunder pointed to all of them as they rode the elevator down.

Once they got to the bottom floor, they exited outside and walked around the emergency room parking lot. After the third time all the way around, Thunder calmed down and sat on the bench by the emergency room entrance.

"Grayhorse?" Thunder stared at him. "How did you do this?"

"Sarah's first delivery was difficult. I felt like you are feeling now. But when I looked at my wife doing all the work, I knew I needed to support her. The best way to do that was to grit my teeth and follow the nurse's orders. I straddled the bed behind her and let her squeeze my hand as tight as she wanted. Not gonna lie. Sometimes when a strong contraction hit, it felt like she was breaking every fucking bone in my fingers. Your sister has a powerful grip. But I wanted her to know I was with her every step of the way, so if it made her feel better, I sucked it up like a man and took it. I mean, I might end up with warped fingers, but she was pushing our future out into the world. That was a hell of a lot more important than my whiny ass complaining about my hand."

"So, what you're saying is that I'm a whiny asshole," Thunder sighed and rubbed his face. "Isa needs me and I'm handing out orders as if I know what I'm doing."

"If the shoe fits," Grayhorse shrugged.

George listened to their conversation, not knowing what to say because he'd never been in that situation. When it came down to it, even if he knew how to behave, he still would never call Thunder a whiny asshole. Glancing at Alex, he knew he wouldn't either. Only Grayhorse could make Thunder face his mistakes. They'd known each other for a long time and were brothers more than brothers-in-law.

"Okay." Thunder nodded and stood. "I'm good now. Let's go back in so I can help my wife instead of causing her more pain."

"You're a good man and will be an excellent father." Grayhorse draped his arm around Thunder and led the way to the elevators.

Thunder went straight to Isa and kissed her forehead. "I'm sorry, Isa honey. I lost it, but I'm good now." Then he straddled the bed behind her, pulled her against his chest, and held both of her hands. "I'm here for you, honey. We've got this."

Everyone else moved to the foot of the bed and watched Thunder help his wife breathe through her labor pains. When the time came, the doctor entered the room and asked everyone except Thunder to leave. They all strode to the maternity waiting room. Matteo and Gaby chatted with Skip and Minnie, who cradled baby Lilly, as Tommy, Emmy, and Lucy played cards. Sarah rushed to Minnie, scooping up Lilly in a warm embrace. George and Lizzy said hi to the adults before they sat with the kids and played war. A card game was a great way to pass the time without the kids realizing how long they had to wait. Less than an hour later, Thunder strolled in wearing a surgical gown.

"It's a boy!" Thunder belted out as he stood tall, chest puffed out, and the biggest smile George had ever seen on his face. "He's seven pounds, two ounces and 24 inches long. His name is Thomas Nando Thunderbird. Thomas after my father and Nando after Isa's father's nickname."

"That's so beautiful." Sarah, Thunder's sister, hugged him and kissed his cheek. "Daddy would be so proud that you chose his name. I am so happy for you. When can we see Thomas?"

"The nurse said he will be in the nursery in a few minutes. They are just cleaning him up."

"I'm so happy for you. Lizzy hugged Thunder.

"Congratulations, *até*." Grayhorse slapped him on the back and gave him a tight hug.

"*Lekší, lekší!*" Tommy and Lucy screamed in unison and pulled at Thunder's surgical gown. "We have a cousin, we have a cousin," they continued to shout until Thunder bent down and kissed them each on the cheek. Not one to be left out, Emmy stood in front of Thunder awaiting her uncle's kiss on the cheek.

"Congrats," George and Alex both said and hugged him.

"I can't thank you guys enough for being here and for knocking some sense into me." Thunder laughed and motioned for them to follow him. "Come on, let's see if he's in the nursery yet."

Following Thunder, they waited patiently outside the nursery, listening to the muffled sounds of the babies. The door opened and a baby in a blue blanket was being carried by one of the delivery room nurses.

"There he is!" Thunder hollered excitedly and pointed to the nurse. "That's my boy!"

The nurse smiled and walked up to the glass so they could all look at him before she laid him in a bassinet with the name "Thomas Nando Thunderbird" written on a plain white index card. They were all oohing and aahing.

"Mr. Thunderbird," –another nurse approached them from behind– "your wife is back in her room. You may follow me. We will bring the baby to you in a few minutes."

The entire crew followed Thunder into the room. He approached Isa and kissed her before a nurse brought Thomas and laid him on her chest. George watched as the happy parents pointed out his body parts and counted all his fingers and toes. Thomas looked healthy and was absolutely beautiful.

"You can start breastfeeding if you like." The nurse nodded to Isa.

"I think it's time for us to head out." Alex pulled out his phone. "Let me get a quick photo to show Tori and Maggie."

Thunder bent down, and Isa turned Thomas around so his face would be visible. Alex snapped the photo and headed to the door. George was the last one out. Before he shut the door, he glanced back at Thunder, Isa, and Thomas. Isa was glowing as she pulled apart her gown and held the baby to her breast. George smiled. He was so fucking happy for them.

Chapter 44

Lizzy with Sky in a Mansion

Throughout the day and into the evening hours, more friends and family trickled in to check on Tori and Maggie, as well as to meet Thomas. The nurse, understanding their large family and circle of friends, made an exception, allowing over two guests per patient, with a request to keep the noise level down. She also allowed Sky to lie down at the foot of Maggie's bed. Lizzy stayed with Tori most of the day while George bounced back and forth between both rooms. When visiting hours ended, the staff asked all visitors except Alex, Mark, and Thunder to leave.

While Lizzy gave Tori a last hug for the night, Mark waved George over. The painkillers had taken effect, and Maggie slept soundly.

"Hey, can you do me a favor?" Mark whispered, not wanting to wake up Maggie.

"Name it." George nodded.

"Can you take Sky with you and stay at my house? She's had a long day, and I know she'd be more comfortable at home."

"Of course," George glanced at Lizzy with a look that said sorry.

"Oh shit," Mark's gaze bounced between Lizzy and George. "Were you going to stay with Lizzy at the hotel?"

"Uh." George rubbed the back of his neck. "I'd hoped to."

Lizzy walked to George and rubbed his back. "It's okay."

"You guys can both stay at my house." Mark shrugged. "Lizzy, I'm sure Maggie has something that you can wear. You guys can raid our closet, we don't care. You'd be helping us out with Sky."

Sky raised her head and whined.

Mark rubbed her head. "I know, girl, but if you're home, you'll sleep better and run around in the yard. You can't do that here." Sky made a noise that sounded like a growly okay and dropped her head on her paws.

If Lizzy didn't know better, she'd think Sky was agreeing, but wasn't happy about it like a child that obeyed their parents and didn't argue.

"I'm good taking Sky and staying at your place." Lizzy bent down and kissed the top of Sky's head. Sky licked Lizzy before Lizzy could get her face away from Sky's mouth.

"Then we're all set. Let's go ladies, your chariot awaits." George bowed at the waist.

"Sky, go." Mark motioned to George, and she jumped off the bed. "George, can you stop by in the morning and bring me a change of clothes?" Mark squatted and gave Sky a big hug with lots of kisses.

"Yep, then Lizzy can see Tori."

"Thanks guys, I really appreciate this." Mark stood and gave them the keys to his house. "The gate code is Sky's service number."

"Got it." George pocketed the keys, and they left.

Sky sat in the passenger seat with Lizzy like before while George drove them to Mark's house. Lizzy ran her hand over Sky's head, leaned her head against the window, and closed her eyes. She was glad to have one more night with George before her parents arrived tomorrow at noon.

Sehoy usually gave her parents a room all to themselves, but with all the chaos, Lizzy had forgotten to ask her about the arrangements. Besides, whether or not her parents were in her room, she didn't think they would want George to stay with her at the resort or for her to stay with George at the cultural center.

She dreaded having to tell them everything that had happened to her during the last week and a half. Their disappointment was a bitter pill to swallow, one she'd swallowed many times before. Convincing them she was a better person now, thanks to George, would take some time. She hoped they wouldn't be too angry with her or try to force her to go back with them.

Lizzy didn't want to leave South Florida. Especially now that she was in love with George and Isa'd had the baby. Lizzy's parents had known about her promise to either live with Isa and Thunder or spend most of the day there to help them after the baby was born. Her parents were oblivious to her relationship with George, but everyone loved George. She was sure they would, too. Besides, how could they not? George consistently rescued her from her poor choices? They would love that. They always joked that she needed a keeper.

So, her plan was to take her parents from the airport directly to Tori and delay their conversation until Tori came home. Tori was the peacemaker between Lizzy and their parents. And if the shit hit the fan, her parents loved Thunder and Isa, so she could take them to meet Thomas. Babies always cheered people up.

"Penny for your thoughts." George took her hand and kissed it.

"Just hoping my parents don't kill me when they find out about all the stupid shit I've done since I got here," Lizzy grumbled.

George chuckled. "I'll help you with them. They like me."

"Yeah, but will they still like you when I tell them you took their little girl's virginity and we're still having sex out of wedlock?"

"Not when you put it like that," George muttered.

"I'm teasing. I wouldn't tell them that. It could tarnish your shiny deputy badge and ruin their image of you."

"Babe, you could tarnish and ruin anything I have." George wiggled his eyebrows at her before he pulled up to the security gate at the end of Mark's driveway.

George lowered his window and punched in the code. Lizzy watched the wrought iron double gates open inward toward the house.

"Wow, that's fancy." Lizzy wished it wasn't nighttime. All she could see was the long, treelined driveway, the headlights cutting through the darkness and illuminating their path to the house.

"When Maggie had all those issues with the LRs, Mark bought this house and upped his security." George drove up to the circular driveway and parked.

"It's a beautiful house." Lizzy stared at the two-story stone house with the circular driveway that looked more like a mansion. She didn't even notice George had left the car until he opened her passenger door. Sky ran out first.

"Come on." George shut the car door. "You can look around while I let Sky out into the backyard." George unlocked the front door and followed Sky and Lizzy inside. "They don't have a lot of furniture since they've only been here a couple of months."

Lizzy spun around in the foyer. "Wow, this magnificent spiral staircase, winding upwards with ornate banisters, is breathtaking!" Her voice, ringing with uncontainable excitement, echoed around her. Lizzy loved the way the rough-hewn textures of the rustic elements offset the smooth, modern lines. This house reflected both Mark and Maggie's personalities, a harmonious blend of their styles. As she neared the banister, Lizzy traced the smoothly worn mane of the carved horse's head with her fingers. She was sure there was a story behind the horse's head on the banister. She needed to remember to ask Mark or Maggie.

As George walked by, he hollered, "Yeah, well, don't get too used to it. A cop's salary can't pay for a spiral staircase."

Lizzy giggled and with a bounce in her step and happiness in her heart, she climbed the staircase to check out the rooms upstairs. She'd lost count of how many bedrooms she'd walked through. All of them with adjoining bathrooms and walk-in closets. She saw a theatre room with an enormous screen, an office, a doggie room for Sky, and a master bedroom with a magnificent bathroom and two walk-in closets.

After exploring upstairs, she went downstairs. The kitchen was spectacular with expensive looking countertops and appliances. Past the kitchen in one direction, she entered the dining room. In the opposite direction, the kitchen flowed into the living space, which was two-stories high with lots of windows and a beautiful stone fireplace.

Lizzy sat on the couch and took it all in. Her head was spinning by the time George sat next to her.

"So, what do you think?"

"It's beautiful," Lizzy sighed.

"Yep, Mark outdid himself. Then he had to convince Maggie to move in. She wanted something a little more modest." George stood and pulled her up. "Come on, I'm beat. Let's find a bedroom and crash. Sky already ran up to her room while you were sitting here drooling."

Lizzy slapped his arm playfully. "Did you feed her?"

"Yep."

"And she already went potty?"

"Yep."

"Then I guess I was out of it while I sat here."

"Yep."

Lizzy followed George into the bedroom that was decorated in blue. "Why'd you pick this one?"

"Because it called to me." George waved his hand around with dramatic flair.

"You're crazy," Lizzy pushed him out of the way and went to the bathroom.

"Seriously, though. I'm gonna go borrow some sweatpants and a t-shirt from Mark. Do you want anything?"

"Wait for me!" Lizzy screamed through the bathroom door. She wanted something comfy to sleep in too, whether it was Mark's or Maggie's.

When she finished, she washed her hands, and they raided Mark and Maggie's closet and drawers. She felt like a kid in a candy store. Maggie had so many cute things, but in the end, she grabbed one of Maggie's flannel pants and a soft t-shirt.

"I'm gonna take a shower. You wanna join me?" George said from the doorway to the bathroom.

"No." Lizzy shook her head. "I feel weird doing anything in their house. I'll take a shower after you." Lizzy dropped her clothes on the bed and walked toward the pillows to pull the sheets back.

"Are you serious?" George said from behind her.

Lizzy shrieked and jumped. She didn't hear him behind her until he spoke. She'd thought he was in the shower. Spinning around, Lizzy grabbed a fluffy pillow and swung it at him with surprising force.

"Ooh, pillow fight. I can get down with that." George winked at her, pulled the pillow out of her hands and kissed the living daylights out of her.

"That was not a pillow fight," Lizzy moaned.

"It's the best kind of pillow fight if it ends with me kissing you." George nipped at her bottom lip.

Lizzy wrapped her arms around his neck and melted into the kiss. George's tongue swirled around her mouth, slow and sensual. Moaning into his mouth, he bent down a little, cupped her ass, and pulled her hips flush against his. Lizzy got the hint and wrapped her legs around his waist, clinging to him for dear life. George sat on the edge of the bed.

"I don't think it's right to have sex on their nice, clean sheets. They have family in town, and we don't have time to wash them." Lizzy moaned as George pulled her shirt off and sucked the sensitive spot on her neck.

George got up and walked them into the bathroom, setting her on the counter. "We shouldn't do it here either unless they have disinfecting wipes."

"Woman," George groaned. "We're not doing it on the bed, or on their counter. We're doing it in the shower." George unsnapped her bra and slid it off her body, throwing it to the floor. "No clean up."

"Well, when you put it that way." Lizzy pushed him back and jumped off the counter. As she pushed her pants and panties down, she felt George's intense gaze on her body. His eyes bouncing all over her naked parts. Cupping his shaft through his pants, she whispered, "What are you waiting for, daddy?" She stroked him once before she ran into the shower.

"Now you've done it," George's voice said huskily before he entered the shower. After a few swats to her behind, he brought her to the best orgasm of her life as he fucked her against the cold tile wall.

Chapter 45

Shower Acrobatics

Following multiple showers during the night because of Lizzy's refusal to engage in any sexual activity on Mark and Maggie's spare bedroom bed, they finally lay naked on the bed, with George holding her from behind as the bigger spoon.

George grumbled, "What's that noise?"

Lizzy forgot she had set up a reoccurring alarm for Sunday mornings to help Tori with brunch. With Tori in the hospital, she was sure there wouldn't be a family Sunday Brunch at Savor today. Maybe a Sunday dinner if everyone came home from the hospital, but not brunch.

"It's my alarm for Sunday brunch," Lizzy whispered.

"I'm sure we're not having Sunday Brunch."

"I know," Lizzy sighed. "But I forgot to delete it for today."

"Can you please turn it off, babe?" George rolled over, grabbed her phone, and handed it to her. "Someone made me use all the muscles in my body multiple times last night to hold them up in the shower. I'm exhausted."

Lizzy turned it off and handed her phone back to him. Rolling over into his arms, she wrapped her arms around him. "Poor baby." Lizzy kissed him while her hands massaged his arms and back. She could feel him harden against her pelvis.

George cupped her ass and rolled onto his back, never breaking their kiss. Lizzy would love to ride him cowgirl style, but not on this bed.

"George." Lizzy pulled back from the kiss. "Shower?" She panted as George lifted her higher on his body so he could devour her breast.

"No, stay here with me, Lizzy." George slid his finger inside her from behind.

Lizzy cried out and ground herself onto his finger one time before she pulled away from him and leapt off the bed, racing to the bathroom.

"Dammit, Lizzy," George growled.

Lizzy was sticking to her guns. If he wanted her, he'd have to come get her in the shower. Turning on the water, she stepped in, not caring that it was cold, and leaned against the tile wall with her thighs clenched. Her body was trembling with need for him.

George stepped in behind her and turned her body, so her back was leaning against the tile. "Let me help you." George murmured against her lips before he used his tongue to kiss his way down to her core.

She needed release so badly that her body wouldn't stop undulating forward. George used his hands to spread her thighs apart and drape them over his shoulders until her pussy was open wide and ready for him to taste and plunder. He dipped his tongue inside. But she needed more.

"George, please," Lizzy groaned and grabbed his head, pushing it closer to her. He was driving her crazy. She needed him, not his fucking mouth. She knew if she asked, he'd do it. Finding her voice and leaving all inhibitions behind, she screamed. "I need your cock, George. Stop teasing me and fuck me now!"

George immediately stood, keeping her thighs draped over his forearms. He braced himself and rammed inside of her. "Fuck Lizzy, you know it drives me wild when you talk dirty to me. Babe, you feel so fucking good." George continued to push into her, reaching her pleasure point. She was so close. "Babe, I need you to play with your clit because I can't hold you up and do that at the same time, and I'm so fucking close."

Lizzy reached down and tweaked her clit. She swore she saw fireworks and stars behind her eyelids as her body exploded around him, causing him to pump into her a few more times, prolonging her pleasure until he climaxed inside her and let her legs slide down his body. Both panting, George stayed inside her with his forearms against the tile wall, holding them up.

"And you said you were tired," Lizzy said between breaths.

"Woman, we need to go to my place or yours so I can fuck you in a bed. I do not want to drop your ass in this tub," George panted, and wrapped his arms around her. His cock slipped out, and he murmured. "You're killing me."

Lizzy knew George wasn't in that much pain because he held her tightly against his body until he could regain control of his breath. If he'd been in a lot of pain, he would've had to sit and would let her go.

Lizzy giggled and pulled his head down to kiss him. "I love you," she mumbled against his lips while gazing into his eyes.

"I love you too, babe." George kissed her, his lips lingering on hers, never breaking their intense eye contact. Lizzy had never experienced a kiss so intense and intimate; she could feel his breath on her skin and taste the sweetness of his lips. The love she felt for him was a deep and unwavering, growing stronger with each passing day. She couldn't imagine a day without his laughter, his warmth, his presence beside her.

"Let's wash up." George grabbed the body wash. "We need to get to the hospital to bring Mark clothes, and I still have to let Sky out."

"You go first." Lizzy stepped back. "I forgot all about Sky. I feel terrible. What if she's been holding it this whole time?"

George chuckled. "Sky has a good bladder, but you're right. I'm sure she's ready."

George finished quickly, gave her a peck on the lips, and got out of the shower.

Lizzy washed her hair and cleaned up. By the time George came back upstairs, he found her already dressed and ready, a faint scent of lavender lingering in the air. She'd stripped the bed and carried the used towels and sheets downstairs to put them on top of the washer. She'd have to tell Mark where they were.

"So, you were stripping the bed, anyway?" George leaned against the laundry room doorway with his arms and ankles crossed, staring at her.

"Well, yeah. What if we sweated on them? I didn't want them to stink or have any stains on them." Lizzy was horrified by the concept of having Mark and Maggie find any of their bodily fluids on their sheets.

George burst out laughing before he grabbed her and pulled her in for a kiss. "You are so fucking cute. I love you."

"Are you making fun of me?" Lizzy leaned back and stared at his face.

"Nope." George shook his head and grinned at her. "Just crazy in love with you."

Sky barked at them.

"I think that's our cue that she wants to see her mom and dad." Lizzy turned to Sky and George released her.

"You want to go see your mommy and daddy, don't you?" Lizzy bent down and rubbed Sky's face with her hands. Sky gave Lizzy kisses.

"Okay, you two. Let's go." George grabbed the clothes for Mark and went out the front door, leaving it open until Lizzy and Sky walked out. Then he shut and locked it.

On their way to the hospital, George asked, "What time do your parents arrive?"

"Their flight arrives at noon. Spirit-of-the-Eagle is coming with them, too. He couldn't wait to see Thomas."

"I bet," George snickered. "He thinks of Thunder like a son, especially after what Joseph did and his death."

"Yeah, my mom told me that really broke his heart. I think meeting Thomas will help to lift the weight he's been feeling lately. Who knows? Maybe he'll spend more time here."

"I'm sure Thunder would like that," George sighed.

Lizzy's phone rang. She pulled it out of her pocket and put it on speakerphone.

"Hey, Alex, is Tori, okay?"

"Yep, they're letting us go home. I've told everyone who's called for an update not to come because we're just waiting on paperwork, but now we also don't have a ride home."

"Is Maggie going home too?" George blurted.

"We're all going home. But you don't have to worry about Thunder and Isa because Grayhorse is coming in Isa's car to pick them up because it has Thomas' car seat."

"Good plan, cause none of us have cars with baby car seats." Lizzy nodded.

"Sarah does, but Thunder wanted Thomas in his own seat. Anyway, can you guys go to the resort and get the company van? Holt and Barrett are going to give me shit if I call them back and ask them to come get us after I told them we were good." Alex sighed.

"You know, when we go get the van and the keys, they're gonna find out, right?" George smiled at Lizzy, even though Alex couldn't see him.

"Yeah, I know, but we need a ride."

"We just left Mark's house with Sky. We'll go to the resort first and get the van. It'll be awhile before we get to you." George got off the highway.

"That's okay. It'll be awhile before Tori and Maggie get their paperwork, so no worries. Take your time."

"Sounds good. See you soon." Lizzy hung up.

"He is never, and I mean never, going to hear the end of this one." George laughed.

"They do like to give each other a hard time, don't they?" Lizzy put the phone back in her pocket.

"You don't understand the half of it." George used his blinker and turned. "Alex is the most organized person I know. He plans everything down to the last detail and is always giving Holt, Frey, and Barrett a hard time if they fuck up or don't think something through. It must be a big brother thing. So now that Alex has stumbled in his planning, they are going to ride that high for months, if not years. It'll be fun to watch."

Lizzy and George picked up the van and a few stragglers that just couldn't help themselves. Lizzy hoped Alex didn't get mad at her. When they got to the hospital, she called Alex.

"We're here. Are you guys ready?"

"Yup, just waiting for your call. We're heading down now. Please tell me Holt and Barrett didn't see you?"

Frey reached around the front seat and disconnected the call. "This way you don't have to lie to him."

Lizzy smiled, "Thanks...I think."

Chapter 46

Let the Ribbing Begin

George got out of the car and leaned against the passenger side door, waiting for Alex. Frey, Holt, and Barrett scooted down to the floor of the van. Their plan was to jump out as soon as George opened the door. Lizzy sunk down in her seat and berated herself for not staying at the resort. She wanted no part of them teasing Alex.

"Lizzy." Frey tapped her shoulder. "Alex won't be mad at you. I'll make sure he knows this wasn't your idea, okay?"

"Okay, thanks Frey."

"Here they come," Barrett whispered. "Get ready."

Lizzy saw Alex shake George's hand before George swung the door open and stepped aside. Sky jumped out and headed to Mark and Maggie.

"Surprise, he who never makes mistakes!" Barrett, Holt, and Frey shouted in unison.

Lizzy was surprised by how perfectly in sync they were. They must've practiced.

"Fuck me," Alex grumbled. "Thanks a lot George. I thought I could count on you."

"You can. It's not like I called them or shouted it into a bullhorn. They were downstairs talking to your mom. I tried to ask quietly, but Frey has exceptional hearing."

"Yes, I do." Frey pretended a curtsy.

"Lizzy?" Alex knocked on her window. When she rolled it down, he said, "Et tu, Lizzy?"

"Uh, what?" Lizzy frowned at Alex. *What did he say? She was so confused.*

"It's a Shakespearian quote from the play Julius Caesar." Tori grabbed Alex's arm. "Could we please move on so you can help me and Maggie into the van?"

"Sure, baby. Sorry." Alex put his arm around Tori and glared at everyone else except Mark, who couldn't stop the grin from parting his lips.

The van had three rows of seats. The first two rows had only two seats, but the third row had three. Alex got in the first row and helped Tori into the seat next to him. Mark settled into the second row as Holt and Barrett carefully helped Maggie sit beside him, her leg extending beyond the edge of the seat. Sky jumped in and sat between them. Then Frey, Holt, and Barrett sat in the back row. George shut the door and pulled out of the hospital.

"I see you assholes are sitting as far away from me as possible?" Alex turned to glare at them.

"Uh, we're not stupid." Barrett shouted from the back. "And we didn't forget how much you love to hit Holt and I in the back of the head. We're decreasing our odds."

"Yeah, some of us remember important details which pertain to our loved ones," Frey hollered and laughed.

"Alex, I would never tease you about forgetting such a minor detail as leaving your wife at the hospital," Holt chuckled. "Your siblings are so rude."

"And so it begins." George turned to Lizzy and winked. Lizzy had her visor down to block the sun and could watch them tease Alex.

"Oh, fuck me. Fine." Alex threw up his hands. "Get it all out of your system. I fucked up. Mr. Perfect made a mistake."

"I never said he was Mr. Perfect." Barrett pointed to Holt. "Did you say he was Mr. Perfect?"

"Nope." Holt shook his head.

"I thought I was Mr. Perfect." Barrett then pointed to himself.

"No, I'm Mr. Perfect." Mark joined in the fun.

"No, Surfer Smurf, you're Big Sexy," Maggie smiled at him.

"I'll take that over Mr. Perfect any day, darlin'." Mark leaned over and kissed Maggie.

"Are we there yet?" Alex belted out from behind George, and everyone laughed.

"Hey, Mark?" George shouted from the front. "I'm gonna drop you, Maggie, and Sky off first. I ran into your mom when I was talking with Sehoy and they wanted to meet you at your house. I gave her your key and told her the code so they could get in."

"Sounds good, thanks."

"Maggie," –George continued– "I also called José and told him what happened. He was going to call your aunt and let them know. I'm sure he'll be by sometime tonight to see you."

"Was he upset that I got shot?" Maggie winced.

"Yes, but he was glad that the last two LRs are behind bars."

"I can't wait to get home and lie down." Maggie groaned. "Barrett, what are you doing?"

"Laying on the floor so I can hold your leg up."

"That is so sweet of you." Maggie cooed.

"Really?" Mark growled and Barrett laughed.

Lizzy knew there was an inside joke somewhere in there, but she wasn't privy to it.

"Here we are." George punched in the code. "Mark, text your mom so she'll open the door for us. Wait, no need. They're all waiting on the porch."

George parked as close as he could to the porch, got out, and opened the side door. Sky jumped out after Holt and Barrett helped Maggie out.

"Barrett, that was so sweet of you to hold Maggie's leg up." Janice turned to her husband. "Isn't it dear?"

Mark growled louder. This time, Maggie was the one that laughed and patted his arm.

All the men except Barrett, who kept laughing while Mark glared at him, helped carry Maggie inside. After a few minutes, they came back out and got back in the van. Frey and Holt now sat behind Alex and Tori. Barrett leaned his back on the side of the van and spread his legs out across all the seats in the back row.

"Hey, asshole." Alex turned and pointed at him. "Sit right and put your seatbelt on."

"Oh, sorry. I must've forgotten that I could get hurt in a moving car if George slams on the brakes." Barrett fumbled with the seatbelt like a bumbling idiot before he snapped it in place. "Sorry, I guess I'm not Mr. Perfect anymore."

Lizzy covered her mouth to stop the laugh from escaping.

"For how long am I going to hear this shit?" Alex shoved the heels of his hands against his eyes.

"I don't know," Frey shrugged. "Forever?"

"Okay, everyone shut up!" Tori screamed. "Enough, you are driving him and me crazy!"

Lizzy looked up and saw everyone's jaw hanging down, even Alex. Like she'd thought. They'd never seen Tori mad or heard her yell at them. Lizzy had; she'd heard it all the time growing up. Smiling, she looked at George and cocked her eyebrow. "Now, who's the nice one?"

The van was dead silent until they reached the resort. They all apologized to Tori as they got out. They all looked so melancholy except for Lizzy, who was smiling, enjoying this moment where the nice one switched with the crazy one.

"What's going on?" Sehoy asked Barrett.

"Tori yelled at us," Barrett mumbled and stared at the ground.

"What?" Sehoy stopped Frey. "What is your brother talking about? Tori doesn't yell."

"Yep, she sure does." Frey nodded. "She can be downright mean."

"Oh, for goodness sakes, I just asked you guys to stop teasing Alex." Tori said, exasperated with them.

"Come on, baby. Let's get you something to eat so you can lie down and rest." Alex wrapped his arm around Tori and smirked at Frey, Holt, and Barrett over her head.

"Alex Panther, do not smirk at them." Tori pulled Alex with her.

"I think she's ready to be a mom," Barrett grumbled when he thought she was out of earshot. "She has eyes on the back of her head like *chatski* and Angel."

"I heard that!" Tori yelled without turning around. "I do and I am."

"Sehoy, can we borrow your van again?" George pulled her attention to him.

"Why do we need their van?" Lizzy frowned at George

"Uh, we need to pick up your family and Spirit-of-the-Eagle at the airport." George looked at his watch.

"Oh, my god." Lizzy sucked in her breath and covered her mouth with her hands. "I forgot all about that."

"That seems to be going around today," Barrett snickered.

George punched him in the arm. "Hey, watch it."

"Sorry, Lizzy." Barrett mumbled.

"It's fine." Lizzy grinned. She loved when George stood up for her. "George, what time is it?"

"We have fifteen minutes before they land."

"Go, go, take the van." Sehoy shooed them.

Lizzy and George made it there just in time to pull up and pick them up. Lizzy didn't realize that Spirit-of-the-Eagle had brought his wife, Morning Star. She didn't like to fly and normally when he came; he came alone. Not that it mattered. There were plenty of seats in the van. Once everyone was seated and they got underway, Lizzy explained what had happened at the cultural center. She made sure they all knew that Tori and Thunder were okay. Maggie was in a cast, but was doing well and she showed them the photo Alex had taken of Thunder, Isa, and Thomas.

"Thank you for picking us up, George." Spirit-of-the-Eagle clapped George's back. "And thank you, Lizzy, for showing us the photo of Thomas."

"It's so good to see you, George." Tall Bear spoke up from the back. "How did you get roped into picking us up?"

"Uh." George looked at Lizzy.

"George and I are dating." Lizzy grabbed his hand and turned around to look at her parents. She didn't want to hide their relationship. Dating George was not a dirty little secret. George rewarded her with a big smile and a kiss on her hand.

"That's wonderful!" Spirit-of-the-Eagle clapped his hands. "I'm so happy for you both."

"Good choice, Lizzy. George is a great young man." Tall Bear smiled.

"I'm happy for you both, but we need to talk, daughter." Dyani gave Lizzy the stink eye.

George was already heading to Thunder's house because he knew Spirit-of-the-Eagle and Morning Star were staying with them and he was closer to the airport than the resort. Everyone got out to see baby Thomas. Isa's family was there as well. Thunder and Sarah were ecstatic to see Morning Star. Dyani, Lizzy's mom, didn't want to stay too late because she wanted to see Tori, so they left a couple hours later.

As soon as they reached the resort, Sehoy handed Tall Bear a key to their own suite and winked at Lizzy. Luckily, Dyani didn't catch the wink, but George did, and he mouthed 'thank you' to Sehoy.

"Let's get settled in." Dyani gave Sehoy a hug. "And then call Tori."

George held Lizzy's hand and pulled her a few steps away from everyone. "I'm gonna give you some private time with your family." George squeezed her hand. "I'll call you tomorrow."

"Okay." Lizzy leaned in and kissed his cheek. "Coward," she whispered against his skin.

George smiled and waved to everyone on his way out.

Chapter 47

Best Friend's Help

George

Now that Lizzy had made it official by telling everyone, George was bursting with happiness. Things had been going so well, he wanted to make it official. If they were engaged, Lizzy's parents wouldn't give her a hard time about them staying with each other. He knew it was sudden, but he had already fallen head over heels in love with Lizzy and knew he wanted to spend the rest of his life with her. They could have a long engagement, if that's what she wanted, but he needed her to know he was in for the long haul.

Even though Lizzy drove him crazy, he enjoyed rescuing her from her crazy adventures. He loved a good challenge, and she was just the person to provide one. There was no doubt in his mind, she owned his heart and soul. Lizzy was unlike any other girl; her spirit was captivating, unlike anyone he'd ever met. He wanted to propose to her, but he still needed to buy a ring, and the jewelry stores closed early on Sunday. Besides, he wanted to talk to Sean and see if he would go with him. Because Sean and he shared the same work schedule, he knew that Sean had the day off and wouldn't begin his shift until 5:00 pm the following day. Dialing Sean, he put the call through his car speakers as he drove to the cultural center.

"Hey, how are you doing?" Sean answered.

"I'm good. How was the cleanup after the shooting?" George was glad he could stay with Lizzy and not have to fill out paperwork. Sean had been off too, but he'd driven to the station when he heard the alert. They'd been texting each other with updates, but hadn't been able to talk it out.

"It sucked," Sean sighed. "I should've stayed home and turned off my phone."

"Yeah, right? Like you would ignore all the action." Sean grumbled about stuff, but deep down George knew there was no way in hell he would've stayed away from a shootout when it involved the LRs. After months of setbacks, they were tired of fucking around with them.

"True. Anyway, what's up? I thought you'd be with Lizzy."

"I was. We picked up her parents, Spirit-of-the-Eagle, and his wife from the airport. I drove Uncle Spirit and Morning Star to Thunder's house and then dropped off Lizzy and her parents at the resort. I wanted to give her some time alone with her parents."

"I'm sure she loved that." George smiled at the sarcasm in Sean's voice.

"She called me a coward." George grinned wryly.

Sean busted out laughing. "I love that girl."

George turned to pull into the cultural center parking lot when he saw the police caution tape blocking the entrance and slammed on his brakes. "Fuck!"

"What's wrong?" Sean immediately stopped laughing and sounded alert.

"The cultural center parking lot is closed. I guess they are still processing everything. Shit, I didn't think about not being able to go inside." George pulled up in front of the center and parked on the street, putting on his lights. "I didn't want to sneak into Lizzy's room on her parent's first night here, so I left."

"Come here. You can spend the night at my house. Call the station in the morning and find out when you can return to your apartment."

"Sounds good." George pulled into traffic and turned off his lights. "Thanks, man. I'll see you in a few."

"10-4," Sean mumbled and hung up.

George didn't have any spare clothes in his patrol vehicle, but Sean and he were about the same size. All he would need was a pair of sweatpants and a shirt. He could go commando for a night. Not like he hadn't done that before.

Pulling into the driveway, he saw Sean rocking like an old man on one of his chairs on the front porch. Kerri really had domesticated him. Too bad she had also fucked him over. Sean was a good guy. He didn't deserve what she did to him.

"Thanks for waiting for me, dad." George smirked as he approached Sean.

Sean gave him the finger before he stood and stepped into his house, leaving the door open for George. George locked it behind him. Police training emphasized locking doors. Plus, having lived in a shelter since childhood, he instinctively understood the importance of security. In the living room, he sat on the couch waiting for Sean. Sean walked in holding two beers, one in each hand. He handed one to George before he sat in his recliner across from the couch.

George looked around and noticed several nicknacks and paintings were missing. "Did she come get all her shit?"

"Yup." Sean took a swig of his beer and continued to face the TV. "Whatever she didn't take, I boxed up and dropped off at the thrift store. Good Riddance." Sean lifted his beer like a toast and took another swig.

"I'm sorry you had to go through that. If you'd let me know, I would've come over to help you." George drank some of his beer.

"Nah." Sean grinned at him. "It was the perfect anger management therapy to throw her shit in a box and kick it out of the way."

George chuckled. "I bet. Hey, I have a favor to ask."

"Ask away, my friend." Sean nodded.

"I want to go engagement ring shopping for Lizzy tomorrow and I want you to go with me," George blurted and waited anxiously to see if Sean would go.

Sean's jaw dropped, eyes wide, as he froze, the beer bottle hovering inches from his lips; silence filled the air.

"I know it's soon, but I love her." George grasped his beer in his hands and looked down. "I'll understand if you don't want to go with me since you just had that nasty break up with Kerri, but I wanted my best friend's help in picking it out." Had this been a mistake? Was he putting a dagger in Sean's heart since his girl had turned out to be a bitch? George looked up when he heard the creaking of the recliner.

Sean leaped out of the recliner, placed his beer down, and hollered. "Holy Shit! Of course I'll go with you. I'm happy for you, man, and I feel honored that you'd include me in such a monumental moment in your life."

George stood, and they gave each other a big hug, complete with slaps on their backs.

"Thanks, man." George grabbed his beer and sat back down.

"Let's go early in case we need to go to several jewelry stores." Sean sat and took another swig. "Do you know where you want to go?"

"I haven't really thought about where to go. Any suggestions?"

"Actually, yeah." Sean snickered. "Kerri kept giving me hints about this jewelry store at the mall. We could go there." Sean grabbed his phone and typed something in. "They open at 10:00 am. We could get breakfast and be there when the doors open."

"Sounds good to me."

They settled in to watch the Stanley Cup Finals. George wasn't a huge hockey fan, but he supported his local team, the Panthers, and they were in the finals. At least hockey was fast-paced, not like watching golf. Besides, the Panthers gave first responders discounted tickets to some of their games. That would be a good date night for him and Lizzy. He bet she would love the fights more than anything.

After the game, George slept on the couch. Sean had a spare bedroom, but he was sleeping in it because the master bedroom was where he'd caught Kerri fucking another man. George noticed there was no bed in the master bedroom, but even if it had been there, no way was he fucking sleeping on it. The couch was just fine.

***

Sean must've gotten up before George because when he rolled off the couch, there was a set of clothes on the cocktail table. Perfect. He grabbed the clothes and made his way to the extra bathroom down the hall. With his hand on the knob, he heard the shower running. Fuck! Sean wasn't even using his master bathroom. It was only a matter of time before he sold this house and moved away from his memories with Kerri. Pivoting, he headed to the master bathroom to take a shower.

They met back in the living room and headed to the garage. Sean opened the garage door. The minivan Sean had bought for Kerri was still in there.

"I can't believe you're still driving this," George said as he got into the passenger seat.

"I've been busy, but I'm gonna sell it soon."

"What are you gonna get?" George raised his eyebrow at him. George knew Sean liked hot rods.

"Not sure yet, but I guaran-damn-tee you, it won't be a van."

Sean pulled out and drove them to the mall. He parked near a mall entrance close to the jewelry store.

As soon as they walked into the jewelry store, an elegant-looking woman approached them. "Can I help you?"

The woman's gaze glanced between both of them. Sean pointed at George. George smiled and approached the woman. "Yes, hi. I'm looking for an engagement ring for my girlfriend."

"Oh, how exciting!" the woman beamed. "My name is Natalie and I would love to help you. Let's go to that other counter." She pointed to her right. "All of our engagement rings are in there."

George and Sean followed Natalie.

Sean elbowed him and whispered, "Do you know what you want?"

"No. But I think I'll know when I see it."

All the choices were overwhelming. He wanted something big, but not too big, that sparkled like Lizzy. He'd been saving his money to buy a house, so he had a nice nest egg. Not that he wanted to spend it all on the ring. Lizzy didn't wear any rings, so he didn't think she would want anything too gaudy.

"Is this your first store looking for a ring?" George looked up and saw Natalie's eyes soften.

"It is, and I don't know how to pick one out. Is there something I should know?" George looked back down.

"There are four important things you need to consider when choosing one. It's called the four c's; cut, color, clarity, and carat." Natalie raised a finger as she named them. "The cut is the shape of the diamond. The color ranges from colorless to yellow/brown. Clarity has to do with any internal or external flaws. And the carat weight is the size. Do you see a shape you like?"

"Don't get a plain ring," Sean nudged him. "Lizzy is not a plain girl."

George and Sean had both been listening while Natalie explained everything while looking at rows and rows of engagement rings. Nothing was sticking out until he reached the last tray of rings. There sat a beautiful round cut diamond ring on a white gold setting. It was clear and sparkled. The size looked good, but the best part was the small blue stones set into what looked to be leaves around the stone and on the bands. He knew most Native Americans liked turquoise, but the blue stones looked like tiny pieces of shiny turquoise.

"Can I see that one, please?" George pointed to it.

"That is a good choice." Natalie pulled the tray out. "The best part about this ring is that it is an engagement ring and wedding band." Natalie pulled the center band out.

"This is the wedding band part. It is white gold with blue sapphires." Natalie set it down on the counter. "This would be the engagement ring. This one-carat diamond circular cut has excellent color and clarity. Some leaves on the band have blue sapphires, but the others are hollow. I know the engagement ring alone looks like two rings, but that is because the wedding band slides in between the engagement ring." Natalie showed them how it worked before handing it to George.

"I love it." George held the ring and looked at it from every angle. "What do you think?" George looked at Sean.

"I think it is perfect for her, but shouldn't you check the price?" Sean raised an eyebrow at him.

"How much is it?" George held his breath, hoping he could afford it.

"It's $8,000 for the set."

George released his breath. "I'll take it."

Sean slapped his back. "Good choice."

Natalie rang it up and went over the importance of getting the ring insured. She also explained that if the ring didn't fit, he could bring it back and get it resized at no extra cost.

George walked out, a very happy man, his heart light and his steps springy. Now he had to find the right moment to propose.

Chapter 48

Prison Fight

Numbers

The bullet that hit Numbers went through and didn't hit any vital tendons, ligaments, or bones. After they bandaged him up at the hospital and gave him medicine in case of an infection, two officers came to take him to prison. Numbers kept telling the officers that he couldn't be in the same cell block as Reaper and the rest of his brothers, but they weren't listening. They thought Numbers was pulling their leg. After all, they were brothers from the same MC. It was better to keep them together and away from other gang members.

Following the fingerprinting and mug shot, he was escorted to a room for a thorough and invasive full body cavity search. The officers took his clothes and gave him his prison uniform. Then they walked him into a cell block which contained a shower with no roof, a TV mounted higher than anyone could reach, and a couple of tables with chairs. Behind the living area were four prison cells, which occupied two inmates per cell. Each cell had a set of bunk beds, one sink, and one toilet.

The officer put him in the cell with Red.

"Reaper?" Numbers hung his hands out of the cell.

"What the hell do you want?"

"I just wanted you to know that I tried. I mean, I did shoot Tori, Maggie, and that asshole Thunder."

"Did they die?"

"I don't know, maybe?" Numbers shrugged.

"I'll ask around. If they're still alive, then things don't look good for you."

"Come on, Reaper. I'm your best friend. We've known each other since we were kids." Numbers banged on the cell, not that it did anything. "You're just gonna let me hang out to dry." Reaper didn't answer.

"Reaper!" Numbers called out his name several times, but he got no response. "Fuck!" Numbers mumbled and dropped into his bed.

Red leaned down over the side of the top bunk. "You think he's gonna kill us, boss?"

Numbers closed his eyes. "Not sure. But I'll keep talking to him. Get some sleep. Maybe he'll be in a better mood tomorrow."

The next day, an officer came to escort Numbers to his First Appearance with a judge. He didn't have a lawyer and was told the court would appoint him one. The officer led him to a room that looked like a mini courtroom. He sat on a bench next to other shackled inmates, awaiting his turn, while the officers stood by the door. The only significant difference between this room and a real courtroom was the monitor in the room's front displaying a live video and audio feed of a judge. When Numbers' name was called, it all sounded like a lot of mumbo jumbo. The judge's gavel slammed down, denying bail, the sound echoing the finality of his fate—a fate shared with Reaper, as he stayed in jail until trial.

With a renewed sense of determination, Numbers went back to his cell, silently plotting ways to earn Reaper's trust, the dim light highlighting the grimness of his surroundings. But Reaper's mood never changed. He was still mad at Numbers and usually ignored him even when they were in the living area of their cell block during their downtime. Reaper would play cards with anyone in the cell block but him. Numbers knew he'd fucked up, but they'd been best friends for years. There had to be a way to find out what happened to Tori and Maggie. If they died from his bullet, then he could redeem himself to Reaper and they could go back to being friends.

Numbers and all the inmates fell into a routine. Every day was the same. Wake up at 6:00 am, make his bed, brush his teeth, shower, eat breakfast, hang out in his cell block, eat lunch, hang out in his cell block, eat dinner, downtime in the living area with the other inmates in his block, and lights out at 10:00 pm. His only variation in schedule was an hour of outdoor time, twice a week before dinner.

One evening during their downtime, he was watching TV when Reaper sat next to him.

"Are you talking to me now?" Numbers glanced at him.

"No." Reaper leaned back in his chair, crossed his arms, stretched out his legs, and spoke low. "I just got word that Tori, Maggie, and Thunder didn't die, and that Angel stood right fucking in front of you and you didn't kill her."

Numbers gulped and looked up. He knew someone was always in the tower watching, which was why Reaper was pretending to be relaxed as he delivered that news to Numbers. Numbers debated waving to the guard in the tower and screaming for help. But then he'd never been a pussy before. Reaper was bigger and stronger than him, but he thought he could hold his own. You didn't show weakness in jail; it could get you killed or bent over with a hard cock up your ass.

"I tried Reaper, I really did. I always followed your orders."

"You're a dead man walking," Reaper mumbled before he pretended to laugh at something on TV. Then he got up and went to the other table to play cards.

Red sat down in Reaper's vacated seat. He was jumpy as hell and kept looking between Reaper and Numbers.

"How did it go? Are we good now?"

"Nope, we're fucked." Numbers wasn't sure if Red was hated as much as Numbers, but it was best that he be on the lookout.

"Shit." Red was frantically rubbing his hands over his head. "Maybe I can go talk to him?"

"Be my guest, but I wouldn't." Numbers hoped the kid took his advice, but he didn't. Numbers watched Red approach Reaper.

"Reaper, man." Red was bouncing on the balls of his feet next to Reaper. "Do you remember me?"

"Shoo fly." Reaper didn't look at Red, but made a swishing motion with his hand like he was swatting a fly.

Numbers watched them out of the corner of his eye, but made no move to help Red.

"My name's Red." Red pointed to himself. "I was one of your prospects. Remember, I got you a burger once."

"Get the fuck away from me," Reaper mumbled.

"Aw, come on, man. Give a guy a break." Red threw his arms up.

Numbers was about to call Red over when he saw Reaper glance at an inmate named Charlie, and nod. The expression was so slight that Numbers would have missed it if he hadn't been watching Reaper's face intently. Within seconds, Charlie tackled Red to the ground like a professional linebacker and began punching him in the face. Red tried to block the punches, but Charlie was stronger. Sirens went off and officers banged on the outer cell with their black batons yelling at them to stop and go back into their cells. The non-combatants entered their cells but kept hooting and hollering, rooting for Charlie.

The doors to the cells closed and automatically locked. Then a couple of officers entered the cell block and tried to pull Charlie off Red, but Charlie was too wound up and he punched anyone in his way, including the guards. That's when the officers attacked Charlie with their batons until he stopped fighting and dropped on top of Red. Two big ass officers grabbed Charlie under his arms and dragged him out of the cell block. Charlie wasn't moving, his feet were dragging behind the officers. Hell, Charlie might be dead. Then two more officers got Red. He was in better shape than Charlie, from what Numbers could see, but his eyes were swollen and his face looked like shit.

The last officer brought in a bucket with a mop and pointed to Numbers. "He's your bunk mate, clean this blood up."

Numbers heard him mumble his cell number to the tower, and his cell door slid open. The officer stood by the entrance to their cellblock. Numbers got to work. At least he didn't have to worry about anyone attacking him, because he was the only one in the living area. When he finished, he pushed the bucket with the mop to the cellblock door and stepped back.

"Get back in your cell."

Numbers nodded and once he was back in his cell, his door slammed shut and locked. The officer stepped in and dragged the bucket and mop out. The heavy cellblock door clanged shut with a resounding echo, its lock clicking firmly into place.

Numbers laid down in his bed wishing Red hadn't done something so stupid as to piss Reaper off. Hopefully, the kid was okay and got to rest in the infirmary on a more comfortable bed than the ones in their cell. Because of the fight, their cells never opened back up during their regular downtime. Numbers didn't care; it's not like he was doing anything, anyway. What difference did it make if he was sitting at that fucking table or laying in his lumpy bed? Either way, he was still in jail with a target on his back, thanks to his so-called best friend.

The next day, Numbers felt eyes boring into him from every direction, the air thick with suspicion as he constantly scanned his surroundings. He didn't get the feeling they wanted him to be their bitch. It looked more like they wanted to kill him. Reaper must have put out a hit on him. At dinner that night, he swiped an extra plastic spoon. He didn't know what he would do with it, but at least it was something if Reaper came after him.

Numbers learned to walk with his back to the walls everywhere he went. He had a better shot at fighting someone if he saw them coming. The victim always got screwed by the element of surprise. He refused to be a victim. He would not make it easy for anyone who tried to kill him. That night, after lights out, the only sound was the scrape of plastic on concrete as he lay in bed. Making a tick mark on the wall with his spoon, he noticed how the concrete sharpened the tip. He realized he could make a knife from the spoon; however, he needed to work slowly and quietly, so that nobody would hear the scraping sounds. He was making progress until he heard the cellblock open. Hiding the spoon, he pretended to be asleep.

Red came in and climbed into his bed. How was he going to keep sharpening the spoon if Red was in the room? He got little sleep that night because every time he heard Red snoring, he would slowly scrape the spoon along the wall.

By his sixth day in jail, between the slow sharpening of his spoon, the constant sounds of other inmates, and the thin mattress Numbers was utterly exhausted. He followed his normal routine. The only difference was that this time, he had the sharpened spoon hidden in his underwear. If he got caught, they would take it away, and he'd probably end up in solitary. But on the bright side, he'd be away from Reaper.

After lunch, he'd stepped into the shower. He always went in fully dressed because of the hidden spoon. After he took off his clothes and placed them neatly outside the shower, he carefully placed his spoon in the far, shadowy corner, hoping the tower guard wouldn't see it. He turned on the water. Washing his hair and face were always the scariest times because his eyes would be closed while the soapy suds ran over his face. He always tried to face the opening to the shower and wash quickly in case someone jumped him. But that day, as soon as he shut his eyes, he felt his body shoved into the shower wall.

The jarring alarm blared, but all Numbers could make out through the ringing was Reaper's raspy voice accusingly whispering, "You let me down, Numbers."

A cold dread washed over him as searing pain erupted in his gut, each agonizing stab a fresh wave of terror. "No, I didn't. I did everything you asked, brother!" Numbers screamed as he slid down the gritty, cold concrete. Looking down for the spoon, he saw his blood, a dark crimson, flowing towards the drain. His fingers, trembling with a desperate urgency, frantically reaching for his sharpened spoon.

"No, you didn't. Because if you had, Tori, Maggie, and Angel would be dead, and Steele would be president of the LRs rebuilding my empire!" Reaper continued stabbing him.

Numbers finally grabbed the spoon. Gripping it tightly in his hand, he mustered all his strength and jammed it into Reaper's throat with a sickening thud. Blood spurted out like a hose. Reaper landed heavily on Numbers, the sickening crunch of bone accompanied by a rush of warm blood that flowed into the drain, marking the end of their lives.

Chapter 49

When One Door Closes, Another One Opens

George

Everyone wanted to celebrate the birth of Thomas Nando Thunderbird, but having the party in the resort's wedding venue still left a sour taste in their mouths. Dyani, Tall Bear, Spirit-of-the-Eagle, and Morning Star were staying for two weeks this time instead of their usual one-week stay. Thunder and Isa wanted to celebrate with everyone, so Mark generously offered his house, or as Lizzy called it, his mansion, for the party the Saturday after his birthday, instead of at the resort. Lizzy wasn't wrong. The house he bought for Maggie sat on ten acres of land in Hollywood, Florida. Mark's closest neighbor, Grayhorse, lived just beyond the treeline, his house hidden from view. As that saying goes, you can take the boy out of the country, but you can't take the country out of the boy, explained Mark to a T.

Mark covered all the costs: the caterers, a large bouncy house for the children, and a massive tent complete with fans, all in his backyard, providing shade and a cool refuge from the summer heat. Though Maggie offered little physical help, her bossy nature ensured George, and others, tirelessly carried out her instructions.

George was still on administrative leave and hating every moment of not being able to do his job. Less than a week had passed since the shooting, and he realized a comprehensive investigation could take months. He juggled helping Thunder at the cultural center, assisting Barrett and Holt at the casino, and obeying Maggie. Part of George's party duties included managing the invitations and RSVPs for Thomas' party.

Secretly, George and Lizzy visited each other's apartments at night, hiding it from Lizzy's parents. Her parents knew they were dating, but not that they were sleeping together. George wanted to live with Lizzy and be upfront with her parents, but he still hadn't found the right time to ask her father for her hand in marriage, let alone propose to Lizzy. Every time he wanted to talk to Tall Bear, Lizzy was with him. Deep down, he feared Tall Bear would refuse their union because of Lizzy's precarious employment and his own uncertain career. Being on administrative leave created a shaky foundation for their future. Which was another reason George wanted the investigation into the shooting to be over.

During the day, Lizzy helped Isa with Thomas while Thunder put in a few hours at work. Thunder wasn't working a full day and sometimes he could even make calls from home. Thrilled about her new grandson, Aurora helped for the first few days before returning to her job. Teasingly, George cautioned Aurora about her overly enthusiastic reaction to her grandson in front of Lucy and Emmy, or she would have two very upset little girls to deal with.

Today was the day of the party, and Maggie had been riding George's ass about everything to do with the party. Did he double check his numbers? Was there enough seating for all the guests? Did they have enough food? Did he remind the bartender to come tend the bar? Did he follow up with the DJ? On and on she went. At least when he married, he would have plenty of practice planning an intimate wedding for around fifty guests.

He was so afraid he'd forget something, he'd asked Sean if he could come before the party started and double check him. There was no way he was asking Holt or Barrett after all the shit they gave Alex for forgetting to ask for a ride from the hospital when Tori was released. Sean, being a loyal friend, showed up at lunchtime and offered his help, proving his support was more than just a last-minute check. The party started at three because that's when Thomas would wake up from his nap.

By 2:30 pm, Sean and George had everything under control. The buffet was ready, the rich smoky scent of hot barbecue mingling with the creamy aroma of mac and cheese, baked beans, and buttery toast. Mark wanted Alex to enjoy the party, so he didn't ask him to cook anything. George was sure Alex wouldn't be able to help himself and would bring some fry bread because everyone loved his fry bread. The multi-colored bouncy house, shaped like a whimsical castle, stood inflated and ready for the kids, its cheerful colors promising a fun day. They set up round tables draped in delicate baby blue tablecloths and matching chairs on either side of a gleaming rectangular dance floor, the rhythmic pulse of the DJ's music already filling the air opposite a tempting buffet of pastries. The bartender polished glasses, ready to serve drinks. And as a surprise for Lucy, Mark had arranged a beauty station. George knew Lucy was going to love it, especially the sign on the top of the canopy that read "Lucy's Hair Salon".

George and Sean sat on a couple chairs at the back of the tent admiring their work.

"We did good." George high-fived Mark. "We make a good team, man."

"About that." Sean rubbed the back of his neck.

"You're leaving." George dropped back into his chair and groaned. He was afraid of that since the night he stayed with Sean.

"Yeah, I leave in a couple of weeks." Sean leaned forward and braced his elbows on his knees. "There are just too many memories of her here. I want a fresh start. Someplace more laid back than here. Less traffic. Less trouble."

"Less excitement." George quirked his eyebrow at him.

"That too. Hell, man." Sean leaned back in the chair and looked at him. "I'm getting ready to turn forty and I have nothing to show for it but my job. I'd thought by now I'd have a wife, kids, maybe a dog. But I'm fucking miserable. I need a change of scenery, which is why I took a job north of here. I'll be working for the Haven Island PD. I'll still be a patrol officer, but it's less crime and maybe, just maybe, I can find a pretty little island girl to fall in love with me and marry me."

"Haven Island sounds like a great place." George stared at his hands, fidgeting with his fingers. He didn't want Sean to move, but he understood. "Less stress."

"Well, Sunrise sounded less stressful too and look at everything that's been going on here," Sean said wryly.

"Yeah." George nodded and took a deep breath. "Sunrise has been crazy, but I found my best friend here." George looked up at Sean. "But I get it. I know you haven't been happy for a while. I hope this move and new job are everything you want them to be. You deserve to be happy with a wife and family. I wish you the best."

"Thanks, man." Sean stood and extended his hand to George. "I'm gonna miss my best bro, too."

George stood and pulled him in for a bro hug. "Things won't be the same without you, partner. We'll have to get some beers and celebrate your new job before you leave."

"I'd like that. Honestly, it's a good time for me to bug out. You have Lizzy to keep you out of trouble." Sean nudged him and mumbled under his breath. "Especially after you propose."

"That's true." George rolled his eyes. "But I think it's more like me keeping her out of trouble."

"Yeah, but I know you're up for the challenge." Sean grabbed George's hand and placed his other hand on George's shoulder. "You are the best rookie I've ever trained. I mean that from the bottom of my heart."

"Thank you. I couldn't have gotten through the academy without your help and support." George's eyes watered. He could count on one hand how many people had given a shit about him throughout his life, and Sean was one of them.

"Hey, don't get all teary-eyed and cry on me like a girl," Sean smirked and punched George's shoulder.

George laughed and wiped his face.

"Besides, I'm only a few hours away. We're even on the same coast. You and Lizzy can come visit whenever you need a break from this crazy town."

"Sounds good, man. We might just take you up on that."

"I hope you do. Now, I gotta get ready for work without my partner, since he shot his fucking gun and went on leave. You know, if you needed a vacation, you could've just asked for a couple of days off, asshole."

"I'd rather be going to work than doing this." George motioned all around him.

"Yeah, but you did good. Everything looks great."

Sean's phone buzzed. Pulling it out of his pocket, he read the message.

"Everything okay?" George frowned.

"Yeah, actually it's great news for me, you, and all your guests." Sean looked up and grinned at him.

"What the hell are you talking about?"

"Apparently, Numbers and Reaper got into it in jail, and they wound up killing each other." Sean turned his phone to George so he could read the message.

"I wonder what happened?" George murmured.

"Hey, don't look a gift horse in the mouth. Take the present and be glad there are two less assholes in the world that are after your family and friends."

"You're right about that."

"Why are you both just standing around?" Maggie hollered from her back patio, balanced on crutches. "Guests will be here soon."

"That's my cue." Sean smacked George's back. "Have fun and stay away from the crazy lady barking orders."

George laughed and watched him walk right by Maggie.

"And where do you think you're going?" Maggie asked Sean.

"I'm going to work. Have fun tonight." Sean turned and saluted George before he winked at Maggie and left.

George walked up to Maggie. She was still watching Sean leave as if her party was going to fall apart without him. "Maggie, it's all under control. I'm gonna head upstairs and take a quick shower. I'll be down in ten."

"Okay. Can you help me inside? I hate these damn crutches and Mark went to pay the caterers."

"Sure." George leaned her crutches against the wall, put her arm over his shoulders and helped her onto the couch. Then he grabbed her crutches and left them on the floor in front of the couch, in case she needed to get up before Mark came back. "Can I get you anything before I go upstairs?"

"No, Mark will be here in a minute."

"Okay," George murmured, but Maggie caught his arm before he left. "Did you change your mind?"

"No, I just wanted to say thank you. We couldn't have had this party here without you. You've done a fabulous job." Maggie smiled.

"You've done great." Mark came up behind him, put his arm around his shoulders, and jiggled him. "Especially with the Wicked Witch of the West yelling at you."

Mark released George and stepped back, away from Maggie's swinging punch.

"Ha, with that cast you can't catch me," Mark smirked.

"You gotta sleep sometime, Surfer Smurf." Maggie sing-songed.

"On that note, I'm gonna go shower." George could hear them swapping smart ass comments, but didn't want to get caught in the crossfire. He knew it was their form of foreplay.

Chapter 50

Welcome Home Thomas

George

After he showered and got ready, he glanced out the window and saw their guests had arrived. Heading downstairs to look for Lizzy, he found her talking to Tori, Alex, Frey, Holt, Barrett, and Angel. Sneaking up behind her, he kissed her cheek.

"Hey." Lizzy spun around. "Where have you been? I was looking for you."

"I was taking a shower in our favorite bathroom," George smirked, and Lizzy blushed.

"Me thinks there is a sexy story behind that comment." Barrett wiggled his eyebrows and shoulder bumped Holt. "Did you see how red her face got?"

"Leave her alone, Barrett." Angel smacked his shoulder.

"Thanks, Angel," Lizzy said, while George wrapped her up in his arms and kissed her neck.

"Come with me," George whispered in her ear. "I need to check on things, so Maggie doesn't blow a gasket."

"Okay." Lizzy turned around. "Lead the way."

"We'll see you guys later. Maggie's minion job is never done." George bowed in their direction.

George pulled Lizzy to the jumpy house. "Let's make sure it's fully blown up. Take off your shoes, we're going in." George took off his shoes.

Lizzy giggled. "I think we can tell from out here."

"Nonsense. A good minion checks every angle. Come in with me." George lifted the entrance flap and waited for Lizzy.

When she was ready and stood before him, George hoisted her up and threw her inside. George flew in after Lizzy and began jumping around, pretending to be a monster who was going to catch the kids. Emmy, Lucy, and Bryce were squealing, trying to get away from him while Lizzy tried to protect them from the clutches of George. Tommy and Jimmy, one of the shelter boys, were chasing George, trying to tackle him. That went on until George ran out of steam and dropped into the center of the jumpy house. All the kids piled on top of him.

"Okay, okay, let George breathe!" Lizzy shouted and sat next to them.

Eventually, they all rolled off. "So, is it fully blown?" Lizzy waved her arm around.

"Yep," George was panting. "I think we're good."

They left the kids inside and slid out.

"I can't believe they're still jumping in there." Lizzy slipped her shoes on.

"Me either." George sat on the ground to tie his.

"Did you kids have fun in there?" Thunder stood over George with Isa next to him, holding Thomas.

George looked up. "That was exhausting. I don't know how they do it."

Thunder gave him a hand and then helped Lizzy.

"I'd give anything for a quarter of that energy." Grayhorse approached with Sarah, who was carrying Lilly.

"I've come to hold my grandniece and grandnephew." Spirit-of-the-Eagle wiggled his fingers at Sarah and Isa. They carefully placed Lilly and Thomas in each of his arms. "My heart is full. Take a picture so I can take it with me wherever I go."

George got out his phone, but Isa was quicker. Moms were always quicker with the photo taking.

"How about if all you stand together, and I'll take a photo?" George motioned for them to get close together.

"Wait!" Sarah hollered. "Let me get Tommy!"

"I'll get him." Lizzy screamed his name into the jumpy house and asked him to come out for a second.

Tommy ran over and they all posed surrounding Spirit-of-the-Eagle as he held his two Lakota grandbabies.

"I want a family photo." Aurora said from behind George.

"Lizzy, can you get Emmy and Lucy?" Gaby stood next to Aurora.

George noticed how Emmy ran straight to Tommy, and Lucy followed. Now they had both sides represented, the Lakota and the Cuban.

"Mommy!" Lucy tugged at Gaby's shirt to get her attention once the picture was taken. "Can I open up my hair salon and start braiding hair?"

"Sure, honey."

"Yay!" Lucy jumped up and down. "Mr. Mark! Mr. Mark!" Lucy cried, whirling around in a desperate search for him. "There you are!" Lucy pointed in Mark's direction. "It's time to do your hair! You can be my first customer since you set this all up for me."

"Fuck!" Mark blurted out from behind George.

George snorted. He knew before the night was over, Mark and Maggie would owe Lucy a bunch of money for her cuss jar.

"Mr. Mark?" Lucy held out her hand.

"Yeah, yeah, I know. I owe you money for cussing." Mark whipped out his wallet and gave her a five-dollar bill.

"Mr. Mark, this is too much." Lucy looked between her mom and Mark.

"I'm sure me or Maggie will use it up before the night's over." Mark rolled his eyes.

George heard a loud crashing sound before he heard Maggie cry out. "Shit!"

"See, I told you, Lucy." Mark smiled. "Keep the five. If we don't cuss again, you can consider it a tip for your hair salon."

"But if it's a tip, then I need to do your hair." Lucy grabbed his hand and pulled. "Come on, Mr. Mark, I'll give you a good hairdo to thank you for my salon."

"Yay," Mark said deadpan, and let Lucy drag him to her salon.

"Do you think she has any blue hair color?" Maggie limped toward them.

"I'm not sure what Mark bought for her." George shrugged. "But I think I saw a bottle of every color under the sun. Hey, shouldn't you be resting or sitting in a wheelchair?"

"Not now, mom." Maggie frowned at George. "Don't ruin my fun."

"That's trouble, right there." Isa pointed toward Maggie and laughed.

"Isa, can I hold your beautiful baby boy?" Janice asked. "I love babies."

"Of course," Isa smiled at Uncle Spirit and he nodded. She gently took him from Uncle Spirit and placed him in Janice's arms.

"Is Mark getting his hair braided?" Frank's eyes bugged out.

"It's my daughter's thing," Gaby grinned. "She loves to do hair. Men, women, dolls, anything really. And if she can't do their hair because it's not long enough like her dad," –Gaby pointed at Matteo– "then she likes to paint their nails."

"Yeah," Frey joined the conversation. "Lucy loves to braid long hair like Thunder, Grayhorse, and Alex. Even though Barrett and Mark have shorter hair, Lucy still puts several braids in it. She's fantastic. "

"I've seen her work." Sehoy and Osceola stood next to Frey. "She is very creative."

"I would love for her to braid my hair." Spirit-of-the-Eagle stood tall and proud. "I'm gonna get Tall Bear and she can braid both of our hair." Uncle Spirit handed Lilly back to Sarah.

"Osceola, go with them and let Lucy braid yours." Sehoy nudged her husband. "It would make her day."

"Spirit, hang on, I'm coming with you." Osceola followed.

"That little girl is going to be in hog heaven," Matteo laughed. "With all the braiding, she might not have time to catch those of us with short hair and do our nails."

"Bite your tongue, that's my niece you're talking about." Thunder glared at him. "Man up and go give her some business and a good tip. She's collecting money for her college education."

"And who do you think is going to cover most of that bill?" Matteo smirked at him.

"Mark, because him and Maggie can't seem to clean up their language." Thunder pointed as Mark handed over more money to Lucy.

They all laughed because Thunder was right. At the rate Mark and Maggie were going, they would end up paying for more of Lucy's college than Matteo and Gaby.

"Come on, Holt, George, let's go get our nails done." Matteo motioned for them to follow him.

"Right behind you." Holt kissed Frey and followed Matteo.

"Are you coming?" Matteo stood in front of George.

"I'll be there in a minute." George had seen Maggie's family, and he wanted to say hello, especially to José, who'd been helping the police as an undercover cop. "I just need to go talk to someone."

"Alright." Matteo pointed his finger at his face. "But don't disappoint my little girl or I'll punch you in your pretty little face. You're not a cop right now."

"Come on, Rocky." Holt pulled Matteo away.

George laughed and faced Lizzy. "I'm gonna go talk to Maggie's family. Do you want to come with me?"

"Sure." Lizzy grabbed his hand, her fingers intertwining with his as they walked, their joined hands swinging back and forth in rhythm until they reached Maggie.

Chapter 51

A Broken Family Heals

George

"Hey, George." Maggie was finally sitting in a wheelchair with her leg resting on one of the plastic chairs. "Lizzy, didn't George do a good job?" Maggie waved her arms around.

"He sure did." Lizzy still held his hand but wrapped her other arm around their hands and held tight before she raised up on her tippy toes and kissed his cheek.

"Lizzy, I'd like you to meet my Tía Inez, Tío Thomas, Cousin Nancy, and her husband, Kevin."

"Hi," Lizzy smiled and waved to them as Maggie introduced them.

"Oh, and walking over with my drink is my older brother, José."

"Here you go, *hermanita*." José gave her a pink frozen drink.

"That drink." George pointed at her drink. "Better be non-alcoholic."

"Deputy George, you wound me." José held his chest and staggered back. "I know she's on pain meds."

"I do not need another keeper," Maggie snarled and took a drink.

"José, it's good to see you. Everything going, okay? How's Lola?" George had been worried about him doing a lot of undercover work to arrest the LRs. Now that they were all either dead, arrested, or scattered, he figured José and his club, Los Lobos de Muerte, could continue with their legit businesses.

"She's getting better." José beamed. "She doesn't flinch anymore when I touch her, so that's progress. She wanted to come to see Maggie, but it's too many people for her right now."

"I told you to bring her by anytime she wants," Maggie said between sips. "We can spend the day together."

"I'll tell her," José grinned. "She'd like that."

"José?" Tía Inez gently touched his forearm. "Maybe, if Lola is up to it, we can have another family dinner?"

George watched José's eyes widen and his mouth drop. "I would love that." Then he looked at Tío Thomas. "Would that be okay with you?"

"We can have it here," Maggie blurted. "If you want a neutral location."

"No," Tío Thomas said sternly. Everyone looked at each other and nodded. George knew Tío Thomas was the last holdout in accepting José back into the family, but wasn't it time to let his anger go? José had been doing a lot of good with his reformed MC and the police.

"Daddy, please?" Nancy pleaded with him.

"I'm sorry, I didn't finish." Tío Thomas looked at all of them. George could tell they were all waiting on baited breaths to hear what else he had to say. Hell, he couldn't wait to hear it. That family had suffered enough.

"I would love for all of us to have a family dinner at our house." Tío Thomas grabbed José and hugged him tightly. "And if your lovely girlfriend wants to come along, she is absolutely welcome in our house."

"*Gracias, Tío*," George mumbled.

George saw tears rolling down everyone's cheeks, especially José.

"Let's give them some space." George bent down and whispered in Lizzy's ear.

Lizzy followed him. George headed toward the shelter boys, who were playing Frisbee.

"I take it Lola is José's girlfriend. What happened to her?" Lizzy asked before they reached the boys.

George sighed, "that, babe, is a long story. I'll tell you later."

Tim had just caught the Frisbee. "Hey, Tim, toss it here." George let go of Lizzy's hand and clapped.

"Are you sure you want to play, old man?" Tim teased. "We are just as happy to play with the cute girl next to you. She seems younger and more fit."

"Yeah!" Steele covered his mouth to holler at George. "You might break a hip or something!"

"I see you're fitting right in, Steele!" George hollered back. "Wiseass," George mumbled quietly, so only Lizzy could hear. The last thing he needed was to have to pay Lucy for cussing.

"Don't worry about me, boys." George emphasized the word boys. "Unless you want me to show you what a real man can do?"

George smiled as Luke and Kenny teased Tim and Steele. He could hear them oohing and aahing along with a few, 'oh snap', 'he got you', and lots of pointing and laughing. Even Tim beamed at him and shook his head.

"Alright everybody spread out, let's include the old man and his pretty girlfriend." Tim motioned for them to make a larger circle. "You can toss to whoever you want." He instructed before he whizzed the Frisbee to George.

They played for a while until George's phone buzzed in his pocket. He pulled it out and saw it was a call from the station. George held up the phone and screamed, "I gotta take this! I'll be right back." He looked at Lizzy as he stepped away from the game. She was frowning. George shrugged and answered the call.

"Hello?"

"Deputy Smith, this is Sergeant Grimes from Internal Affairs. Do you have a minute?"

"Yes sir, let me just step away to a quieter spot." George walked around the back of the house to the side, because with all the chatter and the music, it was hard to hear the sergeant. He took a deep breath, preparing himself for either good news or bad news. It was kind of soon for the investigation to be over. "I'm ready."

"Deputy Smith, I've watched several of the witness' videos and read over all the witness statements," Sargeant Grimes sighed.

George stared blankly at the ground, impatiently waiting for a confirmation from him, wanting to know if he'd been cleared. His heart was pounding in his chest, sweat beaded on his forehead. If they fired him, he didn't know what he would do. Although he could return to the dimly lit, boisterous atmosphere of the bar, he much preferred the challenges and camaraderie of being a police officer. He knew some of the public harbored resentment towards officers, a fact that fueled his desire to improve community relations by making a difference. He'd found his calling to protect and serve. George leaned against the wall and braced himself.

"I wanted to call you personally to let you know you have been cleared of any wrongdoing."

As George slid down the damp wall, a wave of relief crashed over him, the sound of his ragged breathing filling the silence.

"We are proud to call you one of our brothers in blue. Thank you for your excellent work in trying to diffuse the situation. I know it must've been very difficult for you after what Numbers did to your friends and family. Our Sheriff's Office appreciates your professionalism and dedication. I checked your work schedule and I want you to take next week off. You can report to duty on Monday, April 29th. None of this will affect your benefits or your scheduled paychecks."

"Thank you, sir." George looked up and saw Lizzy wringing her hands while she paced.

"Have a great day, deputy, and enjoy your party."

"I will. Now I have something to celebrate." George smiled and hung up.

He'd been reinstated without punishment, a surprising turn of events that left him feeling relieved. As the tension left his body like a released breath, George sprung up, snatching Lizzy into a celebratory twirl.

"I'm back, babe. I got my job back." George stopped and ravished her mouth. His life was perfect. He had the girl, a job he loved, and friends that he called family. *Shit, his friends, he had to tell them about Numbers, Reaper, and his job.*

"I'm gonna make an announcement." George gave her a quick peck. "Keep this news to yourself. I want to tell everyone at the same time."

"You most certainly have an announcement. Lizzy, is there something you need to tell me?" Lizzy froze at the sound of her mother's voice behind them. George glanced up and saw Dyani standing with her arms crossed, hip cocked, and her toe frantically tapping the ground. But that was nothing compared to the thundercloud expression on Tall Bear's face.

"Oh, shit," George gulped.

George released Lizzy and stepped aside. "Mr. and Mrs. Tall Bear, how are you?"

"I'd be better if my daughter would be honest with me." Dyani glared at Lizzy. "Since the cat caught her tongue." Dyani pointed at Lizzy before staring at George. "I'd like for you to tell me what your intentions are toward Lizzy? Why are you kissing her so passionately around the side of the house, where no one is around? It seems a little more than just dating."

"I, uh..," Dyani had caught him off guard. He'd always assumed it would be Tall Bear who questioned him. George glanced at Lizzy, but she was no help. She was staring at the ground. He would let no one yell at her, not even her mother. Lizzy had to know; he always had her back. George wrapped his arm around her and tucked her into his chest. "I love your daughter. We are more than just dating."

"Are you sleeping with her?" Dyani blurted.

"Iná!" Lizzy stared at her mom. "Please don't embarrass me." Lizzy buried her head in George's chest.

George had wanted to be direct and honest with her parents. This was his chance. "May I please speak with you both, alone?"

"What are you doing?" Lizzy whispered harshly and smacked his chest.

"Can you please go check on Lucy and make sure she has everything she needs?" George needed to get her away from them so he could ask her parents if he could marry Lizzy. Lizzy wasn't moving. "Please."

"Okay, but I'll be back in ten minutes." Lizzy pointed at all of them before she stormed off.

George waited until Lizzy was far enough away. Dyani and Tall Bear just continued to stare at him. George cleared his throat. "I...I uh, want you to know that I love your daughter. She means everything to me and I would like to ask you both," –George gestured to each one– "if you will give me your permission to ask her to marry me?"

George glanced between them as they looked at each other, puzzled. Clearly, that was not what they were expecting him to say. They spoke to each other in Lakota, which George didn't understand, before they faced him.

"You haven't known each other very long? How do you know you want to spend the rest of your lives together?" Dyani held her husband's hand.

"I know we haven't known each other long, but I knew she was the one for me from the way she makes me feel. She is smart, funny, and loving. I can't wait to experience life with her. She makes my days brighter and my heart lighter. Sorry, that might sound stupid, but she makes me want to be a better man. I've been saving my money for years and I know I can provide for her and take care of her. We may not be millionaires, or live the lifestyles of the rich and famous, but I promise to love and cherish her until the day I die."

Dyani wiped the tears running down her face. "Thank you for saying that. You are a good man, George."

"You have our blessing." Tall Bear pulled him in for a hug.

"When are you planning on asking her?" Dyani hugged him after Tall Bear.

"In a few minutes. I want all our friends and family to witness our commitment to each other."

"Do you have a ring?" Dyani walked back into Tall Bear's arms.

George smiled and patted his pocket. "Yes ma'am. I do."

"Well then, go find your girl." Tall Bear smiled.

"I'll see you two later." Now that he had their approval, he was nervous about proposing to Lizzy. *She would say yes, right?*

George hurried to Lizzy, pulled her into his arms, lifted her off the ground, and swung her around.

"I take it that went well." Lizzy said between laughs.

"It did. They know we're together, and that I love you. What more could we ask for?"

"I guess you're right."

George turned his head and put his hand behind his ear. "I'm sorry. What was that?"

"You're right, you jerk." Lizzy play slapped his shoulder.

"I'll never get tired of hearing you say that. The right part, not the jerk part." George winked.

"Well, enjoy it while it lasts because I'm sure I'll be right more times than you. You know, happy wife, happy life."

George draped his arm around her shoulder and guided them back to the party. "I thought it was happy spouse, happy house, which could mean me." George pointed to himself, but before Lizzy could smack him again, he kissed her. He knew her weakness. "Come on slugger, I have an announcement to make. But first I need to talk to Angel. Come with me. You can hang out with your sister while I talk to her."

*** Angel ***

Angel, Barrett, Frey, Holt, Alex, and Tori were all standing near Lucy's Hair Salon when George approached with Lizzy.

"Angel, can I talk to you for a second?" George stood in front of her with a serious look on his face.

"Uh, yeah, sure." Angel nodded and stepped away with George. "What's going on?"

"I found out earlier today that your father died in prison."

"What?" Angel covered her mouth. "What happened?" *How could this hurt?* Her father was a horrible man who had terrorized her, her son, and her friends. Looking up, she shot her gaze straight at Barrett. She needed him to be with her while she heard the details. *Oh Shit!* Turning around, she found Steele playing frisbee with the shelter boys. *How was she going to tell him that his grandfather was dead? Would he feel remorse or be grateful?* After everything they'd been through, her feelings were all mixed up. Barrett's arms startled her when they wrapped around her.

"Are you okay?" Barrett cupped her face, frowning as he gazed into her eyes. Then he released her and faced George. "What the hell did you tell her, George?"

Frey, Holt, Alex, Tori, and Lizzy all came over to them.

"My father is dead." Angel's voice sounded hollow even to her.

They all glanced at George, waiting for more details.

"Numbers and Reaper had a fight in their cellblock. They stabbed each other to death. I don't know all the details. Sean gave me the news earlier today. I wanted to speak with you privately, before I announce it to everyone, as it directly affects us all."

"Thank you." Angel clenched Barrett's hand. "We need to tell Steele. Can you give us a few minutes, George?"

"Of course. Do you need me to go with you?"

"No, that's okay. I'll let Steele know he can come to you if he has questions."

Angel pulled Barrett along as she thought about all the different ways she could tell Steele. She could remind him of their good times. There was no sense in judging Reaper now. The highest power in the land would judge him. Now was the time to remind Steele of how much he was loved.

Chapter 52

Announcements

George

George waited, watching Barrett and Angel as they spoke to Steele. At first he looked surprised, but then he hugged Angel and Barrett nodded to George. It was time for everyone to heal and embrace the good times ahead. George pulled Lizzy along to the DJ booth.

"Hey." George waved his hand in front of the DJ to get his attention because he was wearing headphones and grooving to the beat.

The DJ pulled back his headphones. "Hey, man, do you want to request a song?"

"Not right now, but can you stop the music and hand me your microphone?" George pointed to the microphone lying next to the computer. "I have several announcements to make."

"You got it." The DJ handed George the microphone and stopped the music mid-song.

Lizzy tried to pull her hand free from George, but he held on tight and dragged her with him in front of the DJ. He wanted her by his side when he gave the announcements.

"Hello everyone. Can I have your attention, please?" George held his hand up with the microphone and waved before he continued. "If everyone can come in here and take a seat. This won't take long." George waited until everyone trickled into a seat under the tent. The shelter boys rounded up all the kids and sat together at a table. Steele, Angel, and Barrett stood next to their table.

"Yeah, yeah, yeah, get on with it." Barrett waved his hand over his head in a circular motion.

"I think he just likes to hear himself talk," Holt said loudly.

Some snickered, while others remained quiet and smiled at George.

"I have several announcements to make, most of which affect everybody in this room." George spoke into the microphone, ignoring the hecklers.

"He is cute, even though he's not showing us his abs. Take off your shirt!" Maggie shouted. "I guarantee you the entire female audience will shut up."

"Why would we pay attention to George if he takes off his shirt, mommy?" Lucy turned to face Gaby.

George's eyes bounced between Maggie, Gaby, and Lucy, ready to make an excuse for Maggie, when Gaby glared at Maggie and said, "Maggie's still not feeling well. She doesn't know what she's saying." George looked at Maggie and saw her mouth 'sorry' to Gaby.

"Really, Troublemaker Girl," Mark growled and covered her mouth.

"Hey, he's not taking anything off." Lizzy moved in front of George and braced her hands on her hips, daring anyone to say anything else about George stripping.

George put his left arm around Lizzy's waist and pulled her against his body while his right hand held the microphone. "Okay, okay, I'll get on with it."

George looked directly at Angel, Barrett, and Steele. She stiffened. "I was notified earlier today that Numbers and Reaper had a fight in jail. I don't know the details, just that they are no longer with us."

The trio stood with their arms around each other for support. Barrett engulfing Angel and Steele while they shed some tears. George knew they didn't love the things that Reaper had done, but they would cry for the good times when Reaper hadn't been such an asshole. Angel cleared her throat, wiped her face, composed herself, looked up at George, and nodded. He was so focused on Angel that when he looked around; he saw several people hugging their loved ones. George was certain those were tears of sorrow for those lost because of those men, tears of relief that they couldn't hurt anyone else, and tears of joy for their future.

George gave them a few minutes as they comforted each other. When they quieted down, he continued. "I was also told just a few minutes ago that I was cleared of any wrongdoing in the investigation against me and I can return to my position with the sheriff's office."

George smiled as everyone hooted and hollered their excitement and congratulations. Lizzy spun around in his embrace, grabbed his face and bent it toward her for a sweet kiss.

"And now for my last announcement." George held Lizzy's hand and got down on one knee.

You could hear everyone's breath leave the tent with an occasional, oh my god.

"George, what are you doing? Is this because my mom cornered us?" Lizzy stared at George.

"No," George chuckled. Holding her hand, feeling the gentle pressure of his fingers against hers, he gazed into her eyes, lost in their mesmerizing depths. With a slight change, he brought the microphone near his mouth, keenly aware of the high-pitched shriek that could result from getting too close. With a rasping clearing of his throat, he spoke from the heart, his words raw and emotional.

"Lizzy, you have turned my world upside down from the moment I laid eyes on you." Lizzy covered her mouth, her eyes watering. "You make me want to wake up every morning and be the best man I can be. You keep me on my toes with your adventures," –several people chuckled, and George heard Sehoy ask, "What adventures?" before someone shushed her– "but I wouldn't want it any other way. I love being your knight in shining armor, saving you from all those crazy people that just don't realize you're always right. What's wrong with them, anyway?" –George squeezed her hand and smirked. He heard more laughter, even from Lizzy this time– "Seriously though," George looked at her with all the love he had inside of him. "Without you, I'd be utterly and hopelessly lost, like a ship without a sail. I look forward to putting a smile on your face every day because when you smile, your inner light shines brighter than any star in the sky. I want to bask in that light with you for the rest of my life."

George released her hand and reached into his pocket. Pulling out the ring box, he opened it up and turned it toward her. "I couldn't wait another single day to ask the most important question of my life. Elizabeth Tall Bear, will you marry me?"

Time seemed to stand still as George waited for her response, his heart pounding in his chest like a drum.

"Yes!" Lizzy threw herself at him, causing him to drop the microphone and ring box so he could catch her.

Her hands cupped his face at the same time her lips crashed against his. George lost his balance, and they both crashed to the floor. Even during the passionate kiss, George still kept Lizzy on top, protecting her from landing on the floor. Everyone was clapping and cheering them on. After their kiss, George grabbed the box and put the ring on Lizzy's finger. She kept staring at her hand in awe.

"I think that calls for a celebratory toast." Thunder yelled and strode to Lizzy and George. "Everyone, please head to the bartender. He's poured some Champagne for a toast! Unless you're underage or on pain meds," –Thunder pointed at Maggie– "then you get water or apple juice in a fancy glass."

Maggie smiled sweetly, but George noticed her middle finger rubbing her right temple. Since she was the person sitting furthest away to the left of the stage, not many people would catch her reaction to Thunder's comment. Thunder smiled at Maggie and raised his glass, as if he hadn't noticed her non-verbal response.

George got up first and held his hand out to help Lizzy before he asked Thunder. "Where did you get Champagne from?"

"I brought it. I wanted to toast to my son. Now, I get to toast to my son and my brother." Thunder beamed at George.

Isa approached them with three Champagne glasses on a tray. One for George, another for Lizzy, and one for herself. After George and Lizzy took theirs, she grabbed hers and set the empty tray on a nearby table.

"Congratulations." Isa hugged Lizzy and reached for her hand to look at the engagement ring. "It's beautiful. I'm so happy for you both."

Isa stood next to Thunder while Lizzy stayed next to George. When everyone settled down again, Thunder spoke. His voice was so loud and deep it commanded everyone's attention. He didn't need a microphone.

"Welcome, family and friends. Today, my beautiful wife and I wanted to do a celebratory toast to the birth of our first son, Thomas Nando Thunderbird. The first of many yet to come." Thunder put his arm around Isa and kissed her temple.

"Uh, how many are yet to come?" Isa mumbled so only the four of them could hear.

"Many," Thunder chuckled. "So, let's raise a glass and honor our first-born Thomas Nando Thunderbird!"

George, along with several people, shouted. "To Thomas Nando Thunderbird!" while others shouted. "Here, here!"

"Don't drink it all!" Thunder's booming voice bellowed. "I now have another toast to make!"

"*Lekší*, is this going to take long? I have a lot of hairstyles to do."

Lucy was standing like Sehoy had stood earlier when she'd caught George and Lizzy kissing around the side of the house. Arms crossed, hip cocked, and toe tapping. It must be a girl thing.

Thunder chuckled and raised his hand. "I promise this won't take long and no one is leaving until you fix their hair." Thunder glared at all the guests.

Lucy stopped tapping her foot and jumped up and down, clapping her hands. "Thanks, *lekší*. I love you."

"I love you, too, Lucy," Thunder grinned.

George looked around, hearing the murmurs of approval and seeing the shining eyes focused on Thunder and Lucy. Except for Mark and Maggie, who were angrily whispering to one another. Mark's voice broke the silence when he hollered, "Fuck woman, what now?"

"Mr. Mark?" Lucy scolded him with her finger, then held her hand out palm up.

"Yeah, yeah, yeah." Mark set his glass down and pulled out his wallet. He walked over to Lucy and placed a bill in her hand. George couldn't tell how much he gave her, but her smile was infectious.

Lucy pulled on Mark's shirt and when he looked at her, she said loud enough for everyone to hear. "Thank you, Mr. Mark. I love you, too."

Mark picked her up, gave her a big hug and said, "I love you, too, Lucy."

Mark didn't set her down, he just shifted her to his hip and held her while she laid her head on his shoulder and watched Thunder.

"She has all you men wrapped around her little finger," Isa mumbled.

"Yep." Thunder agreed with Isa and cleared his throat. "I would like to toast to this fine young man standing next to me." Thunder motioned to George. "When I moved here to start the American Indian Cultural Center, I never in my wildest dreams imaged that not only would I love my job, but I would be a part of such a wonderful family. I consider all of you, my family. But it all started with this young man." Thunder placed his hand on George's shoulder. "Some of you might not know that I was a teacher before I moved down here. I missed my students after my move and wanted to find other kids that I could mentor and guide like Uncle Spirit did for me and Sarah after our parents died." Thunder smiled at Uncle Spirit, who was holding Thomas.

"I walked into a shelter for homeless boys and knew I wanted to help each and every one of them. See, I was blessed to have my parents until I was in college, but some of these boys lost their parents much earlier in life. I sat and talked to them, but one boy who sat quietly in the corner grabbed my attention. His eyes were so sad when I caught one of his glances. He looked like he carried the weight of the world around his shoulders. His sadness haunted my dreams, and I vowed to get to know him and let him know that someone loved him. That's all we ever want, really, is for someone to love us and make us feel like we belong. It took a few weeks, but eventually, he would join some of the other boys and me in the park for a game of basketball."

"In a short amount of time, our bond became stronger, and I didn't think of myself as his mentor, but as his older brother." George nodded, tears blurring his vision. "I watched him grow from a scared, shy little boy to a confident man who is an incredibly dedicated officer of the law. Not only does he protect the innocent, but he goes out of his way to help and mentor all those other scared little boys out there." Thunder faced George and stared into his eyes. He spoke loud enough for everyone to hear, but George knew the next words he spoke were just for him. "I am so proud of the man that you have become and feel blessed that you have chosen me to be a part of your life. I love you, little brother." Thunder raised his glass. "To Deputy George Smith!"

Thunder took one sip before George embraced him. George's Champagne sloshed out of his glass, but George didn't care. Dropping the glass behind Thunder, George clung on tight as overwhelming emotions coursed through his body. Hearing how much Thunder loved him broke something inside. So much made sense now. He had never realized how many walls he kept around his heart when it came to family. He'd always been afraid of being left behind, and Lizzy had left him behind when she went back home. But his need to be forgiven and accepted was probably why he had needed to apologize to Lizzy so badly after that crazy night, when he was afraid he'd hurt her. His sense of urgency to want to take care of Lizzy at all costs because the thought of losing her was unbearable. Deep down, George longed for the comforting embrace of belonging, the warmth of connection, and the sweet relief of being loved. All things he'd found in Lizzy's arms.

As an officer, George always wanted to help those who couldn't help themselves, like Thunder had helped him. No wonder he loved being a police officer. It fulfilled his drive to make things better, so no one had to go through what he went through growing up. No child should ever feel like they are a burden, unwanted, or unloved. And no parent should abandon their child.

George stood back, and they both wiped their tears.

"Thank you for not giving up on me," George murmured.

"Thank you for giving me the chance to help you and love you, little brother."

"I love you too, big brother."

Chapter 53

Special Thanks

Neri

I hope you all enjoyed my first series, the Path Series. I love these characters and have lived with some (Thunder and Isa) for thirty years! So, who knows, maybe some of them will show up in my next series, Haven Island PD, bringing their unique quirks and stories with them. A prequel, bridging the Path Series and Haven Island PD, will star…Deputy Sean O'Reilly. His short story prequel will be free to my readers via email or Amazon. For the Path Series, I never did pre-orders. However, I will do them with Haven Island PD.

Thank you to all my readers – You are the BEST! I appreciate all your support.

A special thank you to Michelle K. who not only reads all my books before they are published but also buys them to help me. She is my best friend and personal assistant who travels with me to book signing and craft shows. I couldn't do everything I do without her.

I could not have written this book without the help of several people. If I got anything wrong or applied creative license, it is my doing. Their insightful feedback and extensive knowledge helped shape my story into something better.

I feel blessed and honored to know the following first responders. As I write my chapters and questions arise, I reach out to them via text, email, or phone call and they ALWAYS respond with answers as quickly as they can. The Best Men in Blue Support Team ever: Sergeant TJ Williams, K9 Deputy Bryan Wright, and Corrections Deputy Nathan Lebon.

In this book, I had to research what firefighters and paramedics do to help someone who's been roofied. I was lucky enough when I was volunteering for the Sheriff's Department to meet an awesome firefighter named Gabriel Lopez, who was kind enough to answer my questions.

To all the first responders out there, the ones I'm blessed to call my friends and those I haven't met, please stay safe out there. It can be a little crazy. Thank you, thank you, thank you, for what you do for all of us in your community daily.

Thank you to everyone who joined my reading circle for this series and read pre-published copies of my books to help me make them better before their launch date: Tony D., Michelle K., Amy H., Catherine F., and Michelle Z. As always, I must express my gratitude to my previous editors, McKenzie Gibel and Deb Krickovich, for helping me write my first series.

I know my books are hard to find because I lack many reviews, but if you follow me on Amazon as one of your favorite authors, you'll receive alerts when I release a book.

Chapter 54

About the Author

Neri

Neri Lopez has worn many hats as a stay-at-home mom of triplets, graphic designer, and high school teacher (Spanish, Art, and Graphic Design). She lives in Florida with her husband, grown kids, and their fur babies, Mocha and Chewy. She is a crafter of all trades, including making jewelry, scrapbooking, knitting, crocheting, sewing, and painting.

Neri loves to hear from her readers. You can contact her at: sirenbookandcraft@gmail.com

Visit her website: **sirenbookandcraft.com**

and get on her mailing address for emailed newsletters and updates. (When you sign up for her newsletter, you will receive a FREE downloadable bookmark of Red Path.)

Or follow her on:

Facebook: Neri Lopez - Author

Instagram: Neri_Lopez_Author

The Path Series

Book 1: Red Path (Amazon Link - https://a.co/d/7NgFsGI)

Book 2: Unconquered Path (Amazon Link: https://a.co/d/dVu2Nmy)

Book 3: Wagering Path (Amazon Link: https://a.co/d/bVgZT8n)

Book 4: Unexpected Path (Amazon Link: https://www.amazon.com/dp/B0DR7GRP9Q)

Book 4.5 Novella: Double Trouble Path (Amazon Link: https://www.amazon.com/dp/B0DTGTN7D3)

Book 5: Twisted Path (Amazon Link: https://www.amazon.com/dp/1963995171)

Book 6: Blue Path